THE CREEP

THE CREEP

MICHAEL LaPOINTE

Random House Canada

PUBLISHED BY RANDOM HOUSE CANADA

Published in 2021 by Random House Canada, a division of Penguin Random House Canada
Limited, Toronto. Distributed in Canada by Penguin Random House Canada Limited, Toronto.

www.penguinrandomhouse.ca

The author acknowledges the Canada Council for the Arts, the Ontario Arts Council,
and the Toronto Arts Council for their support.

Library and Archives Canada Cataloguing in Publication

Title: The creep / Michael LaPointe.
Names: LaPointe, Michael, author.
Description: Random House Canada edition.
Identifiers: Canadiana (print) 20200328123 | Canadiana (ebook) 20200328131 |
ISBN 9780735279629 (trade paperback) | ISBN 9780735279636 (EPUB)
Classification: LCC PS8623.A734 C74 2021 | DDC C813/.6—dc23

Text design: Matthew Flute
Cover design: Matthew Flute
Image credits: (steel texture) © Katsumi Murouchi / Moment,
(halftone dots) © Hollygraphic / iStock, both Getty Images

Printed and bound in Canada

2 4 6 8 9 7 5 3

Penguin
Random House
RANDOM HOUSE CANADA

THE CREEP

THE BYSTANDER

1.

The girl from *Vice* stands at my office door. I left her no choice, she says. She tried calling, e-mailing. "Can we talk?"

I know she's a novice by her posture of defiance. She's worked herself up to this.

"I'm sorry," I say, "I didn't mean to leave you hanging. It's been chaotic." From behind my desk, I motion for her to come in. "Just close the door."

The girl drops into the chair, cold cheeks flushed, snow melting in her hair. She's maybe twenty-five. Without asking, she takes her iPhone out and starts recording.

"Sorry," she says, catching herself. "It's okay if I record?"

I nod and she roots through her tote bag for her notepad. By the time she produces it, scraggly white headphones pulled along, she's out of breath and has to reset her focus. Then she takes out the heavy book and sets it on my desk: *The Complete Bystander, 1999–2003.* They've printed all thirty-three of the magazine's issues to scale.

"Can I begin with a confession?" she says. "The *Bystander* was huge for me in high school, your work in particular."

I loft a smile over the desk.

"In fact you're one of the reasons I wanted to get into media."

"How have you found it?"

"Obviously we're living in a different time." She glances quickly at her phone and then at me, at the bandage on my wrist. "Like Gordon Stone writes in the introduction, the *Bystander* was maybe the last magazine of its kind, the last to start up, I mean, and go all-in with print. What was the minimum rate, like, two-fifty a word? It feels like a million years ago."

"How much are you getting for this?" I ask.

"One-fifty."

"A word?"

"God no. A hundred-fifty bucks. It's online only. I hope that's okay."

"Of course." After a pause, I ask, "Do you regret becoming a journalist?"

"Every first of the month." She laughs. "You get into it thinking you'll have a life like your idols, but the economics have shifted. I guess that's why so many people have gotten out."

From my office at Diamond Communications, you can see the Hudson's cobalt crawl between buildings. If you'd asked, when I was at the *Bystander*, what I'd be in fifteen years, I would've said editor-in-chief or even publisher, not some associate consultant. But it wasn't money that drove me from the business.

"It's funny, because we're needed more than ever, don't you think?" she says. "We have to sift the facts from the fiction."

I nod in the direction of the book on the desk. "That's what Mort Brewer always said."

"It's the truth, don't you think?"

I wish I could talk about my years at the *Bystander*, my last in journalism, with such pride and self-importance, like some grand old dame of media. But I can only think of all the people I failed, all the dead.

The girl opens *The Complete Bystander* and begins asking about my pieces—profiles of John Malkovich and Madonna, reviews of *Eyes Wide Shut* and *All About My Mother*, a two-part essay on Napster.

"The *Bystander* seems like a golden age," she says.

"It didn't feel that way at the time."

"Then take me back."

I look at her phone. There would be room in there for everything, for the story I never wrote, the one I can never tell.

If I were being real with her, I'd begin with the bandage on my wrist. How on a night when I seemed nothing more than hair and fingernails and one cold skull, I'd sprawled on the couch with glass after glass, the untold dead pushing out. The glass dropped from my hand, it broke on the floor. I saw the shards on hardwood and chose one.

Then came the blood, and with it, a thought. It couldn't happen like this. Slathering red over the screen, I managed to call 911.

And I would tell her about surfacing in the ambulance as they began the transfusion, how when I grasped what was happening, I yanked the IV from my arm. The medic lunged for the drip as it swung, dribbling blood.

They had to hold me down, there wasn't much time. But by then I'd seen the color of the blood. It was red, it was fine.

2.

"The attacks were, for me, a personal catastrophe," said Daniel Eastham. "*Rogue Winter* hit shelves that same morning. Do you think anyone bought novels on September 11?"

I glanced out the window at the snow falling over Brooklyn. You wouldn't normally have been able to see the Towers from Eastham's brownstone, but now there always seemed to be an absence in the sky. I'd arranged this interview months ago, but given the attacks, it had been put off to December. My first assignment back on the *Bystander*'s culture file, it was supposed to have been a coup. At thirty-seven, Eastham was the youngest, most adroitly aloof member of an exciting generation of New York novelists, and *Rogue Winter*, a 900-page postmodern comedy set several years in the future, was positioned to be his grand affirmation. But then, in just a single morning, it became clear that 2003 wouldn't be like his version at all, the America he'd purported to capture had changed, and none of the jokes were funny anymore.

Eastham reached for his glass of red wine and said, "No one's reading fiction right now, let alone author profiles."

In the days immediately after the attacks, it had been all hands on deck at the magazine to cover the only story that mattered. With bridges and tunnels closed, we needed everyone on the streets reporting, including me, a culture writer. At first I panicked at the thought of asking people to describe what they'd seen, who was missing. I hadn't done much hard reporting since my early days in Seattle. But once I entered the stream of events, I felt this other energy. The world around me crackled, true stories were everywhere. There was always someone rousing from their daze with a fresh account, using the presence of a journalist to reconstruct the catastrophe, pin it down with words. The pit still steaming downtown, I was a witness to history unadulterated.

I never got started with alcohol when I still had reading and writing to do, but Eastham poured more wine for himself and said, "Maybe a book like *Rogue Winter* has to be sacrificed for the Towers to be redeemed."

I squinted at his overreach, but this is what people were capable of in their ill-fitting new sincerity. I understood the need to get serious. Ever since reporting on the attacks, I felt it every day at the *Bystander*. I wanted to get out of the culture file, into the rush.

"Please," Eastham added, with a frightened glance at the recorder, "don't print that."

·

I went to the *Bystander* office in Chelsea to transcribe the tape and type up my notes. The freight elevator opened, and though it was late, I saw my colleagues still working to put the issue to bed before the winter holidays.

I greeted Ross Briggs, back from covering Enron in Houston, and Ben Hassan, making a rare cameo from his usual perch in Washington. I checked the window of Mort Brewer's office and, as always, our editor was there, phone clenched between ear and shoulder, scribbling on a yellow legal pad.

In 1998, I first heard a rumor that Mort Brewer was leaving *Harper's* to form a monthly magazine. He started giving interviews about the conglomerated state of media, singling out Rupert Murdoch's greasy empire but not sparing Hearst and Condé Nast's fine feelings. The media ecosystem was increasingly homogeneous, he said. It was time for a new, totally independent magazine.

He may have been on the back end of his career, but people listened to Mort. He'd trained half the journalists in New York at Columbia and given countless others their breaks, first at the *Nation* and later at *Harper's*. His reputation was spotless. It was said he'd thrown Bob Bartley from the *Wall Street Journal* down a set of stairs at a party in the '80s.

Mort's name brought journalistic integrity, literary sophistication, and money. Donors wanted to be involved with a magazine that would compete with his former employers. It would be a New Economy insurgency. A dot-com entrepreneur provided start-up cash—his site was some kind of cut-rate jewelry retailer, I think—and when his fortune vaporized, a real estate magnate's nephew stepped in. Now I know how precarious the magazine's money was, but at the time, it seemed as if anything Mort wanted in New York was just a seductive phone call away.

I remember receiving one of those calls myself. At the time, I was freelancing as a culture writer. I was surprised that Mort called at all, and even more so when the venerable editor lauded my work not only in the *New*

Republic and the *Village Voice* but also some old pieces for the *Seattle Post-Intelligencer*, where I'd cut my teeth after college.

"The piece you wrote about the igloo," he told me over the phone. "That was a breakthrough for you, wasn't it?"

For a few months, the *P-I* had run a weekend series of personal memoir pieces. I'd seized the chance to run a little deeper than my usual work, frivolous city-life stuff—Nordstrom execs who played high-stakes Texas hold 'em, Midwestern tourists who came for *Sleepless in Seattle*–themed weddings— that the editors commissioned in a futile attempt to seem as cool as the *Stranger* and *Seattle Weekly*, the city's alternative papers.

The memoir I wrote about the igloo inspired the best reception of anything I'd contributed to the *P-I*. Before that, my work profited off my easy generational access to a '90s attitude my older bosses found mystifying, as if sarcasm were a confusing new technology that only young people could operate. But Mort was right. With the igloo, I dug deeper. Along with a few of my snappier clippings, it's the piece I sent out when first trying to secure freelance work in New York.

"Thank you, Mr. Brewer."

"Not to disparage your cultural writing," he added. "That's why I'm calling today. I intend to have the best culture file in the country, Whitney. I want you to think about writing for the *Bystander*."

It was the first time I heard the name of the new magazine, and it instantly resonated. I attached myself to the word, like a logo.

If I was going to join Mort's staff, however, I had to elevate my work. Over my first two years at the magazine, I'd never stopped seeking to impress him. As I sat at my desk that day in December and transcribed the Daniel Eastham interview, the author's voice droning in my ears, I kept glancing over at Ross Briggs. His Enron piece was his second 12,000-word article of 2001. That's what I wanted to do, something that mattered, not a profile of a soon-to-be-midlist novelist, as if I were just an extension of the publisher's publicity arm. I wanted something to exceed what Mort expected of me, a story that would make him say, as he'd said about the igloo piece, "That's when you reached a new level."

3.

In the igloo, I went mute.

That's how the story began in the *Post-Intelligencer*.

Mom never liked to talk about the accident, but over the years, I extracted enough from her to plug the gaps in my memory. By the time I wrote about it for the *P-I*, it was as if I remembered it myself.

When I was five, Mom and Dad took me to visit my grandparents in a Pittsburgh suburb over Christmas. Of the many cousins also visiting, I was the youngest, only barely tolerated in their group, which included some kids from the neighborhood. None of them could've been older than ten or eleven, but at age five, they seemed to me like the keepers of the secrets of adulthood. I allowed them to do what they liked with me: paint me like a clown, put me in goal to face slapshots, send me downhill on a trash can lid, it didn't matter.

A few days before Christmas, my dad finally coaxed Mom away from the family to go to a bar in the city. He was always trying to get her to loosen up and quit organizing other people's time. While my grandparents dozed by the TV, I followed my cousins to the front yard of one of the neighborhood kids. It was late afternoon. The dead stalks in the garden speared the crusted snow. The kid wanted to show off his igloo. At least that's the word he used for a tunnel he'd burrowed into a tall snowbank that had been plowed off the street. He envisioned the igloo as a kind of clubhouse, but none of my cousins wanted to crawl into its cold black mouth. Whether I volunteered or was coerced, no one later confessed, and I don't remember; there wasn't any difference.

I see myself on hands and knees, wriggling into the hole, the attention of my cousins pushing me forward like a wind. In my purple snowsuit, it was a tight squeeze, but then the tunnel gave onto a shapeless cavern. The light of day faintly soaked the frozen walls, turning everything blue.

I lay on my stomach, I wrote, *and pressed my cheek to the floor. It was soothing. I thought of the older kids, too afraid to follow. I had a glimmering sense of my courage.*

And that's when the roof fell in. A heavy rush, all the air clapped out of me, and then only dark, and weight.

Later, Dad's family rallied around the cousins, protecting their version of events. The igloo simply collapsed, they said. One of my aunts went so far as to suggest I'd compromised the structure from within. But Mom said somebody must've gone up on the roof.

"Whitney!"

Very dimly, I remember someone shouting my name, how the sound struck my ears, warped by ice. I made no answer, dirty snow filled my mouth. I can taste the car exhaust, the rocks in my teeth.

"Whitney!"

My tongue went numb. I sucked the snow and swallowed, smothered, and that's how it started. At the outer edge of perception, aged five, I knew I would die, that death was the name of this coldness and this darkness, and how good it was simply to lie there, let it happen—seep into the snow.

There came the circling sound of sirens. Adults had converged and were digging me out. Soon they uncovered my body and I was hoisted from the snow. It fell from my mouth.

Only when Mom and Dad got home tipsy and asked me what happened did anybody realize I hadn't uttered a word since the accident. When they couldn't coax me to speak, they took me to the ER, but there wasn't any concussion, no problems with my chest or throat—just a blank where all my words had been.

You can see the change in photographs. Before the igloo, I seem energetic, natural. Unlike Mom, who always glanced away from the camera, as if the whites of her eyes were her most alluring feature, my tiny teeth shone, the blood-red orbs of my eyes open wide. But after, I look more like her, elusive, vague, as if the shutter always snapped at the moment I moved, blurring my face.

I stayed mute almost a year. I've asked myself a million times and still have no explanation. Or rather, I have too many—a crowd of expert opinions. Mom's solution was to entrust me to science. She took me to speech therapists, art therapists, play therapists, and surely this was when I acquired the basic skills of my career, as I lay waiting behind the mask of my face, observing each attempt to explain me. It was guilt for having caused so much fear. No, it was a desire to punish my parents for neglect. No again, it was an anxious reaction to my mother's expectations. No—

The sessions exhausted and confused me and didn't change anything. Mom was disappointed, and I remember the disappointment being trained on me, as if I weren't cooperating with the experts, as if I didn't want to get better. She'd lose all patience and start pleading, furious: "Say something, anything—Whitney, make a sound."

Dad would shelter me, that's what I remember. When Mom wasn't around, he'd ridicule the experts. It's okay, he'd tell me, just hang in there, take your time. There wasn't much worth saying anyway. As if to prove it, he began speaking to me in plain sound, subverbal, like a crude clay from which words were shaped. He'd make monkey talk in the grocery store or at the public pool, frustrating my mother, who found this whole approach unproductive. But I loved my constant jabbering companion—he made me comfortable being in the world. Sometimes he'd just hold me, his breath on my neck, muttering in our private language.

It seemed like nothing could unfreeze my tongue—not until the day at the hospital. Dad had always been a healthy, active man. He'd jog in the morning, play hockey in Burbank, dribble basketballs between my legs, a blood clot worming toward his heart.

He survived a few days after the attack, unresponsive in a hospital bed. Mom told me later that she debated bringing me to see him, but the doctors thought it might be worthwhile. I was told to put on my best black shoes, with the little gold buckles, and then Mom drove me to the hospital.

In the room, her hands on my shoulders, we approached the bed. I don't recall any tubes or machines, just his open eyes, the face of my companion. That's when I began to speak, softly at first, then louder—nonsense words, primordial sounds—Mom's hands springing off my shoulders. Thinking I was having a fit, she rushed me from the room. I never spoke to him again.

As I wrote in the *P-I*, in the piece Mort liked so much, I've come to believe that whatever voice I developed—whatever readers heard as their eyes moved over my words—carried forward from the hospital, when I reinvented speech from scratch.

But there's something else I didn't write, something I could never admit.

I wasn't the girl I'd been before, the girl who crawled into the igloo. Mom observed it first, a certain mischief on my tongue, a tendency to elaborate and embellish.

About a year after the hospital, a teacher called my house to report an obvious lie I'd told in class, something about witnessing a bank robbery downtown, an image off TV. Once I'd spoken the words, they seemed as good as memory. I loved everybody's reaction. Suddenly my classmates wanted to get close to me, near to the source of excitement. It was the seriousness with which I told the lie that apparently troubled my teacher. I overheard Mom explain to her on the phone, "It's a way she has, a creep toward fabrication."

That's what I came to call it, the creep, as if an unwelcome visitor were playing with my tongue.

It was only when I followed this passion for storytelling into journalism that I realized the scope of my problem. With excruciating clarity, I remember a professor at USC calling me into her office one day in junior year. My most recent assignment was on her desk. I'd written about a drunk driving accident involving some students. They'd survived, but the accident had sparked a broader discussion about the severity of campus drinking. The classmates I'd shown the assignment to all agreed I'd captured the terror of being in that car as the driver lost control.

"Heck of a story," said the professor.

"Thanks."

"So good, in fact, that I circled back on some of your reporting—like the minutes before the crash, and who said what, and when."

She slid the paper across her desk. It was streaked with red lines, the creep diagrammed.

"You can see where this is going," she added.

I had no words.

She got up and closed the door behind me, then sat down again. "What happened?"

My instinct was to spin another lie around the lie, but with a gulp, something cleared, and I broke. At first I covered my face. I'd heard Mom talk about crying students and assumed my professor would react with similar scorn, leaving me stranded with my weakness. But to my surprise, the professor came around the desk, kneeled in front of me, and held my hands.

"It's okay," she said, very softly. "Take your time."

I looked down at my hands, her thumbs stroking my skin.

"That's not me," I said. "I promise, that's not me."

I still wonder what my life would be like if she hadn't given me another chance.

The professor quietly placed me on academic probation, and I finished my time at USC actively fighting what had become an automatic, invisible force. From a certain viewpoint, my work declined—classmates weren't amazed by my stories anymore, nobody was drawn to be near me—but I was writing solid, factual journalism. It was a start.

After my confession in her office, the professor took me under her wing, and when I graduated, it was she who recommended me for the internship in Seattle.

"You'll have to claw your way into a permanent position," she told me. "It won't be easy. Make every clipping count."

When we shook hands, I felt her searching my eyes, seeking last traces of the creep.

"Get it right, Whitney."

I said, "I will."

4.

By the time I finished transcribing the Daniel Eastham interview, I'd worked my way into believing there might be a story in it after all. Maybe I could fold *Rogue Winter* into a survey of various cultural artifacts fatefully deprived of marketing velocity by the attacks. The essay could be a commentary on that velocity, its necessity, what that says. But then I felt myself projecting my own recent anxieties onto the subject, as if I could disguise my desire for a serious story with Eastham's desire for an audience. Only a truly bad article could emerge from such confusion.

Still, I stayed late at the *Bystander*, helping out where I could with captions and headlines. We'd recently lost a couple fact-checkers, and some of the interns had gone home for the holidays, so I also assisted with checking Ben's last-minute report on the Bonn Agreement.

Toward midnight, Mort emerged from his office with plastic cups and a case of cheap wine Lewis Lapham had sent him, along with a card on *Harper's* stationery: *Standing by, for your return . . .*

He stopped at my desk and poured out a cup.

"What have you been working on, Whitney?"

I told him I'd just interviewed Daniel Eastham.

"A fascinating writer."

Mort had such a bottomless appetite for reading, for all I knew he'd found time, in some inexplicable recess of the 24-hour day, to actually consume *Rogue Winter*.

"Anything there?" he said.

I wanted so badly to say yes. Mort inspired that in you—think harder, apply pressure, squeeze the story out. Already the details of the interview were coalescing into new, convenient images. Eastham's copy of *Rogue Winter* had been open on the table, but perhaps it was closed, off to the side a little, as if shunned. He'd only had two glasses of wine, but maybe he finished the bottle. The better story crept into my memory.

"No," I said, fighting it off, "there's nothing."

THE TOMAHAWK

1.

I'd planned to go home to Los Angeles for Christmas, but Mom was having a couple good months with her MS and wanted to spend the holidays on her friend's ranch in Arizona. She asked if I'd bought my ticket yet and I said no.

"Good," she said. "I'm glad it's okay."

I didn't really take days off—even the flu just meant less writing—and with all this extra time, I wanted to prep some projects for 2002. I couldn't endure another story meeting without a hit idea. But I didn't have any leads, and soon I knew I'd made a mistake by not getting out of the city. Subjects I would've once found appealing—movies, TV, books—held only a dim luster. I craved something else, something serious.

At loose ends, I was reminded of how I didn't have any real friends in New York. I had a name, a decent reputation, but no friends. Of course men were always around, and here and there they could tide me over. I felt at peace in the aging male ambience of my local bar, for instance, where I could watch the Lakers and make savage comments about the opposing team. But as for men my age, men of shared interests and maybe experience, I found it too exhausting to navigate their obvious desires, their readiness, if not necessarily eagerness, for sex, as if sex were higher than friendship.

And despite my best efforts, I'd never made female friends in New York. With depressing regularity, I arranged plans with women that followed the same abortive pattern. Take Annette, for example. Two, three, four times she canceled, citing something vague like *not feeling social.* It seemed as if the slightest obstacle, just a frigid gust of wind, would deprive Annette of this precious social feeling and set us back for weeks. When at last we got together, the night unfolded with a hyperactivity alien to my idea of friendship. We conversed with terrific vehemence, drinking very hard. Everything had a rushed, wasteful quality, and I came away feeling the night had functioned as a kind of purgative, a way of getting friendship over with. It generated no real intimacy. We never did it again, though when I'd run into her, Annette unfailingly said, "We should get together soon."

The sheer consistency of the pattern was almost funny, and I could feel a certain pride in how I continued to put myself out there, as if I were taking the high road. But then I was always lonely. In some crucial way I didn't understand, I remained the youngest cousin, ready to do something dumb for even a false sense of acceptance. I could almost cry at my hairdresser's tenderness, massaging shampoo into my scalp.

And so the call from Roland that empty winter holiday came as a relief. I knew what it meant. We only spoke when we found ourselves within a hundred miles of each other. This wasn't about friendship. Unless we could fuck, there was nothing to discuss.

"I've been transferred," he announced. "Just landed in Charleston and have to be in San Diego next week."

"You're coming to New York?"

"Actually, I was thinking, what if we hooked up in Colorado? You like to ski, Whitney?"

Among the scant details I knew of Roland's life, I recalled he grew up in a small Colorado city where his parents settled after arriving from Martinique. The name of the city had stuck with me: Arcade. Roland enlisted in the army out of high school and was deployed with NATO forces in Bosnia before being posted in Germany. I'd met him just before joining the *Bystander*, waiting for a train back to the city from Philadelphia, where he approached me on the platform. Getting picked up by a soldier felt like something from another era. He stayed with me for a weekend before he had to rejoin his comrades and ship out or whatever.

Roland had never heard of any of the places I wrote for. I tried explaining that even the president read the *New Republic*, and he was impressed without really caring. I'm a goner for simplicity. I could give myself to Roland without going through the complex strategizing I applied to my career. Someone else might take offense at how he always assumed I was single and ready, but he was always right, so who cares? After we'd fucked, it was always Roland who elaborated fantasies of our being together, spending more time, getting beneath the surface. I came away from our encounters with the impression of having broken his heart a little, until he'd call up out of the blue again.

"You're not scared to fly or anything, are you?" he asked.

"No, why?"

"Just the terrorism."

"Oh, just that," I said.

"Well, you could fly in for the weekend. I know all the slopes."

I told him I'd think about it, hung up, then booked a flight to Denver and called him back.

"Already?" he said, as if amazed by the freedom of civilians. "You mind booking the hotel too? I know good places, but if you could use your card."

"No problem."

"If it's too much, you can just tell me."

"I'm sure it's fine."

"And Whitney," he said, "could you book it for tomorrow, in my name?" He laughed. "I don't have a place to stay in Arcade anymore."

2.

Over the snowbound valley, the plane tilted in its final approach, and we touched down in Denver. I rented a black Jeep Cherokee and hit Interstate 25, a brush of charcoal in the sky. As the elevation rose, snow began to fall. It whirled over the highway and blew hard across the hills with their caps of rusted rock. I remember wondering why I didn't do this more often, get out into the world in a clean-smelling car.

I arrived in Arcade and found the Antlers hotel, its glass facade pink against the blue mountains. A million tons of toxic dust had scattered over Manhattan when the Towers fell, and the air of Arcade struck me as sweet and sticky with pine. I wanted to have a shower and I wanted to get laid.

A few guys in fatigues were lounging in the hotel lobby, not Roland. He'd said there was an air force base nearby. One of the men was trying to wrap a present with a copy of the *Arcade Ledger*, precut Scotch tape stuck to his lip.

When I told the concierge my name, he said he had a message for me and placed a scrap of paper on the counter.

There's been an accident, I read. *I'm at Ascension Hospital. Wait in the room. I'm not sure how long I'll be. Sorry.*

I read the message again and said, "There's nothing else?"

"I guess not."

I went up to the room and took a shower, a bit worried about Roland. Wrapped in a white bathrobe, white flakes sweeping the window, I looked over his gaping suitcase. He hadn't hung anything up or put anything in drawers. Even the collared shirts were still rolled together like towels.

I turned on CNN. The Shoe Bomber was under suicide watch in Massachusetts. Soon enough I started having work anxiety again, a sense of events swirling past, unobserved.

I got dressed and headed for the Jeep.

3.

The American flag didn't wave outside Ascension Hospital. It was draped on frozen elm branches that had grown too close to the pole, squirrels' nests balled up in the overgrowth. Ambulances were bouncing into the lot and a line had formed all the way out of the emergency room, the automatic doors hesitantly closing partway and then shuddering open again.

I saw Roland on a concrete bench by the entrance, smoking a cigarette and staring at the curb. It was the first time I'd seen him in a private moment. He looked stunned, overwhelmed. I stood before him and watched those wide eyes narrow as they climbed to my face. I knew I looked good: broad shoulders filling out the jacket, light-brown hair cut sharp below the ears, my high forehead mercifully unblemished. He got up and hugged me, close, cigarette still in his lips.

"Are you okay?" I said. "What's happened?"

"Oh, yeah. Nothing's wrong with me. It's Floella."

He must've seen me flinch, how behind my eyes the story unfolded from the name: another woman, a wife?

"My stepmom," he added.

Now he flicked the cigarette away.

"I should head back in," he said. "Why didn't you wait at the hotel? They have an Olympic swimming pool, like really Olympic, with an Olympic flag and everything."

"I wanted to see you," I said, looking over his shoulder at the people waiting outside the ER. "Can I come in?"

"I don't know," he said. "It's ugly."

"That's okay."

He didn't insist I leave. He wasn't hiding the situation, exactly, as it turned out. He just really hated Floella.

He didn't know where she came from, he told me—Texas someplace. Only ten years older than Roland, she'd met his father in Vegas and married him when he had about a year to live. His father had left her the bungalow in Roland's old neighborhood, but Floella had problems. Liquor was the least of it; she never could've blown everything on liquor. The real money-suck was Vegas. She'd get on a junket to the desert and come back broke. His father had gambled too, it was true, but he'd been a lucky guy. In just a few years, Floella lost the house, and that was the last Roland had heard of her.

"I never should've looked her up," he said. "I only did it out of loyalty to my dad. She was really good to him after the stroke, when I couldn't be there. The least I could do was check in when I came back. He would've wanted that."

Roland had asked after Floella in the old neighborhood, and the new tenants of the bungalow informed him that she was last seen in the Tomahawk, the poorest district of Arcade. She didn't have an address, they added, but he could try looking for a blue Chevrolet Celebrity.

He wasn't prepared for what he found down there. Poverty in the Tomahawk had always been bad, but for the first time in Roland's life, his hometown had seemed unfamiliar, like one of the combat zones he'd been sent into, armed to the teeth. It didn't matter whether a bomb blew up your house or the landlord kicked you out, the stooped shuffle of the homeless was the same in every country.

He spent the afternoon asking anyone who'd listen about Floella. When he finally got someone to talk, he heard she'd been bitten by Cristóbal's dog.

"I pictured like a little terrier chewing on a postman's leg," he said.

We were standing outside Floella's room, which was locked. With a cross expression, the nurse said she'd have to ask the doctor for clearance.

"But you can't stay for long," she said.

"We don't want to," Roland said.

"Dr. Massengale might be busy."

When it was clear we wouldn't leave, she finally went off.

Cristóbal was a dealer in the Tomahawk, Roland finished. Everyone down there knew him, and everyone knew not to cross his pit bull. The way Roland said it, you'd think Floella was just too stupid to internalize such basic information.

When the doctor turned the corner, I could tell he was surprised to see me.

"Dr. Massengale," Roland said. "This is my wife, Whitney."

I put my left hand in my pocket.

"You can't stay for long, I'm afraid," the doctor said, swiping his card for the door.

"I just want to say goodbye," said Roland, and I knew he meant for the last time.

I was struck by the size of the room, given the cramped quarters I'd seen everywhere else in the hospital. Its edges were shadowy, the lights dim. A half-dozen patients could be accommodated in here, but Floella was alone.

We approached the bed. One side of her face was shorn away. Crusted stitches held her scalp on like a swim cap. She'd lost her right eye, but the lid remained, a bit of wrinkled skin over the socket.

The worst was the damage to her throat. Dr. Massengale hovered over my shoulder as I took it in. Sprayed with teeth marks, the throat looked like a sleeve without an arm in it, hardly enough to join the torso to the head. I'd never seen injuries like that.

Cristóbal took the dog home, Roland told me, and hosed it down in his yard.

I turned away, nearly colliding with Dr. Massengale.

"Your mother-in-law is very fortunate," he said. "The artery was severed. She should've bled to death, right in the street."

"Why didn't she?"

"As I explained to your husband, when we understood she qualified for emergency research, she was the beneficiary of a clinical trial here at Ascension."

I'd never heard these words before. "Emergency research?"

"Well, if we'd known she had family, the protocol would've been different. But in her condition, you understand, the first responders made a determination. The trial saved her life."

"Trial," I repeated. "What sort of trial?"

The doctor's little eyes glimmered, like the idea was in his mind, fully formed. I knew he wanted to put it into words.

He smiled and asked us, "How long have you been married?"

"Not long," said Roland, who leaned toward Floella, whispered something in her ear, and came away from the bed.

As Dr. Massengale led us to the door, I noted the details: the locked room, the impatient nurse. There was something here.

"I'd like to know more about the trial," I said.

"I'm afraid I can't get into it now." Dr. Massengale jotted something on a pad. "But if you call me at this number tomorrow, we can chat."

He ripped off the page, handed it to me, and, with a salute to Roland, closed the door behind us.

4.

Roland knew how to fuck me. I could only come one way, eaten out slowly then pounded from behind. After that I'd do basically anything, for however long, but my way first.

Back at the Antlers, we got naked quick. Roland put so much effort into fucking me, his asshole got a little pursed, and I gave it one clean lick. At that he got so hard I thought his cock might break off, and I sucked it until he came over my tongue, onto my chin.

Then we ordered pizza and champagne and watched my Lakers crush the Nuggets. I could feel my heartbeat in my vagina. During timeouts, Roland spoke of Paris: the boulevards, the apartments, the Seine. I knew the beauty of his description came out of his disgust with the Tomahawk. He'd seen too many ruins for a guy his age.

Soon he was folding me into a fantasy of what we could do there, on the boulevards of Paris. Had I ever been to Paris?

"Yes," I said.

"Wouldn't it be amazing to live there?"

"I'm too New World."

"Even a beggar could be happy there," Roland said.

5.

The men I dated always described a certain limit in me, a check against intimacy. I think Keith was the last one I let in. After that, I contained a wall that no one ever scaled.

I'd met Keith on campus when I was a freshman at USC. He was wheat-pasting posters for a show his band was playing, and I caught his eye. It's not that I'm unattractive, though my style back then was unspeakably bad, but I remember feeling confused about what drew him to me. It would take time to realize that what enticed him wasn't beauty.

He had the unnaturally green eyes I'd come to believe, from various movies and books, to be portals into extrasensory dimensions, and he spoke with an ease, present in the moment, foreign to my horny male peers. I went to his show that night at Small's K.O. and passionately admired how he became lost in the songs, which weren't any good, his flat, hairless stomach thrusting against the keys.

We started seeing each other every day at his apartment in West Hollywood. I wasn't a virgin when I met him, but he made me realize I'd been having pretty indifferent sex. He set about learning my body with an intent that I thought sweet, and would make me come again and again, almost against my will. It was the first time sex surpassed the pleasure of masturbation.

After that night at Small's, I didn't go to his shows anymore. Keith was really trying to make it as a musician—what kind, he didn't seem to care— and so his bands were often just groups of strangers assembled by some semi-connected impresario trying to turn a buck. He kept a Sony Handycam in his apartment and would film audition tapes of himself playing one instrument or another.

Things started going badly after those first sex-comatose weeks. For one thing, we were always, always high. As soon as I walked in the door, before anything else, Keith would spark a joint, and when we woke up in the morning, he'd light one and watch me smoke it before class, as if it were my vitamins. Soon he was bringing back coke after the shows. We stayed up all night with it, and I'd have to give him endless blow jobs just to get him hard enough to fuck.

Around this time, I started wondering exactly how old Keith was. I guess part of the rock 'n' roll fantasy is that your talent gets discovered a little before, not a little after, its flowering, so I understood why he was sensitive about his age. But after a certain point, it seemed like he was actually hiding it. And he was. I snuck a look at his driver's license while he slept, only to discover that the man lazing there in the early morning, burned out on cocaine, dried semen on his leg, was twice my age.

Soon we were fighting all the time. I'd try breaking up with him, but he always found a way to talk me back, to turn my resolve into mere confusion. By the time we got done fighting, I was too stoned and exhausted to go home, and his bed would swallow me in cotton folds.

Over time, the fighting also ceased to be exciting. Finally I told Keith I was leaving for real. That's when he smiled, as if his face were slowly unzipping, and brought out the videotape.

"Before you make up your mind," he said, "you should know about this."

I think I already sensed what was on it, but I let him slide the tape into the VCR and saw myself snort a line off the bedside table and spread my ass for him. I watched as he shot come on my back. I still feel sick when I recall the delirious sound of my orgasm. It's horrible to admit, but these are the only permanent images I have of myself in the act of sex.

Keith had copies. He told me that almost offhand.

Not a single choice occurred to me. With the tape, he'd simply outmaneuvered me, so I stayed, I did the drugs, I took him in my body. Those are pitch-black weeks. I remember feeling like a skull staring out through skin, and sensed—with indifference—that this was the precondition of a suicide. I was nineteen years old.

As the weeks wore on, Keith started drinking with even more rock-star exaggeration. Maybe the remnant of his conscience was afflicting him, I don't know. One time, blacked out, he sleepwalked and took a piss in his acoustic guitar. I awoke to the sound of urine singing off the spruce. In the morning, he sat down to strum something and it sloshed out the hole.

There came a night when I stayed on campus until the facilities closed, trying to finish an assignment due the next day. The deadline had already been extended. In fact the prof had taken me aside, and I thought he might ask how I was doing, if something was wrong. The story was right there, ready for his merest inquiry. But all he did was tell me that if I couldn't wrap my head around the concept of a deadline, I had no future in journalism.

It was past two by the time I got to Keith's place in Hollywood. He didn't answer the buzzer, but someone at the lobby pay phone recognized me and let me in. The blood-red light of an Exit sign filled the hallway, where I found the door to Keith's apartment ajar. Keys dangled from the lock.

My first thought was I was going to find him with another girl. I wasn't sure how I'd react. I thought I'd probably just sit on the couch and wait for them to finish. But Keith was sprawled in bed, alone, still wearing his clothes. The standing lamp had toppled, all the shadows were misplaced. Yellow vomit covered his shirt, down to his crotch. It smelled of beer. I could see pepperoni.

I thought maybe he'd died a dumb rock 'n' roll death. But then I saw he was breathing. There was no relief when I realized this. It struck me powerfully that his death wouldn't have been shocking, or unwelcome, he meant nothing to me, all this meant nothing.

I crouched beside him, observing, and saw the chunks blocking his nostrils. I didn't pick them out. I left him in bed, not closing the door behind me, and caught the bus home.

I lived in a daze for weeks, hair coming out in the shower, but never heard from Keith again. Still, just his presence in Los Angeles, the existence of the tape, helped convince me to take the internship in Seattle after graduation. Even with the distance, it took a long time for the feeling to fade that he was watching me on a permanent loop.

6.

In the morning, Roland went to swim laps in the Olympic pool, and I took the opportunity to call Dr. Massengale. Yesterday he'd seemed barely able to restrain his enthusiasm, so after introducing myself as Floella Bailey's daughter-in-law, I thought he'd dive right in.

"How can I help you?"

"You said if I called, we could talk about the trial."

"Right." He cleared his throat. "I'm sorry, Whitney, but that's not going to be possible after all."

"Why not?"

"It's not within my authority to speak about the trial."

My instinct was to make it seem like I thought this was a normal shift in direction. I was, after all, just a Colorado soldier's wife.

"Well, is there anyone I could ask?"

"You'll have to talk to Rubicon."

"What's that?"

"Rubicon Tech," he said. "It's their trial."

"And you, what, administer it at Ascension?"

"You'll have to talk to Rubicon about what I do. Okay, Whitney?"

"Okay, Dr. Massengale."

I didn't think anyone would answer on a holiday weekend, but to my surprise, a receptionist picked up: "Rubicon Tech."

I explained I'd just spoken to Dr. Massengale, that I was the relative of a patient, and that he said I should call this number. She transferred me to a man with a lightly Southern accent.

"This is Baker Watt."

Again I explained who I was, why I was calling, though my curiosity was beginning to confuse me a little.

I said, "Dr. Massengale told me—"

"Dr. Massengale doesn't have the authority to speak for Rubicon."

"I don't understand."

"Who did you say you are again?"

"I'm related to a patient in your trial."

"And you have documentation to that effect?"

"Well, no."

"It's my understanding this was an extremely desperate situation," said Watt. "It's my understanding she'd been more or less abandoned by her family. Is that accurate?"

"We're still entitled to some explanation."

"I'm not sure that's true."

I could tell he was just going to bully me, the soldier's wife, so I said, "Mr. Watt, I'm a journalist." It's impossible to count how many rooms I've entered through the magic of these words. "Ever since I got to that hospital, I've been getting the runaround. The nurse didn't want us in the room, Dr. Massengale got us out of there ASAP. All I know is, Floella's part of a trial—otherwise she'd be dead—and you won't tell us the first thing about it."

I could almost hear his mind calculating.

"What did you say your name is again?"

"Whitney Chase."

"And what paper are you with?"

"The *Bystander*, in New York. It's a magazine."

"Never heard of it."

I named some other publications I'd written for. He hadn't heard of those either, but I guess they still sounded impressive.

"Why don't you come down to the office tomorrow morning," he said. "We'll get on the same page then."

Roland came through the door in Antlers flip-flops, a fleecy white towel over his shoulder. I was looking into his eyes when I said to Watt, "I'll be there."

Roland didn't ask who was on the phone. He showered off the chlorine, pulled on his fatigues, and said he had to take care of something.

"What?"

"Floella's car. It's still parked somewhere in the Tomahawk. I want to find it, see if she's got anything of my dad's in there. You don't need to come. We'll go skiing later."

But something had changed, and I realized I was looking at Roland with the journalistic eye. He was a lead.

7.

We drove around for almost an hour before finding the car. A blue Chevrolet Celebrity, all the glass smashed in, tires blown out. The trunk was open and looked like it had been on fire at some point, the metal misshapen and charred. Contents were scattered around the car—loose clothing mainly, and some black plastic electronics broken into bits. It was parked beside a lot that ran out toward pines, and in the shadows of the trees I could make out tents under blue tarp. Huddled around a fire, I saw cloaked men and women, like mounds.

Across the street stood small houses, curtains closed against the day. Snow ripped off the roofs in sudden squalls, fine as fiberglass. Two men in parkas watched us from the corner as Roland reached through the window of the car and opened the door. Beads of glass covered everything inside the Celebrity. I could hear them shift and spill as he rooted around.

"Fucking disgusting," he muttered.

One of the men stuffed something in the other's parka and they started walking in opposite directions.

Roland pounded the glove compartment until it fell open. He found some candy wrappers and an envelope full of photos. Still on all fours inside the car, he filed through the photos like a deck of cards, flicking the shots that included Floella onto the seat.

I picked one of these up, just to see what she'd looked like before the attack. It was her and Roland's father on their Vegas wedding day. In a baby-blue tux, white hair bunched about his ears, the groom looked more like the father of the young, energetic bride, her bouquet gripped too tight. I slipped the photo in my pocket.

Now a woman with an overcoat cinched around a hoodie came crunching over the plastic bits, her dirty woolen socks stuffed in sneakers. The dull daylight just caught the screwdriver she was clutching. I tapped Roland on the back.

"What're you doing in my car?" she said.

When Roland withdrew from the driver's side and she saw his fatigues, she hid the screwdriver behind her back. "Officer."

"This isn't your car," he said, "it's Floella's."

"Floella's gone. It's my car now."

Roland held out the envelope. "I just want these photos," he said. "She was married to my dad."

The woman eyed the envelope. He turned it over for her.

"That's fine."

"Can I ask you something?" I said. "Where did it happen, the attack?"

"Cristóbal's dog?" She gestured vaguely up the block.

"Did you see it?"

"Everybody saw it." She glanced at Roland. "There was nothing we could do."

"I really don't care," he said.

"We stayed with her, though, till the purple truck came."

"Purple truck?" I said.

"The ambulance."

The ambulances I'd seen at Ascension had been white like any others. But we were a long way from the hospital now. Maybe things were different in the Tomahawk.

"You want me to show you the place?" she said.

"No," Roland said, and gripped my arm.

I'd only felt his strength during sex. I resisted as he tried moving me along.

"Officer," she said, "I can keep the car?"

Roland made no reply. The woman started throwing clothes back in the Celebrity.

As we drove away, I saw burnt houses, the concrete stoops orphaned on empty lots, the ground black beneath the ice. A man was walking his dog along one scorched block, the animal straining the taut leather leash.

"You think that's Cristóbal?" I said.

Roland didn't slow down. I played with the photo in my pocket, trying to hold the details true and clear before they crept.

Already it felt like the day was ending. The sun had never really emerged and now a darkness seeped into the afternoon.

"We could still hit the slopes," Roland offered, "under the lights."

He'd been right. I should've stayed at the Antlers, done laps beneath the Olympic flag. In another life, I was taking a vacation.

I said, "That was my editor on the phone this morning. He wants me back in New York by tomorrow morning."

The leather wheel slid under his palms. I wondered if he knew I was lying. There was no show of surprise or disappointment, nothing of his usual sentimental cast when it came time for us to part. He'd just hit the wall in me, and it was done.

We said our goodbyes. I packed my things in the Jeep and told him I was going back through Denver. In truth, I drove around Arcade until I found another hotel.

It wasn't nearly as nice as the Antlers. The window of the room faced the brick of the building next door and the sheets felt grainy when I got into bed. But here, alone, I became excited, energetic. I leaned the photo of Floella's wedding day against the bedside lamp, turned on CNN, and wrote my notes.

8.

Rubicon Tech had offices in a building just outside downtown Arcade, its windows reflective gold glass. I could still see the glue marks from a previous tenant's logo beneath the sign in reception. *RUBICON* was rendered in leaning black text, underscored with red, blue, and green lines, to emphasize momentum, efficiency, and dynamism. The receptionist was listening to Jewel on a little CD player. After I signed in but before I could sit down, she'd summoned Baker Watt.

He insisted I call him Baker or Bake. A few inches shorter than me, his sideburns shaved up too high, he wore a dress shirt with vertical white-and-salmon stripes and a pair of loose-fit khakis. On the filing cabinets that flanked his desk, he displayed Ole Miss Rebels footballs.

Watt told me he'd been in Arcade five years—"Married a mountain woman," he half lamented—and with Rubicon Tech for two. They were a relatively new corporation, or rather a new offshoot of an old corporation.

"I think I owe you an apology," he said, once I had my notebook out. "I was pretty rude on the phone yesterday. Thing is, we get competitors calling all the time, trying everything they can to get something out of us. I thought you were another lame attempt. But I looked you up, read some of your work, and I think it's good stuff. I can always tell where the brains are."

"So you won't mind my asking a few questions."

"We've never had a journalist come around," he said. "To be perfectly honest, we're not really equipped to handle the exposure. We don't even have a director of communications. We've just been going about our business."

"And what is your business?"

"We save lives." He smiled. "And we're going to save a whole lot more."

"Like Floella's."

He glanced at a paper on his desk. "That's the subject at Ascension. Tell me something. Are you really related to her, Whitney?"

I leaned back from my notebook and said, "Not exactly."

"That's what I thought."

"I dated her stepson."

"I see."

"Someone told me she was picked up by a purple truck. Do you know what that's about?"

Watt brightened and said, "Common Dreams. That's the charity we sponsor. Now, if you wanted to write about Common Dreams, that would be terrific. They don't get enough recognition."

He slid a page across his desk. It was a map of Arcade, the districts shaded different colors. The Tomahawk was pale red.

"The Tomahawk is what we call a health care desert," Watt explained. "There just aren't services there for the people who need them most. Let's be honest, most of the time, an ambulance won't even bother answering calls to the Tomahawk. On the one hand, I can't blame them: people down there often refuse treatment, thinking they'll end up in jail. On the other hand, it's a disgrace. People die too often, and pointlessly—people like Floella. So we fund Common Dreams, and they service the places others won't."

"That's very generous."

"We take the idea of corporate citizenship seriously, Whitney. You don't last in the health industry without building trust."

"And Common Dreams," I said, "they're part of your trials?"

"In Floella's case, yes. But if you asked Common Dreams what their day-to-day job looks like, I wonder if they'd even mention Rubicon. As far as they're concerned, we just cut the checks."

I scratched it all into my notes, wishing I hadn't left my tape recorder in New York.

Watt eyed my notebook, hunched over the desk. "Look," he said, "I got on the phone last night and put the feelers out to the top brass. They're not completely, absolutely against talking about this in public. You can feel it on the tips of their tongues, you know? Whitney, how long are you staying here?"

"I'm supposed to fly back tomorrow."

"There's not a whole lot more I can tell you," he said. "If you could open up my head, you'd find more questions than answers. But I'm sick of the secrecy too. Even my wife wonders what we're doing. So I'm advocating hard for you, and I think it's going to happen. I think I'm going to get you an interview with Dr. Kriss."

THE SOLUTION

1.

The journalist from *Vice* shuts her copy of *The Complete Bystander*. The edge of daylight has traversed my office and she's settled into the interview. Now there's space for silence, like the one that falls over the two of us, the iPhone still recording on the desk.

"What made you want to be a journalist?" she asks.

It's the right question at the right time. I'm pleased to be drawn away from the *Bystander*, all the way back to Los Angeles.

"It's temperament before it's anything else," I answer. "My mom says I wanted to be a flight attendant. When I was ten or so, we took a plane to visit her relatives in Vancouver, and something about the nomadic life of flight attendants made a deep impression on me. I suppose I was attracted to drifting careers, where it's never certain where you'll be next week."

But my primal vision of journalism, I tell her, arrived in the form of my uncle's girlfriend. All my family had entered into sensible marriages by their early twenties, but my uncle remained a bachelor. He was a simple, handsome man, borderline beautiful, and he often punched above his weight with women, at least for a while, until they figured out the only thing he understood deeply was the roster of the Dodgers.

"For a couple months, when I was maybe eleven or twelve, he dated a reporter," I say. "He always brought new girlfriends over to see my mother, to show them off or gain approval. I remember the first time I saw her, it was like she'd touched down from another planet. She worked for KTLA, her hair immaculately sprayed. Everything she said struck me like a psychic blast, like there could be no higher form of life."

Even then, I could tell the reporter didn't like coming by our house. She didn't like Mom and me—at all. In our backyard, she'd sit beneath the jacaranda tree, drinking gin and soda, and smoking, watching us from behind her Ray-Bans. But I secretly adored her. I think I admired her contempt for us. It hinted at a world beyond the tightly controlled zone of my mother.

One day she rattled the ice in her glass at me. I looked back at the house, but Mom was in the kitchen with my uncle. I approached, wanting to scale the cold peak of her sophistication.

"Do you know what this is?" she asked, holding out the sweaty glass.

"Your glass."

"Will you fill it for me?"

"With what?"

"On the counter, there's a bright-blue bottle and a silver can. Give me this much from the bottle," she said, holding her pointer finger and thumb at maximum distance, "and a little splash from the can."

I took the glass in both hands and made for the sliding door. I looked down into the glass, so transfixed by spent lime on watery ice, the kiss of lipstick on the rim, that I didn't put one foot before the other, and tripped. The ice spewed over the earth and the glass fell and broke.

I glanced back at her, horrified. In this house, you didn't make mistakes like this, out of control. But she was smiling, inexplicably, and I started to laugh.

The door slid open: "Whitney."

Mom saw the broken glass and muttered, "Bimbo." I don't know which one of us she meant.

Not long after that, I saw the reporter on TV, on the steps of a courthouse. She wore a perfect deadpan, an objective face, personifying the public record. I tried to set my face like that and picture myself on assignment, the satellite dish unfolding from the news van like a huge venomous flower.

"From then on, I told people I was going to be a journalist."

"Then you went to USC," says the girl from *Vice*.

"Yes."

"But you didn't go into television?"

"No."

"And from USC you went to Seattle."

"Right."

"That seems strange," she says. "Most people would stay in LA, try to break into the local market."

"I wasn't proud of being from Los Angeles," I say, unable to avoid the correction—I hate when people say *LA*. "I think I internalized other people's stereotypes of my city—a criminal wasteland beneath that rosy haze of death. It seemed cooler to hate it there. But now, when I think back on my childhood, all I remember are wildflowers and succulents. I think you could rip a piece off those plants and heal any sort of wound."

I catch her glancing again at the bandage on my wrist.

The girl starts removing printouts of my old articles from her bag, some all the way back to the *Seattle Post-Intelligencer*. My tongue goes cold.

"I adore these pieces," she says. "Even in this early work, I see traces of your future style."

When I pick up one of the pages, I notice my thumbnail against the white of the paper. Blood still stains the underside. I'll have to hack the nail down to pick it out.

"There's something I want to say," I don't say. "I made this story up."

My professor at USC had sent me off to Seattle with that warning about having to work hard to vault from the internship to a permanent position. As my contract progressed, I realized she was right. No one was paying attention, let alone advocating to hire me. I'd resisted the creep all year, but the work only came out okay, nothing special, nothing that mattered.

So gradually, I began backsliding on my promise. While I don't count myself among the worst journalistic fabricators, like Stephen Glass or Jayson Blair, I allowed the creep to finesse the edges, correct the fine connective tissues, and give the stories an artfulness real life never had. Sometimes a character had to be invented, but it was always a composite character, a merging of true elements in a more perfect vessel, and that's as far as it went.

I learned how to cover my tracks, so what happened in J-school wouldn't happen again. If an editor asked for my notes, I'd carefully comb through to make sure they reflected what was in the story. If I needed a particular detail, for instance, I'd dig deep for some true but irrelevant observations I hadn't written down at the time, then manufacture a page that tucked my invention in among those observations. Once, I spilled coffee across the margin where a source's number had been written, so I said—the digits washed away in brown. After enough practice it became like an instinct, or a method, or an addiction, and the further I traveled down the path, the more the secret seemed unspeakable. I lived in the shadow of the creep.

Sure enough, my stories started attracting positive attention. People at the *P-I* talked about how much my work had improved. I became a writer of promise. I got offered a position, and eventually built a portfolio big enough to make a go of freelancing in New York.

It was in New York that I discovered my niche in culture. I found that if I limited myself to frivolous subjects—books, music, movies—I could hold the story firmly in place. Perhaps I misread a novel, or let my analysis of some lyrics run amok, or overburdened the screen with my own pet theories, but it could never be said that I was wrong about the facts. There were no facts. Culture wasn't a current event with its own objective reality, it was a protean phenomenon, a set of omens available for any half-decent writer's elucidation. Soon the creep seemed to disappear. I told myself I'd just been writing about the wrong things.

But I knew I had to stay vigilant. That was especially true when I strayed near hard reporting. The journalist from *Vice* wants to talk about my profile of Courtney Love, for example. It appeared in the *Village Voice* in 1998, and I got a call from Love's publicist shortly after publication.

"It's just a small thing," she said, "but Courtney's curious. This scene where you're in the East Village."

Love had ditched her entourage and we'd wandered until she found a store she'd heard about, some nameless spot that sold T-shirts screen-printed with Dadaist collages. Soon a man entered the shop in neon-yellow Skechers, carrying a clipboard. He started posing questions to the girl working there— like what bands she liked, what restaurants, what shops.

Love called the guy a trendspotter, sent to suck young blood for some corporation, and was pissed. I used the scene as a springboard to discuss her obsession with selling out, a theme she'd been confronting head-on in the aftermath of her role in *The People vs. Larry Flynt*.

"In the piece," said the publicist, "you say Courtney confronted this guy, really scared the shit out of him. It's a hilarious moment, perfectly written."

"Yes, thank you."

"But Courtney doesn't remember it going down like that."

"That's funny," I said. "What does she say?"

"Just that she talked to you about the guy, but that she never said a word to him."

"I don't understand. Does she not like it?"

"No, she does. We all do. It's just, she doesn't remember it like that, so she was wondering if you could—"

"I don't know what to tell you."

"You have fact-checkers and stuff, yeah?"

"Absolutely," I said. "I can have my notes photocopied—"

"No, that's alright, I trust you." She yawned. "Between you and me, I'm just crossing off these queries she gave me. It's a whole list. She reads everything, you know, watches everything."

"I understand."

"Thanks, Whitney. Really great piece."

I remember poring over my notes, panicked, and the weird thing was that I couldn't find the fabrications. I thought back on the scene I'd written and the memory seemed to wobble. It was like the creep had retreated to a hidden position, but still subverted everything.

"This is the best thing ever written on Courtney Love," says the journalist from *Vice*.

"Oh, that," I want to tell her, handing back the page. "I made that up."

And as I'd learn, a public lie is never really over.

2.

By the time I got back to New York, I had a message from Baker Watt. Good news, he said. I'd been granted an interview with Dr. Eva Kriss. She'd be in New York next week for meetings with Rubicon's parent company.

"I'm really excited for you to meet her," he said on the voice mail. "She's got the brains to answer anything."

I arrived at the *Bystander* office with an excitement that made me impatient. The story meeting was scheduled for tomorrow, but I couldn't wait. I knocked on the door of Mort's office and he called me in.

A man I didn't recognize was sitting across from him.

"This is Lane Porter," said Mort, "our new fact-checker."

When he stood up, Lane rose to about my chin, with bushy orange hair and a dense orange beard. He wore a cherry-red bow tie and navy blazer, and his blond lashes fluttered as he offered a small, soft hand.

"Lane comes to us from *Vanity Fair*," Mort said, "very highly recommended."

"Nice to meet you," I said.

"It's an honor," said Lane. "I've admired your work for a long time."

"That's very gratifying."

"We were just wrapping up here," Mort said, and he looked to Lane. "Got everything you need?"

"I think so."

"We're a tight-knit group, so pitch in where you can. We always need a johnny-on-the-spot with research. When you're not fact-checking, feel free to float around, okay?"

"Okay, Mr. Brewer."

"And bring me some mint from that garden of yours. I want to make tea."

"I certainly will," said Lane. "It's good to meet you, Whitney."

"You too," I said.

He shut the door behind him.

Now that I was in front of my editor, I wondered where to start. My eyes roamed over the cedar bookshelves where, among all the atlases and dictionaries, Mort kept a caricature of Nixon, a postcard from Václav Havel, a photo of Katharine Graham at the Black and White Ball.

"So what's up?" he said.

"I think I've got something."

I brought out my notes and began telling him about Arcade. Mort liked a story that began between the coasts. As I described Floella's accident, the scene at Ascension, my meeting with Rubicon, I knew I had him. His eyes were looking past me, out to where the story curved like a beautiful landscape.

"This could be a medical breakthrough, Mort."

I wanted uncritical enthusiasm, but when I finished, he only rocked in his chair and stared at me. I'd never detected chauvinism in Mort, but now he seemed to appraise me almost physically.

He said, "You're ready for this?"

I felt two cold drops of sweat leave my armpits and scurry down my sides. "Why not?"

"It's a very different kind of story for you. Would you feel more comfortable teaming up with someone?"

I could easily imagine one of my more experienced colleagues commandeering the story. But I'd brought it back from the heartland myself, it was mine.

"No," I said, "I want this one, Mort."

He observed me, deciding, then stabbed the yellow pad with his pen. "Alright," he said. "Follow it, Whitney, and tell me what you need, money-wise."

In the life of a magazine writer, there are no sweeter words.

"We've had happy news," he said. "An investor renewed for another year. We're flush. I'll miss you on the culture file, but it sounds like you've got to pursue this. In the meantime, do me a favor and chip in copy where you can."

"You got it."

"And ask for help if you need it, okay?"

"Okay."

He extended his hand across the desk. "You're making me a promise."

"I am."

And we shook.

"Very exciting, Whitney. Very nice."

I floated back to my desk. I had to research Dr. Kriss before the interview, I had to learn what I could about Rubicon, and it would be nice to check in with Dr. Massengale, at Ascension Hospital, for news of Floella. Once I knew more about the trial, he would probably be candid with me.

While I was compiling the to-do list, Lane Porter's orange head dawned over my cubicle.

"Can I help with anything, Whitney?"

"Not at the moment."

"How about a cup of coffee?"

"Maybe later."

With a smile, the fact-checker was gone.

3.

Over the coming days, I printed off articles about Rubicon Tech and took them to the Donut Shop. That was a place on 8th I liked for no better reason than it was the first place I'd gone after starting at the *Bystander*. Everything you could buy there was bad, the coffee harsh, the donuts dry, the tomato slices stiff as Frisbees in the sandwiches, but it had such a supreme basicness, it felt like the donut shop you'd find in a perfect democracy. I'd order one large coffee and one shredded coconut and sit at a table, its red laminate flaking at the edges, feeling totally serene in everlasting fluorescence.

Rubicon Tech was a subsidiary of Inland Medical, a mammoth corporation that had been part of American health care since the Second World War. The largest cache of articles on Inland concerned their troubles in the late '80s. The corporation manufactured medication for slowing the advent of AIDS in HIV-positive people, and came under fire for the exorbitant price of the drugs. I found dozens of pieces about the protests, photos of ACT UP activists hanging pink triangles, *SILENCE=DEATH*, on Inland's corporate headquarters on 3rd. I guess the bad publicity taught Inland what Baker Watt called corporate citizenship.

Only one piece in *Medical Businessweek* covered Rubicon Tech's quiet establishment in 1998, dubbing it "the high-risk, high-reward incubator of Inland Medical." The article had quoted Kenneth Sample, the CEO of Rubicon, who'd come out of retirement to helm the enterprise for Inland:

"If someone had asked me to run just any start-up biotech company, I wouldn't have been interested. But we might have the best doctors in the world."

I assumed he thought Dr. Eva Kriss was one of them—"she has the brains to answer anything," Baker Watt had said—but there was next to nothing on her in the public record. I found an archived website from when she'd taught at Duke in '94. It said she'd earned her medical degree at the University of Washington and had been a resident in emergency medicine at the University of Pittsburgh and Boston Children's Hospital before enlisting in the navy in 1990. Then she'd been deployed in Desert Storm. The lone photo I found was from a scanned navy brochure. Dr. Kriss wore fatigues and a surgical mask, blond hair pulled back from her forehead. The caption identified her as being assigned to the USNS *Mercy*, which had been positioned off the coast of Saudi Arabia. "Every member of the *Mercy*'s crew has been blood-typed," said the brochure. "The crew can function as a walking blood bank at a moment's notice."

After the Duke appointment, news of Dr. Kriss ran dry. I could only assume that at some point she'd been headhunted for Rubicon Tech, but exactly why they wanted her, what made her one of the world's best doctors, wasn't on the record.

I considered putting Lane Porter on the case. He'd unpacked a row of action figures on his desk—shirtless he-men, ghoulish villains—and I watched him flit around the office like a bumblebee, pollinating stories with freshly gathered facts. My *Bystander* colleagues seemed to find him useful. It was sort of cute how he worked behind those toys and then sprang up with some complex question unraveled. Every now and then he'd come by my desk and ask if I needed anything, and the offer was tempting. But I hadn't told anyone except Mort what I was following, and didn't want to jinx it.

In the meantime, I called Dr. Massengale a few times, but it kept going to a robot that intoned his phone number and then said his inbox was full.

When I finally called the main switchboard at Ascension Hospital and asked for him, I was told he'd been reassigned.

4.

It surprised me to hear that Dr. Kriss wanted to meet in a Midtown Irish bar. I had every reason to believe Rubicon had reassigned Massengale just for talking to me, so I'd expected some corporate cloister built for secrecy. I'd forgotten it was possible for someone like Dr. Kriss simply to be kind of lame and not know anywhere good to meet in the city.

It was January, the sun glaring from a bald sky, and it took my eyes a moment to adjust to the bar's interior, sticky with beer. Dr. Kriss was the only one in there. She'd arrived early and eaten a burger. The big white plate sat between us through the interview, smeared with ketchup.

The doctor pulled out the headphones of her iPod and placed the all-white object beside the plate. She seemed about a decade older than me, her eyes like light passing through cola, her blond hair dark, as if some soot had been rubbed in.

When I took my jacket off, she said, "We're twins."

We'd both worn white blouses and red skirts. I smiled, a little uncomfortable with the coordinated look, and asked if I could set the tape recorder running, an ungainly black box beside the iPod. You can often detect a flicker of hesitation when the tape starts and the subject knows they're being recorded, but she just nodded as her voice ran on.

She had her laboratory in Arcade, she said, but had just come from Florida, a city called Retreat, to meet with executives at Inland Medical.

"I'll be honest with you, Whitney, my superiors are pretty nervous about this interview. They'd hoped I'd finish my trials before we started bringing in the media. But I read your stuff, and the fact that someone who profiled

Madonna wants to write about me and my work—let's just say I pressed them for permission. I can fit all her albums on here."

She tapped the iPod.

"What's your favorite?" I asked.

"*Ray of Light.*"

Anyway, she went on, if her superiors thought they could keep the media out, they were being naive.

"But there's an understandable need for discretion," she said, "and I should warn you, if you're going to do this story, you'll have to get comfortable working around corporate protocols. Rubicon protects its trade secrets. Every medical technology company in the world wants what we have."

"And what do you have?" I asked.

"You're ready?"

"Sure."

It was like a line she'd always wanted to say: "We have all the blood in the world."

Later, I'd transcribe her word for word.

"Every two seconds, someone needs blood in this country," she said. "The stats are terrifying. About 40 percent of Americans could donate, but less than 10 percent do. Do you?"

A brief silence as I shook my head.

"That leaves us with about seventeen thousand preventable deaths each year. That's forty-six people per day lost because of a lack of blood, and we're only talking about the US. We've taken to calling it the permanent drought. So many have tried, and failed, to find a solution."

"And you have?"

She nodded.

"What is it?"

"Do you have a scientific background, Whitney?"

"Some," I said, though that wasn't really true. Mom had taught organic chemistry, that's all.

"Nanometer-sized dendrites," said Dr. Kriss, "a perfect equivalent to natural hemoglobin in terms of O_2 and CO_2 transport. The solution maintains arterial blood pressure and pH, and has intravascular persistence. It won't overload the reticuloendothelial system, won't react with oxygen. And it's stable at room temperature, of course."

When she saw my pen had stopped moving and I was just watching her lips, she laughed and said, "It's plastic, basically."

"Plastic blood."

"Put very, very simply."

"And it works?"

"We wouldn't be in the final stage of the trial if it didn't. We've jumped through a million hoops to get here. Your interest was sparked by a trial subject, right?"

"Yes," I said. "Floella Bailey."

Dr. Kriss reached for a laptop bag, withdrew a manila folder, and dropped a pair of purple-framed reading glasses on her nose.

"I brought her case file. My understanding is that her throat was severely traumatized, and the artery was severed."

I remembered how the dog's teeth had twisted the flesh. "It was horrible."

Dr. Kriss made a sympathetic clucking sound. "The transfusion was performed before she got to the hospital," she said.

"By Common Dreams."

"That's right." She licked her thumb and turned the page. "Were it not for their intervention, Floella would've died of blood loss before arriving at Ascension. As it stands, she's still in critical condition, but the solution is flowing."

"You think this will be possible with all those people," I asked, "all seventeen thousand?"

"It will never be possible to get there in time all the time. But we're going to save millions of lives."

"And make millions of dollars."

"Well"—at last her focus broke from the page—"that's what my bosses think, and that's why they slap these protections on everything we do. But would you believe me if I said I don't care about the money?" Before I could respond, she said, "Don't answer, sorry. It doesn't matter."

Dr. Kriss took the napkin, already balled up, from the plate. She unfolded it and balled it up again.

"I was awake half the night thinking about what I'd tell you," she said. "Not about the solution—talking science is easy—but about myself. It's the first time I've seriously considered how to present my life alongside my work, you know, what story to tell. And then I started going through your articles. Like I said, I was impressed, so I kept going back and back, all the way to some of your earliest work. You're from Seattle?"

"Los Angeles," I said, "but I did an internship in Seattle."

"The *Post-Intelligencer*, right?"

I made a pointless note, underlined it twice. "That's right."

"I found the piece about the igloo," she said. "It was very moving. It's incredible what you went through."

I didn't want this to become about me. "Everything turned out okay," I said.

"There's a passage I kept going back to. It's at the end, after you've described your father in the hospital, how the sight of him strangely opened up your speech again. You talk about how unlikely it seems that you're a writer now, that you made a profession from your voice. But it's all tinged with this sadness, this regret, that you lost the last year of your father's life, like you just assumed he'd still be there when you were ready to speak again. That piece was very personal for you, wasn't it?"

I said yes, it was, and she said, "Then I want to say something personal too. Is that okay?"

"Of course. Please, go on."

She'd grown up poor in the Pacific Northwest, she began, mostly because her father was bad with money, hilariously bad. He'd head off to get groceries with the last of their savings and come home with some frivolous gift. And so she and her mother would starve, but they'd starve in brand-new scarves, or with a crystal fixture shining over the table. They'd starve in love with him.

"He could make you laugh so hard, you didn't remember you'd eaten nothing but peanut butter for days, or that your shoes were too small, or that the Christmas tree had been hacked from the side of the interstate."

But while Dr. Kriss was on scholarship, studying medicine at the University of Washington, he came down with a degenerative disease.

"MS?" I asked.

"We never found out. If we'd had more money, we could've had better doctors, a clear diagnosis maybe. I'm still not sure."

He'd have agonizing abdominal pain that didn't respond to conventional treatment, she explained. Then it would migrate to his throat and he couldn't speak, as if his breath were coming through a chewed-up plastic straw. His whole body racked with fever, he'd be bedridden for days.

She told me how a young Eva Kriss undertook to penetrate the mystery. He'd always told her she was the best, the brainiest. She skipped class to study him, she stayed up through the night, she dug obscure texts out of the library, seeking anything, ancient or modern, that resembled his symptoms.

"But nothing worked," she said. "And one day, he was gone." She looked down at Floella's case file and seemed to read the words: "Something went out of my life."

Later, as I transcribed the interview, the hiss of the tape seemed to seep into the foreground, as if a shroud had been thrown around the two of us.

"Do you understand?" she said.

"Yes."

"Then understand this. I made him a promise, a long time ago, to reach for the very highest. You could say the impetus behind my whole career has been to make good on that promise. Because in his case, it wasn't enough. I wasn't enough." She looked down, embarrassed by the tears in her eyes.

"It's okay," I said.

Since his death, she told me, she'd made a vow to herself: the moment a patient awakens, she'll be there, the doctor, to tell them they're fine, that it all went well, everything is okay.

"I can see him in their faces," she said, "and it's like I have those last weeks back again, and I'm enough, smart enough and good enough, to find the solution he needs."

There are times when a journalist only knows in retrospect, through a close inspection of the transcript, that a cohesive story will emerge. And then there are times like this, when even in the moment the journalist knows what the story will be, as though written in advance.

I glanced at the recorder. The white spokes turned.

When our time ran out, I paid for her burger and she volunteered the invitation I'd hoped for.

"Come to Retreat," she said. "Don't just write up what you have and what you saw in Arcade. I pushed my bosses, and they've authorized me to let you observe the trial, step by step."

We shook hands. Dr. Kriss popped in the iPod earbuds. I thanked her, told her I'd be there, definitely.

She said, "We're going to make a great story together."

THE TRIAL

1.

"In those months immediately after 9/11," I tell the journalist from *Vice*, "you could sometimes observe an unusual ceasefire with the Bush adminis- tration, even in the offices of the *Bystander*, where everyone voted Gore, maybe Nader. The guy who'd spoken of nothing but butterfly ballots all year was silenced when Bush threw the opening pitch at Yankee Stadium and delivered a perfect strike."

She's asked what it was like at the magazine in the run-up to the invasion of Iraq, and first I want her to understand this weird interlude. She looks like she was still in junior high in September 2001, so her entire political education was conditioned by the bald rapaciousness of the Bush years. It might be impossible for her to grasp those tender in-between months, after the attacks and before the invasion, when the world actually liked us, pitied us, and wanted us to heal. Can she imagine the goodwill we enjoyed then, so much that it was almost as if the world had forgotten Vietnam? Looking back, I'm reminded of those fugitive minutes after the first plane hit, when everyone thought it was an accident, like it had a chance to be an accident until the second plane soared into the picture.

In January 2002, I tell her, I watched the State of the Union Address with my colleagues at the *Bystander* office. The squandering of international goodwill was swift and truly American. After praising the troops in Afghanistan and pledging that terrorists wouldn't escape, Bush addressed a broader enemy.

"Our cause is just," we watched him say. "And it continues."

Continues?

The jaw of war gaped open, and suddenly it wasn't just about terrorists, but states—the Axis of Evil.

"After that night," I say, "Iraq seemed like all anyone talked about."

As the winter of 2002 wore on, Mort's office transformed into a kind of geopolitical salon, with writers dropping in from the *New York Times* and the *Nation*, *Vanity Fair* and *Foreign Affairs*, to debate the prospect of war. It was like a macho smoking club. You could only dimly perceive the men through a nicotine haze, but you could hear them, as cool debate devolved into shouts. Then the men would burst from Mort's office, dazed and furious, like a gang of hockey goons who'd thrashed each other on the ice.

The girl from *Vice* smirks and makes a note.

"Do you remember Daniel Pearl?" I ask.

She shakes her head.

He was a reporter with the *Wall Street Journal*, I explain, who was kidnapped in Pakistan. Mort took his abduction as a personal attack. The kidnappers released a photo of Pearl holding up a newspaper, and Mort taped it to his office door. He was horrified by this kind of extremism, but never on the fence about the war. The *Bystander* immediately assumed a posture of dissent.

Still, there was no denying Mort relished the atmosphere of combat. It must've taken him back to the '60s, when everyone's career got made in the heat of the moment.

"I think he believed objecting to war in the most strenuous possible terms would cement the legacy of the *Bystander*," I tell her, "but I'm willing to wager the countless pieces we ran about Iraq will be among the least-read in this book."

"I admit I couldn't get through them all."

"They're of sociological interest only."

"Yeah," she says. "I know how the story turns out."

2.

When I arranged my trip to Retreat, Mort authorized my expenses, but he didn't take the sustained interest in my story that I wanted. Everything with him had become WMDs, Al Qaeda links, oil reserves.

In my corner of the office, I dove into what Dr. Kriss had sketched in the interview. I began by researching the history of artificial blood. I read about the experiments of T. Gaillard Thomas, an eminent nineteenth-century gynecologist who'd devised the method of *lacteal injections*: intravenous infusions of cow's milk. Dr. Thomas recorded three cases in which he injected a patient with eight ounces of milk. One survived, two died, and Dr. Thomas concluded that in order to be successful, the injections should be made with fresh, not settled, milk. No one developed his theory any further.

In the 1950s, the navy treated some anemic soldiers with a hemoglobin solution, resulting in everything from renal problems to what researchers called *untoward side effects*. And most recently, a corporate developer of *highly purified bovine hemoglobin*, a bizarre echo of Dr. Thomas's milk experiments, canceled their trials after 50 percent of the subjects died, having developed various pulmonary, cardiovascular, and neurologic dysfunctions.

I phoned an expert at Washington University in St. Louis and told him I was working on a piece about artificial blood. We roamed over the historical attempts before he told me, "It's the Holy Grail of medical science."

I underlined the quote in my notes.

"The words 'artificial blood' don't really describe the current candidates," he continued. "At best, they have only limited applications, like carrying and delivering oxygen or augmenting blood volume. We're years away from something like true artificial blood." When I didn't immediately answer, he added, "Unless you know something I don't."

It was taking so much time to reverse-engineer scientific expertise that I asked one of the unpaid interns to research Rubicon Tech. When all he gave me was a sophomoric scrape of the Internet, I finally enlisted Lane, the new fact-checker. The other *Bystander* writers gave him such rave reviews, it felt foolish to let the resource go to waste.

A day before my flight to Florida, Lane caught me by the elevator. There was such a giddiness about him, he actually rocked on his heels. "I've got something for you."

"I'm headed to lunch."

"Can I join?"

A little more than I didn't want to be friendly, I didn't want to be rude, so I invited him to the Donut Shop. I ordered a coffee and one of their $1.75 BLTs. I don't know what Lane ordered, but it arrived as gnarled corn beef and a pool of relish on a kaiser.

"What's with this place?" he asked.

"It's my spot."

Lane scraped the relish off with a plastic knife and said, "Any particular reason?"

"Its total indifference to self-improvement."

"Have you ever been to BurritOasis?"

"No."

"Next time, my treat."

I said, "Thanks for looking into Rubicon."

He'd dismantled his kaiser and started carving up the corned beef.

"The subject is a bit of a departure for you," he said. "Corporate medicine, serious stuff."

"That's true."

"I've only ever seen you cover culture, in the *New Republic* and the *Voice*, except for a couple things for the *Post-Intelligencer* in Seattle."

I revealed more surprise than I wanted to.

"I love your writing, Whitney, I've read every last word. I think you have a fascinating mind."

I really don't respond well to flattery, unless it comes from an editor in writing. I kept my head down, chewing through the rough white bread and jerky-like bacon. I popped a fallen scrap of iceberg lettuce in my mouth and it broke like a potato chip.

"So what have you got for me?"

"Well, there isn't a whole lot out there," he said. "But I think I found something that suggests a minor human resources problem."

Lane swept sandy crumbs off the table and laid the pages out. He'd printed them off the website of the *Retreat Examiner*, the city's local paper. Last year, the *Examiner* had run a perfunctory article about the opening of Rubicon's office and the arrival of the Common Dreams charity, *which aims to serve our most downtrodden citizens*. In the Web 2.0 pivot every newspaper attempted in those years, the *Examiner* posted the article on their Community Forum and invited comment. Lane said no one had commented on the Rubicon item for months, until one user, SunshineRay, started using it to vent about the company.

> *I worked as a Jr. Technician and let me tell you R-con*
> *is 1000x worse than Enron*

> *Why won't the Examiner ask Real Questions???*

Klausmeyer is on the take

What you don't know could FILL A BOOK!

SunshineRay posted a dozen comments of this variety, his only contribution to the *Examiner* forum, Lane reported.

"Interesting," I said. And it was. So far, I hadn't read a bad word about Rubicon.

Lane pulled a slip of paper from his pocket. "I went a little deeper, and found the e-mail associated with the username: rrix@aol.com. Turns out there's a Raymond Rix who lives on Snowy Egret Place, in Retreat. If it's the same guy, he could be a good source for you."

"He sounds like a crank."

"Some local color, then."

Lane reclined in his seat, the lowest buttons of his shirt distressed against his gut.

"You know, I've always been curious," he said. "Why Seattle?"

I gathered the pages together and told him I should really get back.

Things were strangely quiet at the office. When I asked what was going on, someone told me the *Wall Street Journal* reporter Daniel Pearl was dead. His killers had released a video on the Internet called "The Slaughter of the Spy-Journalist, the Jew Daniel Pearl." They had him recite some prepared lines before they sawed through his neck and held his decapitated head up by the hair.

Mort and a few other writers had watched it. Now they sat huddled together, mute.

That crime was the first I can remember of—for lack of a better word—a new genre: the Western journalist on his knees, reciting propaganda before an online decapitation. Later, the image would become almost commonplace, orange jumpsuits on the burning sand, but the Pearl video came with the shock of the new. The murder wasn't by a stray bullet. It was deliberate, meaningful, like the war zone had no border and journalists were all unwitting soldiers—unarmed, fair game.

When I boarded the plane to Tampa the next day, I felt a new fear. I told myself it was just anxiety about the reporting, the dread of not nailing a story outside my expertise, but I kept thinking about Pearl, how the day of his capture began like any other on the job.

3.

I awakened to the silver wing cutting clouds over blue-green water, and then I was in Tampa. After renting a Ford Escape, I headed down the coast. I wondered if this was gator country, if I should keep an eye out. All I knew about alligators was you're supposed to run away in a zigzag.

I wasn't impressed by my first sight of Retreat, despite the city's placement on the water. The homes were shady and sunken, the palms hairy and unkempt. I passed through downtown and it didn't boast a building over four stories, some vultures rotating above it.

Once I stepped outside the Escape's AC, the air pumped down my throat like hot soup. My hair went greasy, my clothes stuck, and I had to wipe the sweat off my eyebrows before knocking on the bungalow's door.

I'd found the sublet in the *Retreat Examiner* classifieds. It was cheaper to rent it for a month than to take a hotel room for ten days, and anyway, I didn't relish the thought of a few weeks eating at restaurants and sleeping in recycled air. I planned to be here well into March, and the reporters I knew who spent a long time on the road were always in ruinous condition.

The house belonged to a middle-aged woman named Candy who'd gone to Chicago for the month to sit with an ailing brother. Her son-in-law was the one who opened the door, then gave me the keys and a perfunctory tour.

It wasn't much to speak of, just a few rooms and a backyard of chickweed. Weirdly, Candy had hung mirrors on all the walls, so every time I turned a corner, I spooked myself.

I unpacked my clothes. When I profiled a celebrity, I usually wanted to appear at least vaguely in their milieu, and I'd decided to apply the same tactic to Retreat. I'd brought my most conservative items, plus a Tampa Bay Devil Rays ball cap I'd picked up in Times Square.

Dr. Kriss had invited me for a briefing at Ocean General, the local hospital where Rubicon was conducting the trial. I took a cool shower and was heading for the Escape when a dog caught my eye. It came limping up the block, hind legs rigid, a pale tongue drooping out one side of its mouth. I looked around, but there was no one on the street, no obvious owner. The dog paused in front of me, crusty eyes twitching. The sun flogged the two of us. I didn't want to be late to meet Dr. Kriss, but I couldn't just leave the dog like that. I gathered her into my arms and headed up the path to the back-yard. The dog was light and pliant, bones jutting out. I set her down beneath the Spanish moss and she watched me trot back to the bungalow for a bowl of water.

She lapped it eagerly. She wasn't wearing a collar, and so, while I generally don't like calling animal rescue—the first step toward the crematorium—it wasn't my place to keep a dog here. I found the number in a phone book in the kitchen.

A woman answered dully, "Retreat Wildlife Services."

I said I'd found a dog. She asked me what kind, and I gave a description, a mutt with short hair, blondish, pretty sick-looking.

"Can I ask if you're a visitor?"

"I just got here from New York."

"That's what I thought." She exhaled. "You found a stray."

"Stray?"

"It's a problem here. Get out into town and you'll see. They're all over the place."

I looked at the dog through the patio door. Now she was dozing by the water bowl, green flies flicking past her ears.

It was then I felt a bite, and looked down to see black dots prancing on my arms. I yelped and dropped the receiver, sweeping off the fleas. They scattered and leapt back onto my legs.

I heard the woman: "Ma'am?"

I picked up the receiver and started pinching the fleas individually, lacerating them between my fingernails until they popped with greasy blood.

"What should I do?" I said.

"We can send somebody, but we have orders to shoot strays on sight. And anyway, they'll be a couple hours."

"That won't work for me."

"Then I'd try scaring it off. Grab a stick."

I broke one off the sweetgum tree and made my way toward the dog, thrashing it through the grass quite menacingly, I thought. But she just lifted her head and regarded me steadily. I'd have to actually strike her, but all I could muster was a prod to her ribs. The dog didn't budge, though she did look annoyed. I could annoy her. I considered taking away the water bowl, but instead refilled it and left her in peace in the shade.

4.

The woman from Wildlife Services wasn't kidding about the dogs. When I drove to Ocean General, I saw them everywhere, sometimes wandering alone, sometimes in packs that galloped along the side of the road, lean muscles working in the sun. They tumbled and jawed, black and white and freckled brown.

I wondered if the dogs were why I saw so few people on the streets. But then I got through downtown and emerged into west-side Retreat. With its sparkling view of the Gulf, the west side was stately, pristine. All the dogs were leashed. Tropical deco architecture, everything hot pink and lime green, and newer buildings of blinding white, like salt, lined the boulevards, along which the elderly moved so slowly they seemed as still as bronzes, and the palm fronds shimmered and swayed.

At Ocean General Hospital, I found Dr. Kriss in a state of excitement. She wanted to show me a new subject. He'd been brought in late last night with ballistic trauma to the abdomen, a gunshot wound. Like the Tomahawk in Arcade, south-side Retreat was plagued by violence of the sort that made it ideal grounds for the trial.

The subject's name was Quinn. He was about twenty years old and his chest, sparsely sprouting blond hair, was exposed, a damp bandage on the entrance wound.

I introduced myself as a writer from the *Bystander*.

"I'm not saying anything," he muttered.

"He's like this now," Dr. Kriss told me, "but you should've seen him when he first came to—he was like a kitten."

"It's true."

I turned to see that another doctor had arrived.

"This is Dr. Behniwal," said Dr. Kriss. "He supervises the trial here at Ocean General."

I mentioned meeting Dr. Massengale in Arcade.

"Who?" he said.

"Your colleague, Dr. Massengale. He runs the trial in Colorado."

"I don't know him," said Behniwal, taking up the patient's chart. "You're a lucky guy, Quinn. You would've bled to death."

"Better than you put that shit in me."

I asked Quinn how he was feeling, but he turned away from us, staring at the curtains across the room. They were drawn and full of light.

·

Dr. Kriss led me to her cramped, windowless office. It was messy, unadorned, no diplomas, no photos, the fluorescent light loud on the walls. She lifted a stack of files off the chair for me and sat behind the desk. I pulled out the recorder.

"I was sorry you missed the action last night," she said. "Quinn's an ideal subject. It could be a while before we have another like him."

"It sounds like he's hostile to your project."

"That's pretty common."

"It must be hard to get consent for something like this."

Dr. Kriss paused a moment, then met my eyes and said, "I should get this out of the way."

"Alright."

"We operate in a regulatory gray area. A lot of your readers won't like it, I'm warning you."

I nodded.

"About five years ago, the FDA created an exception in the informed consent laws. They wanted to leave room for emergency research."

I recalled Dr. Massengale using these words in Arcade.

"What does 'emergency research' mean?"

"It means if the subject isn't in a condition to provide consent, and if available treatments are unsatisfactory, then experimental treatment becomes an acceptable course."

"So you look for someone who meets these exemptions," I said, "and they become subjects in the trial?"

"Like I said, a lot of people will think we're out of bounds. They'll say we're using human beings as guinea pigs. I know you haven't written on science before, but if you do some digging, you'll find that guinea pigs have it a lot better than humans in most medical trials. Let me explain a typical setup. The corporation hires out the work to a CRO—that's a contract research organization—which rounds up ex-cons and alcoholics for the trial. The CRO pays a physician a small fortune to lend their imprimatur, even though the doctor usually doesn't have any research training whatsoever. And the physician, in turn, delegates the trial's day-to-day operations to a monitor, usually some low-wage nurse, who treats it as an audition for a better job at the corporation that hired the CRO in the first place. This is how corporations acquire the results they need to get past the FDA. It sounds like it should be the biggest scandal in the country, but in fact it's happening all the time."

"So you're saying your trial is more ethical?"

"There is no perfect trial," said Dr. Kriss. "But in our case, the subjects are dying, one second to the next. There are no services for them, period. We're not replacing some other, more conventional treatment they'd otherwise receive. While they're here, they receive the very best care, I supervise absolutely everything, and of course we throw in a small amount of money when we discharge them as well."

My initial reaction was that it seemed exploitative, targeting these health care deserts to bypass informed consent.

"Couldn't you just bring them a regular bag of blood?"

Dr. Kriss must've shadowboxed this argument a million times in her head. "In the permanent drought," she said, "subjects like ours are not prioritized, to put it kindly. If Americans want to donate more blood, and get more of these people medical insurance, I'd be overjoyed about it. But that's not my cause. My cause is the trial. We're presented with a unique opportunity to advance medical science. We'd be killing untold millions if we didn't seize our chance."

I jotted down her remarks, and said, "How long will Quinn be here?"

"Another obstacle." Dr. Kriss sighed. "The short answer is, as long as we can keep him. I prefer fifty days, to monitor his health and collect data, but I'll settle for three weeks. A lot of our subjects, as you can imagine, wrestle with their mental health or substance abuse, and it isn't easy to keep them in bed. I do everything I can to persuade them to stay, though, because once they're out those doors, there's a good chance we'll never see them again. It's extremely difficult to perform follow-up testing. These aren't citizens in a conventional sense of the word."

The trial was up and running in three cities, she told me: Arcade, Retreat, and somewhere in California called Mimico. It amazed me to think that, coast to coast, there were people walking around with plastic blood in their veins.

Dr. Kriss had arranged a series of ride-alongs with Common Dreams for me. It was her hope I'd be able to observe a subject's progress after intake.

"As long as you have a strong stomach," she added.

"I think I can handle it."

I told her that the experts I'd talked to thought this was impossible, that we were still years away from the breakthrough she was claiming. Dr. Kriss let me finish, then rooted around beneath her desk and produced a small plastic sack of white liquid. She tossed it on the desk and it bounced into my lap. The bag was cool. The liquid sloshed from side to side, like cream.

"Forget what people say, Whitney. You're going to see it for yourself."

5.

As I followed her around Ocean General that day, everyone seemed in awe of Dr. Kriss, an awe tinged with fear. She almost never made eye contact, and when she did, there was a sense that she avoided it for your sake, her gaze opening onto an intelligence that saw through everything, especially you.

Personally, I was prepared for it. My mom also had a confidence that came across as intolerance. I remember sitting in on one of her organic chemistry classes at USC. In front of the students, all the impatience and superiority that I dreaded at home were amplified to cartoonish proportions. There was no generosity toward the silly question, every sentence was punctuated with a crisp, rhetorical, "Yes?" Then on to the next slide. She wasn't very popular. I once found a stack of her student evaluations and was startled by the anger, the hurt: *rude, unfair, dangerous.*

After we'd left Ocean General and Dr. Kriss had brought me to her favorite bar on the roof of a pale-peach west-side building, I asked her about the source of that confidence. Our table had a view of the Gulf, the sun on the water like a platinum sheen. When the waiter approached, he asked Dr. Kriss, "The usual?" She nodded, and because this was my last piece of business for the day, I ordered gin and soda. But when he returned with our orders, Dr. Kriss's usual turned out to be a 7UP, so I was the only one drinking.

I set the tape running, but the recording wouldn't turn out well, clogged with nearby chatter and the breeze swooping into the mic.

"From early on, I had to be confident," she told me. "I didn't have a choice. I'm an only child, and all the neighbors had older boys, so there wasn't much room for girlishness, whatever that means. I aped the boys while avoiding their real stupidity. At the University of Washington, we were told again and again what a great time it was to be a woman. Just look how many there were, they said. But in reality, women made up, by a generous estimate, 20 percent of the class, and fully half burned out. No one wanted them to succeed, so they didn't. As for my time in the navy, I constantly had men with rank and authority coming on to me. I had to maintain situational awareness."

"What do you think," I said, "are we going back to Iraq?"

"I hope so."

I felt a strange disappointment in her.

"The things I saw," she said, "the things Saddam did—nothing we could do in Iraq will ever touch that."

Another gust blew over the recorder, but later, listening to the tape, I thought she said, "War is good for medicine."

6.

My first ride-along with Common Dreams began early the next morning. I plunked ice cubes into my coffee and waited on the stoop of Candy's bungalow, jays rousing in the trees, and read the *Retreat Examiner* until the purple truck rolled up.

It was a repurposed ambulance, taller and rounder than the standard ones at Ocean General. COMMON DREAMS COMMUNITY OUTREACH swooped across the side like a comet, beneath which was tucked: A RUBICON TECH INITIATIVE.

Vince and Gwen sat up front in matching purple polos. He was almost bald, with the exception of a ponytail, brown with some wiry gray, and she had a painful-looking piercing on her lip. Both were out-of-work paramedics from Tampa who'd found a Rubicon job listing and been assigned to Common Dreams.

"Is there not a demand for paramedics in Tampa?" I asked.

Neither wanted to answer at first, but finally Vince said, "Let's just say they filter out guys like me."

"You too, Gwen?"

She picked at the piercing and said, "I took a couple things I shouldn't have. I was in a bad place."

But they loved Common Dreams, which they saw as a social justice effort.

"That's really what attracted me," said Vince. "It's not often you find a truly progressive initiative on the coast."

"Common Dreams puts the human subject at the center of care," Gwen said. "That's a real step toward equity."

"I'd love your article to spread the word about that," said Vince. "It would be brave of you to write something positive about these communities, as opposed to the usual kill-kill-bang-bang."

"We were talking about this on the way over," Gwen said.

"We were talking about how the best outcome for a story like yours is for people to say, 'Hey, maybe this is something we could do in our town.'"

"If I'm picturing my future life," said Gwen, "I can't think of anything better than trying to set up more Common Dreams across the country. I'd even transition into an administrative role, if that was possible."

"Not me," said Vince. "If I don't get my hands dirty, it's not a proper day in the trenches."

I glanced at the tattoo on Gwen's forearm, cursive letters that said *live life laughingly.*

We cruised into south-side Retreat, scattering a pack of strays in the road. The streets had the same barren tension as the Tomahawk, and in the shade you could see tents under tarps, sunburnt feet protruding. A woman emptied a bucket of waste into a sewer.

But there was one major difference. Here, a massive plot was being developed. Construction workers were erecting huge wooden frames for new houses that stretched almost all the way up to the tents. Fronting the site was a billboard advertising the development: THE GLADES.

"When I got here, this was all burnt-out houses," Gwen told me. "It's crazy how fast these new ones are going up. What was it, Vince—a month?—since they poured the foundations?"

"Feels like even less."

"It's hard to think they'll hold up in a hurricane," she muttered.

Suddenly Vince said, "Bastards," and swerved the truck to the curb. We all got out.

As if sleeping at its master's feet, a dog was curled up, the blood around it dried black. I thought it was a trick of the light, how the fur seemed to bristle with brown waves, before I realized it was ants pouring over the body. Vince nudged it over with a foot and you could see where the bullet had passed through, bright pink entrail poking out like a thumb.

"I swear to god, these guys," said Vince.

"The construction workers shoot them," Gwen told me.

"What makes you think it's the workers? I hear everyone shoots them."

"Nobody who lives down here would waste a bullet on a dog."

Vince put on some gloves and retrieved a bag. Gwen held it open as he lowered in the corpse, then he shook the ants off his hands and put it in a cooler in the back of the truck.

We spent the rest of the morning in charity work. The first task was to run a quick needle exchange. Hepatitis A was a scourge among the south-siders. They knew the drill. Yawning, anxious, they ditched syringes in a purple plastic bin, then Gwen issued a baggie with a fresh needle and cotton swabs. When that was over, we drove around the corners where sex workers gathered, handing out condoms and bottled water, Gwen and Vince chirping, "Courtesy of Common Dreams."

When we drove by the workers at the Glades, who were on break, Vince leveled a scowl that made them laugh.

I asked the paramedics what they thought about the Rubicon trial.

"Honestly, I don't pay much attention to it," Gwen said. She was dabbing her piercing with hydrogen peroxide.

"Me neither," said Vince. "Only when we're actually performing a trans-fusion."

"And then I'm like, 'White blood, that's weird.'"

"But if it works, it works," said Vince. "In Tampa, only the chopper carries blood reserves, so this is pretty awesome as far as I'm concerned. It's the first ambulance I've ever seen fully prepped for emergency transfusions."

"Why's it so rare?"

"There's never enough O-neg to go around," said Vince, "so it'd be too costly to stock it in a whole fleet of ambulances."

"And besides," said Gwen, "you're usually just a few minutes from the hospital, so you can permit a certain amount of hypotension and focus on driving."

"The problem is, some of your patients are goners by the time you get there."

"Right," said Gwen. "If you're really bleeding out, the window's super-small."

We stopped at a Burger King near the water and took some food to the beach. Pelicans hunted, suspended in the wind. The dogs knew to follow us. Vince always brought along scraps from last night's dinner, and with every bite he took, he heaved something out to the pack, who scrambled over hot sand to rip it up.

We talked about Quinn, the subject at Ocean General.

"The call came in just after midnight," Gwen said, munching onion rings, the grease polishing the piercing. "He was unconscious when we got to him. Actually, I thought we were going to pronounce him right there. It's a certain way the headlights catch flesh sometimes and go straight through—you can tell. But he was breathing. It looked like someone had been putting pressure on the wound, but they'd run off, maybe when they heard us coming."

"He'd lost a ton of blood," Vince said. "You had to basically splash through it to get to him. Obviously an ideal candidate for the emergency research protocol. There's no doubt the transfusion saved his life."

As we got back in the truck, I remarked on how astonishing it was that the hospitals wouldn't service the south side.

"I think if you did your research, you'd find it's not so unusual," Gwen told me. "I've seen poor and homeless turned away from hospitals a million times. This is just turning them away before they even arrive, like, don't even bother."

"They keep putting those houses up," said Vince, "and I bet you'll start seeing service down here again."

"This is why we need Common Dreams all across the country."

Now began the punishing hours. There was hardly anyone on the streets in the afternoon heat. The hammers and drills of the Glades carried for blocks in every direction. It felt like there used to be a lot more people around, Gwen told me, when she first started working here.

I was barely listening. With the ambulance turning onto block after block, and the Whopper sitting uneasily, I was queasy. My head was light, my wrists went weightless. I hadn't felt motion sickness in years, but we'd been driving around in this unrelenting heat for hours.

Gwen noticed. "You're looking kinda green," she said. "Why don't you lie down in the back?"

"We do it all the time," said Vince. "It's the nicest room in the neighborhood."

"No thanks."

There was no way you could get me into the back of the ambulance, packed with the body of the dog. I closed my eyes and imagined cool white sheets draped over me, a moist towel on my forehead.

Soon we stopped again. Gwen and Vince went out to assist an elderly woman, her dress printed with sunflowers. She'd taken a seat on her walker, and Gwen gave her oxygen while Vince dabbed her head and neck with water. It looked nice.

Gas had a lot to do with how I was feeling, and I could let it out while they were working. A little lighter now, I took notes on the equipment in the back: surgical masks, intubation kits, electrodes, and a dozen sacks of white blood.

"Sunstroke," Vince reported.

That was the most dramatic thing we encountered all afternoon.

7.

Over the next few days, my ride-alongs didn't produce a trial subject. Not that Gwen and Vince cared. It was a good shift when the worst thing they dealt with was chest pains, asthma, or the shape-shifting symptoms of withdrawal.

As I was sitting in the shade one morning, watching them conduct blood pressure tests, I heard rustling in the dead grass behind me. My mind went to an alligator, if I should take off in a zigzag, but it was just two girls.

"You're a writer?" one asked.

She was sixteen tops, her Alonzo Mourning jersey long, like a dress. The other was no older and hung back, gnawing her nails.

"That's right."

"You've been writing about us?"

"Just looking."

She eyed Gwen and Vince. "At them?" she asked. "At the purple people?"

"Yes."

The other girl cut in: "You know where they took Jules?"

I glanced at her bruised legs.

"Not Jules, retard," said the girl in the jersey. "Julia, Julia Rawls?"

"I'm sorry," I said, "I haven't heard anything about her. What happened?"

"This guy Deck—"

The other girl said, "Don't," and told me: "They took her in the truck."

"When?"

"A couple months ago. December."

I said I was sure they'd brought Jules to the hospital, Ocean General.

"Why hasn't she come back?"

"I don't know. Want me to look into it?"

"Don't say we asked, okay?"

"Okay."

The girl reached into her jersey and brought out a photo of their friend. It was the face of a small white girl—her smile still looked full of baby teeth—two ponytails cinched with white scrunchies.

"She's a bit older now," said the girl in the jersey.

"How much older?"

"Like two or three years, maybe."

I was about to hand the photo back, but the girl said, "Keep it."

I pocketed the picture and said I'd do what I could. The girls gave their names, Tori and Lina, and the address of Tori's grandmother. I could find them there, if I heard anything.

I'd packed a light lunch of fruit and cold cuts. As we ate by the water and Vince fooled with the dogs, I took out the photo and asked Gwen about Julia Rawls.

"Sure, I remember her, the little one."

"Was she in the trial?"

"Yeah," said Gwen. "We never got the whole story, but when we found her, one of her breasts was nearly severed. I think it was a pimp thing."

"What happened to her after that?"

"Once you discharge them, you can't really follow the patient anymore," Gwen said. "It's too much, too heartbreaking. You have to detach a little, you know? You probably aren't close with everyone you write about, are you? It's not like they're your friends."

8.

I dropped by Ocean General after that day's ride-along, and had just parked the Escape when Dr. Behniwal, the trial's supervisor, emerged from the hospital. Both hands compressed his bald head, as if to crush it. He staggered into the parking lot and suddenly started running.

I called, "Dr. Behniwal!" but he didn't stop. By the time I hustled through the parking lot, between cars, he'd driven off.

In the hallway, nurses cleaned and sorted and evaded each other's eyes. When I knocked, Dr. Kriss's shout pierced the office door: "What?"

She was embarrassed when it turned out to be me.

"Whitney, sorry, sit down. What is it?"

"What's going on? I just saw Dr. Behniwal—"

"Quinn got out, that's what."

"Got out?"

"Sometime last night. Dr. Behniwal was on duty. I had to let him go."

"Just like that?"

"I have to present my findings to Inland," she said, "and cases like Quinn's are key to the data pool. It's unacceptable that Dr. Behniwal would fail to secure him."

I brought out my notebook and inquired about the patient named Julia Rawls, who'd been taken to the hospital in December. "Her friends on the south side are asking about her."

Dr. Kriss relaxed. "Julia was a milestone in the trial," she said, "the young-est patient to receive the solution, just fourteen."

"They say she didn't come back."

"Jesus, I'm sorry to hear that," said Dr. Kriss. "I really hate to admit this, but we get stories like that all the time. We've had a lot of debate over giving out money when the subject leaves. Sometimes they just go on a bender with it, and that can spell catastrophe."

"Julia Rawls was a little young for a bender."

"I'd like to think so too. More likely, she hopped on a Greyhound and got the hell out of there. Whoever hurt her in the first place is probably still on the south side, after all."

A pimp thing, Gwen had said.

"You know what's funny?" asked Dr. Kriss.

"What?"

"When I was persuading Rubicon to give you access to the trial, one thing they were scared of was you writing about Common Dreams. They don't like the idea of everybody knowing they sponsor a needle exchange and hand out condoms. Anything progressive is embarrassing, it leaves them vulnerable. Meanwhile, they have no objection to the idea of you exposing a situation like Julia's. Can you imagine that? I mean, god bless Rubicon, honestly, for their commitment to the trial, but—off the record?"

"Sure."

"Sometimes their priorities make me sick."

9.

Vince and Gwen advised me never to visit south-side Retreat alone, never to leave the car, and certainly, at all costs, not at night. And so, naturally, I was curious to do all these things. After another ride-along failed to produce a subject for the trial, I became restless, unwilling to spend another night in Candy's bungalow, staring at myself in a mirror.

I prowled around in the Escape. Windows down, I listened to the empty south-side streets, insects shooting through the headlights, and when I saw maybe two dozen people gathered on an empty lot, I parked and got out. On the rubble by a broken wall, some south-siders were having a party. Laughter bounced off the nearby houses, where lights glowed behind drawn curtains. I'd already had occasion to observe the stark social division between the south side's homeowners and the sort of vagrants at the party, even as people elsewhere in Retreat saw them all as part of one communal problem.

I recognized some faces from the ride-alongs, and they nodded at me. This wasn't anyone's home, and everyone was welcome. Rusted tire rims had been fashioned into grills, and a cook, his gut overflowing a tank top, barbecued some scrawny pink meat. It smelled pretty good. Whenever another piece was ready, the cook impaled it on a stick and handed it out, then tossed some scraps to one of the stray dogs lurking nearby.

"You look hungry," he said to me. "Bring something for my barbie?"

"Sorry, no."

"Won't hold it against you. What'll it be?"

"What kind of meat is it?" I asked.

"All kinds."

He laid a carcass on the grill and the smoke took flight.

"Maybe in a little while," I said.

At the edge of the barbecue light, a couple slow-danced to LeAnn Rimes, whose voice persevered through the fuzz of a radio. I watched them, crisp shadows on shuddering orange, her cheek flat against his chest, his nose buried in her hair. Between songs, they lazed on a blue bench seat torn from an Oldsmobile and shared a cigarette. I sat on the ground in front of them, and they introduced themselves as Lorie and Mitch. About forty, they wore matching blue jumpsuits. When Mitch heard I was a journalist, he was eager to talk about Lorie's disability. She'd been with a maid service for almost five years, until the chemicals messed up her system. Now she got sick all the time—"the little hairs in her nose are gone"—but no one at the company would take responsibility.

"Some of the chemicals aren't even legal," he told me.

A stray stepped between Lorie and Mitch on the bench seat, circled a few times, then flopped down so they had to make room. Lorie French-smoked the cigarette, eyes elsewhere, as if bored by her own story.

They'd been on the south side about two years, Mitch told me. They liked it here.

"It's not like we don't have problems," he added. "The other day, this fucking rat ate a hole in our tent and ate all our stuff."

But there were a lot of people in similar situations, he said. You could get by thanks to nights like this, friends like these.

When another song came on, Lorie seized him by the wrist and they danced some more.

I wandered around the party, thinking that my job was to represent scenes like this, people carving simple pleasures from a night that provided them nothing. I had to give this place, these people, the story they deserved.

"Here you go, little miss."

The cook held out a stick, steam curling off the meat. It must've been some kind of bird, the skin studded with pimply pores. I said thanks and found a place to eat off to the side, by the broken wall. At first I leaned against it, then realized the wall had been burned almost black and soot had flaked onto my shirt.

My teeth were just drawing off the skin when I thought I heard: "Hey."

The whisper struck my ear like a dart. I looked around.

"Hey."

I realized it came from behind the wall.

On the other side, the dark of the night had no dimension, no depth. I couldn't discern the source of the voice.

Squinting, I said, "Who is it?"

The shape came nearer, and the dimmest light of the grill touched the eyes, the shadow of a nose.

"Quinn?"

"Get me something to eat?" he said.

I stepped forward.

"Don't come close."

I froze and held out the meat. "You can have this."

He snatched it away and tore into it, the cartilege cracking. As he ate, the glow of the fire faintly touched his face. My eyes widened, horrified. In what must've been a trick of the light, it seemed as if his mouth couldn't close—or no, as if there weren't any lips, just bald bone, a black juice running from his chin.

"Quinn?"

I touched my lips and drew closer. I heard the air gurgle in his throat.

"What happened?" I said.

For a moment I could see the wet shape of eyes before he slipped off into the dark.

THE SUBJECT

1.

In her office the next morning, I told Dr. Kriss I'd seen Quinn.

"Where?"

"The south side."

"Specifically where?"

I tried describing the lot with the broken wall, but the geography eluded me. Still, she produced a map and I managed to circle the general area.

"Alright, thanks," she said. "Did you talk to him?"

"Not really."

I hesitated to mention what I'd come to think was shadow play, but said it looked like he'd suffered some kind of injury.

"What kind?"

"To his face."

I gestured around my mouth, but as I tried to put the vision into words, it seemed to creep, like a stepping stone that wobbles underfoot, and I broke off with a grimace.

"This is your first time doing a story like this, isn't it?" said Dr. Kriss.

The question startled me. "Yeah, why?"

"A science reporter might not find what you saw so strange."

"How so?"

"Quinn's blood came back positive for amphetamines," she said. "You'll see it in the report. What meth does to your facial musculature, your teeth and skin, can be horrible."

The night before, I'd debated whether even to write down what I'd seen. I wanted to follow Vince and Gwen's advice, tell a positive story about the south side, and maybe it would be better to let readers imagine Quinn thriving, to have them see the south side as a place where a person could flourish. But I'd shaken it off, put everything on paper, solid.

Dr. Kriss asked me to call her immediately if I saw him again, but I never did, and she seemed to forget all about him when we found the next subject.

2.

Everyone knew Zeke. Even I'd seen him before, during my ride-alongs. You couldn't help but notice a guy stalking the streets in black leather pants, a black leather jacket, and Nikes wrapped with electrical tape. On a black ball cap, he'd used bleach to inscribe a cross with light beams shooting out. A Walkman clipped to his pants, he kept belting out tracks off *Rubber Soul*, his only tape.

Zeke was a bicycle thief. Right out in broad daylight, he'd use bolt cutters on chains and U-locks, spray-paint the bike frame black, and go looking for a buyer—ten bucks, five for a BMX. Occasionally you'd see someone ride by on one of Zeke's bikes, black paint sticky in the sun, the south side's unofficial transit.

Of course, it was hard to like a thief, but south-siders tolerated Zeke as he and his latest stolen ride cut through the needle-exchange lineup, reeking of spray paint, or as their conversations got drowned out by his tuneless Beatles singing. They also knew not to go too far with him. Any moment, he'd push the bike over and come at you with fists extended in a nineteenth-century boxing posture, eyes rolling, underbite clenched.

The dispatch came toward sunset. All at once, my listless hours on the ride-along gave way to fierce activity. It was a stabbing near the Glades development. Gwen executed a U-turn and we soared over asphalt as stray dogs moaned to the siren.

We pulled up to a crowd of south-siders and construction workers, the unfinished Glades looming over them. Even before I got out of the truck, I heard his brutal, unconscious shouts. But the crowd around Zeke was laughing, like they didn't take the bike thief's bleeding very seriously.

"Get back!" Vince barked.

The people parted. Planks of golden light struck Zeke where he lay, turning the blood black-violet. Two construction workers restrained him while a woman applied pressure to his gut. I'd never seen so much blood, they were all covered in it, you could smell the iron.

Zeke's eyes had fixed on his belly as if invisible flames were spreading.

"He's trying to put his fingers in," the woman said.

"Back! Back!" Gwen called as the crowd kept pressing.

"Get off me!" Zeke yelled.

Vince took over applying pressure, blood pulsing between his fingers, and Gwen struggled to give Zeke oxygen as he violently wrenched his head side to side. Then one of the workers said, "Fuck this," and wrapped his biceps around Zeke's throat. This meant relinquishing one of Zeke's arms, and now I found myself on the ground, gripping the tensed, bony muscle in its cracked leather sleeve.

Blood seeped through the seat of my pants. I could feel him relaxing, or dying.

"Gel," said Vince, who'd peeked beneath his hands. I saw him grimace at the bowel. "Dressing."

Gwen applied hemostatic gel to one of the puncture wounds and used a moist dressing for where he'd been eviscerated. I only learned these terms later, when I interviewed Gwen and Vince about what happened. All of this took only minutes, a brilliant, frenetic competence, and they had him on the stretcher and into the truck.

The Glades receded through the back windows of the ambulance as I rode with Zeke and Gwen. At this point, she explained later, the hypovolemia had resulted in hypotension, low blood volume causing low blood pressure. She got a large-bore IV in an antecubital, and at last I got to see the solution in action. The bag of white blood was hooked up and I watched it flow into his veins, a clean contrast to the red mess on my clothes. In the fury of the moment, I didn't give a thought to anything like consent.

It was a long way to Ocean General. Over the course of the ride, I saw the solution work. His skin plumped, his lungs ballooned, and I could almost hear his heart pound louder. The white blood filled him up and his eyes met mine, sparkling. He was alive.

3.

A nurse allowed me to shower off the bike thief's blood and gave me scrubs to wear. He was in surgery for a couple hours. I sat with Dr. Kriss in the waiting room, staring at CNN on a little TV in the upper corner. It said scientists in Texas had cloned a calico cat.

Sitting with Dr. Kriss for these hours gave me more insight into the story she'd told about her father, and why she felt he'd died because her expertise hadn't been enough. She kept turning every possible outcome over in her mind and worrying it aloud.

"What about sepsis?" she asked a nurse.

"What about it?" he said.

"Zeke, blood poisoning. It could already be happening."

He said that wasn't his patient, but he could check if she liked. Dr. Kriss waved him away impatiently.

"There's always a risk with colorectal surgery," she told me, slumping back in the chair. "Anastomotic leak."

I found myself putting my hand over hers. It was hot to the touch. I managed to hold it about ten seconds before she said, "I should talk to somebody."

Dr. Kriss got up and hurried down the hall.

I took a walk outside, the baggy scrubs swishing. Night had fallen, a hiss of insects in the air. I found Gwen and Vince washing out the truck in the ambulance bay. Vince had changed out of his purple polo into cutoff jeans and a T-shirt that said MUSIC HEALS.

I interviewed them about what happened with Zeke. They assumed he'd been stabbed over a bike with what looked like a pair of scissors. After they explained the various procedures I'd witnessed, I asked about informed consent.

It was the first time I'd posed a probing question, and Gwen immediately tensed.

"You don't know Zeke like I do," she said. "He wouldn't have understood. It would've made it impossible for us to do our job. Anyway, he was totally incapacitated."

"He was awake."

"I don't think so."

"His eyes were open."

"That doesn't mean he was conscious."

I didn't have an answer.

"It's been a long night," said Vince, and he shut the back doors of the truck. "A long few days, am I right?"

I closed my notebook, thanked them both for having me along, and offered my hand. To a lot of people it seems unfeeling, how the journalist pivots from confrontational to cordial. For us, the questions aren't personal, but for the subject, the answers are. It must feel like we're messing with their heads.

Vince shook my hand, but Gwen held hers up as if they were too dirty.

"Enjoy the rest of your stay in Retreat," said Vince, "and good luck with your story."

When I got back inside, Dr. Kriss was gone. I found a familiar nurse, who told me the subject had stabilized and the doctor was looking for me.

I jogged aimlessly along the hallway. Suddenly someone snatched my wrist. I spun around to see Dr. Kriss, who whispered, "I want you to see this," and pulled me into a room. A few doctors were standing around Zeke's bed. He was intubated, eyelids flickering open.

"Do you have your recorder?" she asked. "Take it out."

"Alright," said Dr. Warner, who'd replaced the fired Dr. Behniwal. "He's awake."

I turned the recorder on.

Dr. Kriss stepped to the bedside. "Zeke?"

The subject looked at her. She smiled. I'd never seen a smile so pure. This moment was everything to her.

"My name is Eva Kriss. I'm your doctor."

She explained to him where he was, what had happened. She told him he'd been the beneficiary of a new medical advance. From a pocket of her coat, she produced a bag of white blood and held it up. The solution in this bag had saved his life.

"Everything is going to be alright," she said, turning it over in the light.

As soon as he saw that sloshing white, Zeke's eyes widened, terror pushing up through anesthetic. In an instant he'd yanked the IV from his arm. His doctors rushed forward. With a muzzled scream, as if from behind a rubber mask, he tried ripping out the tracheal tube.

Dr. Kriss was saying something to me. When I looked away from Zeke, I saw she had her hand over the recorder.

"Get out of here, Whitney."

I took one last glance at Zeke as they pushed the IV back in his arm, his legs thrashing like eels. Dr. Kriss seized one and shouted at me: "Leave!"

4.

It was after midnight when I got back to the bungalow. I dropped the tape recorder on my bedside table and crawled under the sheets. In the dark, all I could think about were Zeke's fingers digging into the gash in his abdomen, the damp shock of blood through denim, and Dr. Kriss—*Get out of here.*

There are times when I'm afraid to sleep. I'll lie awake, running my mind down to nothing, and then dip into a half-conscious nightmare. I might have any sort of dream later on, but it's a nightmare first, like a purge, and then I'm back at full attention, dreading everything until I somehow fall back in.

That night in Candy's bungalow, I dreamt of being stabbed over and over without dying, and when I startled awake, I saw him for the very first time. He stood in a corner of my bedroom, dark, a faceless head, as if someone had thrown a black sheet over a body. I remember trying to blink him away—just a shadow on a shadow—and thinking that if this were real, I'd be able to move, call out. Somehow I lapsed into sleep again, and when I awoke next, he was gone. I went around in the dark, still half asleep, placing empty wine bottles in front of every window and door before slumping back into bed.

I retained no memory of this until I saw the bottles the next morning. There was no trace of an intruder—the doors and windows were locked. I felt stupid, spooked. Quinn and Zeke, all that blood—it had crept under my skin, invaded my dreams. That's when I began to have my doubts, hearing echoes of Dr. Kriss—*a science reporter might not find what you saw so strange*—and

Mort's questions about my fitness for the assignment. I began to wonder if I really had the strength to cover a story like this.

5.

A gray gloom crawled in from the Gulf and hung over Retreat for days. Inside Ocean General, Zeke steadily improved, according to Dr. Kriss, who kept me updated on his condition. The surgeons had performed an exploratory laparotomy, she said, and were able to suture the distended loops of bowel. Of course none of this would've been possible without the solution he'd received in the ambulance.

I kept thinking about how he'd thrashed in the bed. But oddly, when I'd gone to review my tape of the incident, it was blank. I chided myself for not double-checking that the machine was recording, too caught up in the moment.

After that initial shock, Dr. Kriss reported, Zeke had grown calm. When she let me into the room, however, I found the bike thief bound to the bed with nylon straps. The nurse was changing the dressing on one of his wounds and he whimpered as her hands moved over him. Dr. Kriss hung back and listened to what passed for an interview.

"How are you feeling, Zeke?" I asked.

He hadn't noticed me come in, and flinched as if I had a needle in my hand.

"I'm a journalist," I said. "Can I ask you some questions?"

"Let me out?"

"I'm sorry, I can't do that."

He noticed Dr. Kriss, then motioned with his chin for me to lean in.

"You're a journalist?" he whispered.

"Yeah."

"What'll they do with me?"

"Just keep you here a little bit longer, run some tests, make sure everything's okay."

"And then what?"

"And then you'll go home."

"No," he said, loud enough that I had to back away. "I mean, and then what? What will they make me do?"

"I don't understand."

"I know all about it," Zeke said. "MK-Ultra, the whole setup. You put that stuff in me, so now what? What will I do?"

In the room next door, a woman started moaning.

"Like her," Zeke muttered. "She's lost her fucking mind."

I'd check later, and it was the mother of a patient unrelated to the trial.

"Lord," he said, and strained against the straps, letting out a gasp of pain. "I'm still me right now. I know I'm still me, today."

I looked to Dr. Kriss. She just stared right back, as if reminding me that this was what I'd asked to see.

There was a little CD player by the limp potted plant on the windowsill. In a stack of CDs—belonging to staff, I assumed, or maybe left behind by a previous patient—I found a copy of *1*, the compilation of Beatles hits.

"How about some music?" I said.

I dropped the CD in the tray and looked at the track list, trying to find something off his favorite, *Rubber Soul*.

I said, "'Ticket to Ride'?"

But I missed the number and the button to go back was broken. "Help!" came on instead.

"Well, this is a pretty good song too, don't you think?"

I adjusted the volume until it overrode the woman's moans next door. Zeke watched me nervously.

"Is this okay?" I asked.

When he closed his eyes, tears escaped.

6.

I awakened the next day to find that Dr. Kriss had left the city. At Ocean General, I was met by Dr. Warner, who told me she'd flown to Arcade on the Rubicon jet. In the meantime, it seemed he'd been instructed to minimize my contact with Zeke. He provided updates, but I didn't get back into the room. When I asked why, he cited Rubicon protocols.

"Dr. Kriss has authorization that I don't," said Warner. "If the company found out I was granting you access, I'd be finished here."

With Dr. Kriss away, I was aimless. I realized how much I'd come to depend on her to organize my time and make meaning out of what I was seeing. I decided to conduct some other interviews, things she didn't know about. For one, I wanted to meet with the mayor of Retreat, Benny Klausmeyer, to get a sense of how Rubicon had been attracted to the city. I thought my interview request would take a few days to process, but he was ready to meet the next day, as if he'd been waiting. But first, I decided, it was time to pursue the tip Lane Porter had slipped me at the Donut Shop: the former employee named Raymond Rix, who'd posted with such anger on the *Retreat Examiner* forum.

I drove out to the address on Snowy Egret Place. The dogs ranged freely in this neighborhood, lounging in front yards as if to tempt gunshots and then bolting off in crazy diagonals. A blue boat called *Funny Valentine* was parked in the driveway, a man up on the deck washing it down. It's always important to remember in which states you can be summarily shot for trespassing. I stood at a distance. Soapy rivulets funneled down the driveway into the road.

I called, "Mr. Rix?"

The man looked up from his brush. Face crisscrossed with acne scars, he wore a Seminoles T-shirt and a green canvas hat. He jumped off the side of *Funny Valentine* and vanished into the backyard. Soon another man came out, flip-flops smacking asphalt. He wore a straw cowboy hat, khaki shorts, and a long turquoise button-up opened to reveal a chest of corkscrewing hair. He held a bottle of Corona loosely by the neck. Like many white people in Retreat, his face was a burnt mask.

I introduced myself as a reporter.

"Who with, the *Examiner*?"

When I told him about the *Bystander*, he said, "Never heard of it."

"It's a magazine in New York."

"You're from New York?"

"Yes."

"What's this about?"

"I want to talk about Rubicon."

Rix glanced at his friend, who'd climbed back onto the boat and was now looming over me.

"I saw your posts on the *Examiner* forum," I said. "I thought you might like to share your story."

He gulped half the Corona and pointed at me, eyebrow cocked. "You're with them, aren't you?"

"Who?"

"Rubicon."

"I'm a journalist with the—"

"We don't play that game here," said Rix. "If Rubicon wants to knock on my front door, that's fine."

"Alright."

"But have the courtesy to tell the truth."

I brought a business card out of my pocket and said, "I'm really not deceiving you, Mr. Rix."

"You people will try anything."

"Here's my card."

I held it out, but Rix turned away. I offered the card to the man in the boat, but he didn't take it either, so I bent down and left it on the driveway, hoping the next rinse wouldn't carry it off.

7.

Retreat's Town Hall put me in mind of a colonial outpost in the tropics. Yellow air bricks let in a salty breeze, the entrance was flanked by squat palms, and everyone inside was a crispy bureaucrat. An assistant led me into the mayor's office. The venetian blinds were drawn, the room illuminated with green reading lamps. The AC gave me goosebumps, and I wondered if Klausmeyer kept it that way so he could sport his herringbone blazer. The mayor was on the far side of middle age, with blond hair thin on his freckled scalp and tiny crayfish eyes.

"Really great to meet you, Whitney," he said. He sat about a mile away, behind his leather-topped desk. "When I heard a girl had come down from New York to write about Retreat, I hoped we'd get a chance to chat."

"I appreciate your taking the time to see me."

"Have you been to Marble Beach yet?"

"No."

"Pelican Key?"

"Afraid not."

The mayor soundlessly slapped his palm on the desk. "Well, where the heck have you been?"

"Mostly Ocean General Hospital," I said, "and the south side."

"Right." He leaned forward seriously. "Rubicon Tech."

"Yes."

"I assume you've met Eva Kriss?"

"Yeah. Do you mind if I record?"

"I'm an open book," he said, and I set the tape rolling, then double-checked it.

"An incredible woman, Eva," Klausmeyer continued.

"How so?"

"She sat right where you're sitting now and sold me on Rubicon in half an hour. I could tell right away it was a win-win."

"In what way?"

"You've been spending time on the south side?"

I told him about my ride-alongs with Common Dreams.

"Heroes," he said. "And we need heroes down there."

"How long have things been bad on the south side?"

"Were you born in New York, Whitney?"

"Los Angeles."

This seemed to solve something in his mind.

"We're small-government folks down here," he said. "I've found it's a radical concept to West Coast types, no disrespect."

"None taken."

"If you have certain inclinations, let's say, certain tendencies, no one's going to stop you from living them out. That's your right. If you want to get carried away, then you can damn well get carried away. But that doesn't mean we don't take care of our own."

"With initiatives like Common Dreams?"

"Now you're getting it."

"The south side is changing," I observed. "The Glades, for instance."

"I'm glad you asked about that."

He got up and motioned for me to follow him to a table on the other side of the office. A color-coded map of Retreat was laid out, labeled *Klausmeyer Administration Major Economic Development Initiatives.*

"We call it Retreat 2010," he told me, "a broadscale revitalization plan for the city. By the next decade, I want Retreat to be the premier real estate market on the Gulf coast."

"Ambitious."

"I play to win."

He touched the small of my back and indicated sections on the map. The south side was entirely purple.

"Target areas," he said. "The Glades are pioneers, but they're only the beginning. You might not be able to see it right now, but that's some of the most beautiful land in Retreat. We've got developers chomping at the bit to get their bids in, and a whole smorgasbord of restaurateurs just waiting to transform the area."

"What about the people who live there," I said, "the ones with certain tendencies?"

"Development has to be consistent with neighborhood character," said the mayor. "We have to balance growth and preservation. But we can't artificially hold back market forces, we have to let them work. That's the ticket I ran on, and in fact I carried the south side by a terrific margin."

"The homeless vote?"

"I work for all voters," he said.

The phone rang on the desk. After he hung up, he splashed me with a smile. "I've got a busy day ahead, Whitney, but this has been a treat."

I flipped my notebook shut and picked up my recorder.

He said, "I hope you'll find room in your piece for Retreat 2010."

"You never know."

As he showed me to the door, two fingers on my ribs, he said, "What are you doing tonight? My sons are having a yacht party off Pelican Key. I'm making the punch. I'd love them to meet a girl of your sophistication."

"I have plans, but thanks."

"Just promise me one thing, Whitney."

"What's that?"

"Get your butt down to the Stowaway on Marble Beach and try the surf 'n' turf. Tell them Benny sent you."

8.

Dr. Kriss must've flown back from Arcade that night, because the next morning I received an invitation over the phone: "Do you play tennis, Whitney?"

I said yes, though in fact it had been years.

The Racquet Club of Retreat was a coconut-white building on the west side, hidden up a long driveway and fronted by huge agave. As I approached, I could hear the hollow pop of tennis balls, and found a series of courts along the cliffside. For the fourth or fifth day now, the sky was pregnant with cloud, but the Gulf was still a gorgeous churning blue and breaking white. It made me want to stop and launch tennis ball after tennis ball into the expanse.

Dr. Kriss looked like a pro in her pressed whites and purple Huskies headband, but she wore a busted pair of sneakers so I could borrow her new Nikes. They cramped my toes a little and ground my Achilles, but I appreciated her sacrifice. As we made our way to the rubico clay courts, she offered me a pair of goggles with those aquamarine lenses that make the ball look like a neon meteor, then she unsheathed her Prince racquet and gave it to me too, opting for an old Wilson with an unraveling grip.

She cracked the lid on a fresh can of balls and took a whiff of petroleum. "I've always been crazy for that smell," she said. "Rally for serve?"

I sensed doom from the start. For someone who'd traveled from Colorado the night before, Dr. Kriss got loose in a hurry, ranging along the baseline without gravity and hooking the ball crosscourt. Back in New York, I was on a low-key exercise regimen, which basically meant I'd do crunches when I wanted a tune-up, or go for a jog when I felt, in a panic after a night of drinking, that I was prematurely dying.

None of this prepared me for Dr. Kriss. As she ran me around with impunity, I felt my knees stress, my hamstrings yank. Sweat blackened my gray T-shirt, and when she had her back turned, I hawked a prickly hunk of phlegm. Meanwhile she covered the court in one or two strides and sent winners up the lines with maddening topspin, clay wheeling off the ball.

We took a break after the first set, which she'd won 6–0. My bottle of water disappeared before I even registered wetness.

"You good?" she said.

I did what I could to nod.

"I'm sorry I had to leave for Colorado like that," she said. "It couldn't be helped. But Arcade was brilliant. I pulled incredible data, just what I need to finish the report for Inland. I'm excited for you to see it."

I still needed a minute.

"I'm going to have to discharge Zeke soon," she continued. "He wants out of the hospital and there's nothing we can do to keep him. He thinks it's all some kind of CIA mind-control plot. He's kind of driving me nuts." She laughed. "Don't put that in your story. Anyway, I'd be a lot more discouraged by his resistance if I hadn't got such good stuff from Arcade, and Mimico isn't too far behind either. I'm more disappointed on your behalf. Zeke hasn't exactly been the most thrilling subject for your story."

"You have to work with what happens," I said, still a little short of breath. "You can't ask for more."

"Ready to go? Your serve."

Lactic acid doused my quads and it felt impossible that I'd get running again. Yet to my surprise, I discovered a viable strategy in the second set.

It all hinged on my serve. For whatever reason, serving has always come naturally. I planted my dead legs, tossed the ball with Statue of Liberty poise, and powered it just over the tape. Dr. Kriss, I found, wasn't so adept at digging out a quality serve, and her return would come back hovering. If I could summon the energy to charge on the follow-through, I had a chance to place the shot shrewdly beyond her reach. I remained defenseless when she could play at her pace, but I managed to prevent her breaking serve and stole the set.

When we took a break this time, there was no talking. I was proud to have made her sweat, and now she focused on hydration, staring at the court's roughened clay.

"Let's go," she said.

It was time to witness excellence.

Dr. Kriss brought out a devastating weapon: a cruel drop shot that either froze me in no-man's-land or sent me flailing to the net. The total effortlessness of this shot was demoralizing.

On match point, Dr. Kriss withheld the drop shot, opting to work me side to side until I was just lobbing it back in despair. Then, with one colossal overhand smash, she finished it.

"Forgive me," she said when she saw me heaving. "I couldn't help myself."

"All good."

The clubhouse sent out glasses of 7UP and fresh towels.

"Do you want a beer?" she said as I took up a glass.

"No thanks."

"They can send one, it's no problem."

"No, this is good."

"So," she said, and took a quick sip, "you think you have what you need?"

I looked into the fizzing cup and said, "It's fine, I like 7UP."

"No," she said, laughing, dabbing her neck. "I mean for the story. I wish I could host you indefinitely, it's a joy to have you around, but I have a mountain of work ahead of me with the report."

It took me by surprise, but I controlled my reaction. After all, I'd been here a couple weeks, what more could I expect?

"I'm sure I can make do," I said.

She zipped the racquets into her bag and slung it over a shoulder. "Come to Ocean tomorrow," she said. "We're discharging Zeke."

"Alright."

"Oh"—she offered her hand—"good game, Whitney."

"Good game, Eva."

9.

I invited Dr. Kriss to have dinner with me that night. "How about the Stowaway?" I said, the restaurant Mayor Klausmeyer recommended. But she said she really had to get writing, with the report deadline looming. I thought I played the rejection off with relative cool.

I decided to go by myself. Just before sunset, I drove the Escape to the groomed blond sand of Marble Beach and walked a path of bleached seashells to the Stowaway. The restaurant was built around the rippled trunk of a banyan tree. The hostess led me to a little table with a view of the beach, where the water stirred beneath a granite sky.

The waiter arrived, and I said, "Mayor Klausmeyer recommended the surf 'n' turf."

"Is that so?"

"He was very emphatic about it."

"The mayor's an old friend of the owner," she said, handing me the wine list.

As I looked it over, the waiter brought a flute of champagne.

"On the house," she said.

"Really?"

"For a friend of Benny's."

As soon as the bubbles touched my tongue, I decided to get drunk. I ordered a bottle of sauvignon blanc with the surf 'n' turf. Why not? Apparently this would be one of my last nights in Retreat.

I pictured Dr. Kriss at home, in a study overlooking a pool, the chlorine light licking her face, writing the report. The image filled me with strange shame, as if I was far behind on my own assignment. I took a drink, washed it from my mind.

Just as I cut into the steak, I felt a cool gust off the water, and moments later the deluge began. That's the only way to describe a rain that fell in thick white sheets. The Stowaway was covered by a metal roof built around the banyan, and I could've yelled and heard nothing but the hammering of rain on tin. The sides were all open air, and I enjoyed my proximity to the storm, watching people flee Marble Beach as I dipped lobster in garlic butter and cleansed my mouth with wine. Soon the bottle was two-thirds gone.

I toasted myself. I'd acquired a wealth of raw material, and grew excited about getting back to New York and shaping it into a story. At the same time, however, I worried about my feelings for Dr. Kriss, and what they meant for how I'd write about her. I recalled with embarrassment how I'd held her hand while Zeke was in the operating room, and the way I'd had to force a smile when she rejected my invitation to dinner.

I thrust the worry aside. I'd paint the portrait as I saw it, I told myself, finishing the wine. I'd write the truth. I could do this.

After paying the bill, I paused at the door, then charged into the rain. I was instantly up to my ankles in water and drenched from above. I made it to the Escape, not really thinking I was drunk. Only when I turned out of the lot did I feel wine behind my eyes. The roads were flooded, the side-walks overflowing. The Escape waded, wipers smacking off the rain. I saw strays cowering under trees. The headlights shocked their eyes like coins. You will be in the story, I told them, like a blessing. In my mind, the story was magnificent, pure concept, no words.

In another minute, I was at the bungalow. I ran in the front door, drenched and drunk and happy. There was half a bottle of pinot grigio in the fridge, and after taking a shower, I finished it.

10.

The next morning, I arrived at Ocean General in sunglasses with a bottle of Jolt, the hangover in my brain stem. I found Dr. Kriss in her office. Even as she said good morning, her fingers chattered away on the keyboard, eyes flitting across her sentences. Her indifference to my arrival made me want to provoke her, like a little girl tugging on her mother's skirt.

"I leave for Tampa this afternoon," I said.

It wasn't true, but it worked. She broke from the screen. "Really?"

"Unless there's anything else to add, my editor doesn't see the point in pouring in more of the magazine's money."

Dr. Kriss stood and took a deep breath. We watched each other for a moment until she smiled, and I mirrored it. I took off my shades.

"You've been amazing, Whitney," she said, sounding genuinely glad to know me.

"Thanks for your hospitality. You've been remarkably generous."

"I can't wait to see the story."

"Just so you know," I said, "I won't be able to get started until you send the report."

"I'll have it ready by the weekend."

So this was it.

"Alright," I said, and took a deep breath.

"There's something I want to say before you go." She seemed briefly shy. I'd never seen that from her before. "I'm glad it was you, Whitney."

I managed to say thank you and extended my hand. But Dr. Kriss didn't shake it, she just held it for a moment until, confused, I let go. I put my shades back on and hurried to the ambulance bay.

Gwen and Vince of Common Dreams were preparing to discharge Zeke. I'd ride out with them to the south side. Sitting on the bumper of the purple truck, Zeke was hardly recognizable. Someone had shampooed him, which made his hair puff up in a bizarre halo, and he wore a fresh denim shirt and khakis. He looked healthier than I'd ever seen him, though he was nervously chewing his lip to the point that it was bleeding.

"Do you need a tissue, Zeke?" I asked.

He ignored me.

"Did they pay you?"

"He got his money, alright," Vince told me. "You won't get a word out of him, though."

"Do you feel you've been mistreated?" I tried.

Zeke flicked his ear and spat on the floor of the bay.

"Alright, we're ready to roll," said Gwen, and Zeke quickly climbed into the truck.

He sat with his knees to his chin until we reached the south side. A few people gathered around the truck to see what we'd hand out, but when the bike thief emerged and shuffled into the blazing afternoon, they took a few steps back, sizing him up in his weird new clothes.

"Alright," said Vince. "You're free at last, bud."

"Good luck, Zeke," I said.

He walked backwards, staring at us. When a woman got too close to him, he pushed her off.

"Get away," he growled, and then lunged at another man. "Get away."

"Easy, Zeke," said the man.

He pointed at us. "I'm one of them now, I'm dangerous."

The people laughed.

"What a guy," said Gwen.

"I like him," said Vince.

I watched the bike thief stalk out past some tents in a field of rubble. His shadow mingled with the trees beyond, a medical miracle reborn into the world.

11.

When I got back to the bungalow, there was an e-mail:

> *Whitney,*
> *Excuse my jackass manners. I checked you out and you seem square.*
> *Look, you want what I've got. Maybe we can work something out.*

I'll be at Salty's Marina today around 3, that's F-dock 12, east pier.
Delete this e-mail, OK?

—Sunshine Ray

I checked my watch—already past two.

I quickly booked a flight out of there for the following morning and called Candy's son-in-law, telling him I'd put the key through the mail slot. Then I threw on my Devil Rays cap and drove to Salty's Marina.

I parked the Escape and found my way to the east pier. There wasn't anyone down by the boats, which nodded in the water. My shoes clapped on the wooden planks as I followed the signs to F-dock. When I turned at a yellow boathouse, I froze. Standing in my way was the man I'd seen at Rix's house. He had a grill sizzling and was petting a few shrimp kebabs with marinade, drips hissing on the coals. A curved blade with a plastic handle sat beside his beer.

I cleared my throat and said, "Is Mr. Rix around?"

He gestured to the boat. The water lapped at *Funny Valentine*, which bumped against the dock. High above, a few gulls headed out to sea, and their cries gave me a strange, lonely chill.

I glanced at the blade. It occurred to me to just say thanks and get back in the Escape. You can write the story without this, I thought, also conscious that no one knew where I was. Through the smoke, the man was watching me.

But I stepped on board. The cabin door swung open and out came Sunshine Ray in his straw cowboy hat. I glanced back to the man at the grill, but he was busy with the shrimp.

Ray said, "Anyone follow you?"

"Follow me?"

"Come in."

Not wanting to show hesitation, I ducked into the cabin and sat on one of the cramped leather couches. Ray opened two Coronas and offered me one. Normally I wouldn't drink on the job, but I needed to level the hangover.

I took a gulp and said, "Cool boat."

"Still needs a lot of work," said Ray, "but she floats. Romeo does a lot of the heavy lifting. When she's finally ready, we're crossing to Mérida."

He'd taken a seat by a table with a bowl of oranges. His veins bound his arms like ropes, all the hairs sun-bleached.

"We don't love what this country's becoming. Homeland Security, Patriot Act—just look at what they're doing. They treat us like terrorists to catch the terrorists. Meanwhile, they won't answer basic questions."

"Like what?"

"Like how does jet fuel melt steel, that's what I want to know. Are people asking these questions in New York?"

"Not really."

"What else is there to talk about?" Ray peeled an orange and started pulling off sections. "Well," he said, "Rubicon, I guess."

"Yes."

He asked how I'd heard about him, and I reminded him about the post on the *Examiner* forum.

"Romeo made me delete that."

"Why?"

"We got a visit from Rainer. Have you met Rainer?"

"I don't think so."

"Austrian guy?"

"Maybe he got fired," I said, thinking of Dr. Behniwal.

Ray laughed. "No way," he said, "not Rainer. He came by the house to discuss my nondisclosure agreement. It was a real friendly discussion alright."

I put the name in my notes.

"What was your role with the company?"

"Junior technician, supervising patient recovery and collecting data. I lasted until December last year. I assume you know about the trial?"

I was startled by the cabin door. Romeo came down with a plate of steaming kebabs and set it by the oranges. Ray sang his name—"Romeo!"—in an operatic burst, then said, "Have a kebab, Whitney."

I wanted to prop up my hungover stomach but couldn't trust this guy to feed me.

"I ate already."

Ray nibbled at the purple onions first. "Tell me something," he said. "As an outsider, what do you think of Eva?"

"I think she's impressive," I said. "Single-minded, of course, but she answers criticism well."

"So you've made up your mind."

"It's not about what I think," I said. "I've seen the trial with my own eyes, and so far no one but you has leveled accusations. Worse than Enron, you said."

Sunshine Ray kissed marinade off his thumb. "Like I mentioned, Rubicon makes everyone sign NDAs, and these are all people who want ongoing careers in medical tech. They won't say jack to you."

"But you're different."

"I got into it late," said Ray. "I was over forty when I got started, so it was never about the career for me. You want another beer?"

I fought the urge to say yes. Ray cracked a bottle. It looked great, sweating on the table.

"You're really crazy not to try Romeo's 'babs."

"I'm alright, thanks."

"Anyway, like I was saying, I bought into Rubicon and the whole Common Dreams initiative. But in the end, I had to quit. She didn't fire me. I'm not some guy pissed about how he got dealt. That's why I don't care about breaking the NDA." He drew a sticky shrimp off the kebab and sucked it from its tail.

"I'm definitely interested in your story," I said, "but if I'm going to include your concerns in my piece, it would be useful to have something more concrete."

What I didn't say was that he sounded a little like Zeke.

Ray walked over to the kitchen, opened a drawer, and withdrew a silver CD-R in a neon-orange case. Written on the metal in black Sharpie was *12/01*.

He rapped his knuckles against the plastic. "I just had time to burn it on my way out."

"What is it?"

"The raw data from the last month of subjects I supervised. It'll show you how they really do things at Rubicon."

He went to hand the CD over and then pulled back.

"No one knows I have this." He looked at me intensely, eyes bloodshot and blue. "You have to promise you won't fuck me. Nothing can happen to me or Romeo."

"I promise," I said.

12.

That night, I scanned the contents of Ray's CD, thinking, is this it? I'd expected waves of data, but there were just three folders, each pertaining to a different subject and containing spreadsheets and photographs. The spreadsheets compiled data from tests that had been run on the subject at Ocean General, the results of which I didn't understand. I'd have to find someone to help me parse them back in New York.

I steeled myself before opening the photographs. Asleep in a hospital bed, an obese black man had his stomach held together with staples. In the next folder, an elderly white man had his cheek ripped off, exposing the black gums and molars and the purple root of tongue.

Then I came to the girl. At first glance, I thought surely she was dead, lying in bed as white as the camera flash, eyes locked in a narcotic gaze. I turned to another image. Her flat left breast was carved around the top, the silver stud in the nipple glinting in a slather of blood. My hand went to my chest.

I rifled through my notes and found the photo those two girls had given me of their friend Julia Rawls. I compared the faces, and it was her.

Scanning the spreadsheet in her folder, I couldn't decipher much, but the record clearly stated she'd been discharged from Ocean General in December 2001.

I found the address the girls had given me for Tori's grandmother's house. I had to be on the road to Tampa early the next morning, but I wanted to tell them what I'd learned about their friend.

13.

Welded metal caged the windows and doors, and the entire bungalow was speckled with mold, lizards darting over the walls. I drove my thumb into the buzzer and waited, glancing at the vacant lot across the way. The one dim streetlight lit the weeds growing over the house's foundation. Soon, I thought, this will all be part of the mayor's Retreat 2010. Someone zipped by on one of Zeke's black bikes, and was gone.

"Yes?"

I could barely see the old woman through the cage, a stooped shadow.

"I'm looking for Tori and Lina."

She muttered something and the cage swung open. I followed her down the hall, the walls lined with family photos, their gold frames dull with dust. She turned into the empty living room. There was only one other door. I knocked.

"What, Grandma?"

The door cracked open. It was Tori.

"Hi," I said. "Remember me?"

Tori was hanging out in her bedroom with Lina and a girl named

Carmen. They were watching the Heat game on a flickering little TV. Tori wore that same Alonzo Mourning jersey and her bedroom was lined with basketball posters and banners, everything slightly outdated, like it had been decorated in the mid-'90s and forgotten.

I perched on the edge of the bed, where Lina sat with her knees to her chin, while Tori and Carmen sprawled on the floor. All three were fixed on the TV. A joint smoldered on an empty can of Surge.

It was nearing the end of the fourth quarter. The Heat were losing to the Magic.

Carmen asked, "You booting for us?"

"No."

Tori told her to be quiet as time expired.

"Clowns." She shut the TV off. "We almost came back."

"Tough season," I said. "Maybe try being a Lakers fan."

Tori laughed bitterly and picked the joint off the can. It seemed huge in her fingers.

"I found out some stuff about Jules," I said, and all three girls looked away. "She left the hospital in December."

"No," Lina said, "she never came back."

"Maybe she left town."

"Why would she do that?"

"To start over," I offered, "without her pimp coming after her."

"Pimp?" Tori coughed, and the girls nervously laughed.

"That's what I was told," I said. "Isn't that who attacked her?"

"Pimp would be, like, a promotion," Lina said. "It was her idiot boyfriend, Deck. He took off for Tampa."

"She better not've gone to Tampa," said Carmen.

"There's no way," Lina said.

"But that would be like her." Tori tapped her head. "Jules isn't so quick."

"Don't diss Jules like that," said Lina, snatching the joint.

"I'm not dissing her, it's just facts."

I explained a little about how Jules was involved in a medical trial, for which she would've been paid.

"If you had some money," I asked, "would you leave?"

"Leave?" Carmen said. "No."

"Hell no," said Lina.

"We grew up here," Tori told me. "Everything is here."

"But I hate the way it's changing, though," Carmen added.

"You know," Tori said, "if my grandma ever moved out of here, they'd tear this whole block down."

"You think so?" I said.

"That's what happened with the Glades," Tori said. "It was just this one old lady who wouldn't sell. They were waiting on her to bulldoze the area."

"What happened to her?" I asked.

"The place next door caught fire and I guess she had to go. I swear it was like two weeks later and they already had workers out there. You know how much they make?"

"No," I said, taking notes. "How much?"

"I was asking you."

I told her I didn't know. "So what happened with Deck?"

"Deck is way old," Carmen said. "And I mean, I like older guys."

"Jules says he has white hair on his balls," Lina said.

The girls laughed, the joint was passed.

"Deck's basically just a mean asshole," Carmen said. "He beat up Jules lots of times, lots. I told her it would get worse."

"We found her," Lina said, "me and Tori."

"Yeah."

"It's us that called the ambulance, the purple people."

"I saw pictures of her wounds," I said. "I'm sorry you had to see her like that."

"It's nothing," Lina said quickly. But there was a silence as each girl seemed to contemplate her friend, weed smoke curling in the air.

"Hey—" Carmen poked me. "Maybe you can get the patties."

Lina gasped, "Tori?"

Tori regarded me with red eyes. "Yeah," she said, "maybe. My grandma keeps them around, but she hates us. Can you ask? Ask for the coconut patties."

I went softly to the living room, where the old woman sat with blue TV light playing on her face. I introduced myself as a writer from New York.

She sucked her teeth and said, "Speak up."

"I'm a writer from New York," I shouted. "I'm interviewing Tori and her friends for a magazine article."

"Good god, really?"

"She said I had to try the coconut patties before I go back."

"When do you go?"

"Tonight."

The old woman leaned painfully over the side of the sofa and pulled up a yellow box. "Fine," she said, "fine. And let the girls have one."

I reached for the patties and she said, "One."

"One," I replied.

Carmen leapt off the bed when I came in, and all three girls bunched together on the floor. I sat down with them, cross-legged, and set the box in the center of our circle. The patties were dense coconut sandwiched in layers of chocolate. The girls took them two at a time. That's how I spent my last night in Retreat, with three teens on the floor, munching through a box of junk until we wanted to puke.

"Maybe there's something I should tell you," Carmen said eventually.

"Don't," Tori said.

"Yeah, don't," said Lina.

"Look, I know," Carmen said, "but what if I'm right?"

"You're not."

"Yeah, you're not."

"What is it?" I asked.

Carmen glanced at her friends, who looked away, jaws working through the coconut.

"I thought I saw Jules one time."

Tori shook her head.

"It was back in January."

"That would be after she left the hospital," I said.

"I guess. If you say so. Anyway, it was late, and I was pretty wasted."

"She blacks out," Lina told me.

"Yeah, but not then. And so what? I saw what I saw."

"Tell me," I said.

"I was walking home, just a couple blocks from here, and saw a girl crouching on the street. I thought it was somebody shooting up, but then I saw it was Jules."

"It couldn't have been Jules," Lina said.

"Why not?" I asked.

"When I spoke to her, she just ran off," said Carmen.

"Jules wouldn't run away from you," Lina said.

"But I saw her face."

"And it was Jules?" I said.

Carmen chewed a knuckle. I could see teeth marks on her finger.

"Carmen?" I said.

"Look, I don't know. Her face, it was all messed up."

"Did she do drugs?" I asked, thinking about Quinn.

"Like what?"

"Meth."

Carmen shook her head and said, "Anyway, that's not what I saw."

"What did you see?"

"Don't spread lies," Tori said.

"Her lips," Carmen said, "it was like they'd been eaten away."

"Eaten away?"

"Carmen—" Tori said.

"Like she was eating her face."

THE FACT-CHECK

1.

"My friends and I have this conversation all the time," says the girl from *Vice*. "We wonder if it's possible to have a family and still succeed in media. Everyone has their own opinion, and no one knows for sure, but I like to bring you up as an example. You never married, never had kids. Did you have a partner back then?"

"Nothing serious."

"That's what I thought. Of course, there are counterexamples, but my own instinct is that you have to keep your distance. Maybe if you could have kids at fifty, you could still do what you need to do in your prime. But considering the obstacles we already face, it's too much to overcome."

"I was just unlucky," I say. "I wasn't taking a position."

"Would you rather not talk about this?"

"We can talk about anything you like."

"I have a boyfriend," she goes on, "and he's pretty progressive on these questions. But he eventually wants a house, a kid, a lot of our parents' stuff, you know? I wonder how long he'll last in the city. I tell him I want to be like you."

"Don't say that."

"But it's true."

"Be like Oriana Fallaci."

"Wasn't she a racist?"

At a glance, I can tell this journalist will have a house, and kids, and she won't live in New York forever. At some imperceptible point, in a moment of awesome relief, a kind of homecoming, she'll surrender to what she once considered her opposite. I've seen it a million times.

"Stay true to your own path," I tell her, "and follow where it leads."

Who knows, maybe love would've come for me too, had I not strayed from the culture file. But after what I saw, and what I did, it wasn't possible anymore.

2.

The terror risk was orange for elevated when I returned to the city from Florida. While I'd been gone, the Iraq fixation had intensified at the *Bystander*, but Mort had suspended the debates in his office. Everywhere he looked, he sensed a pandemic of misinformation, and didn't want his magazine contaminated. The latest outrage was that Cheney had gone on CNN and said Saddam was developing nuclear weapons.

"They've already got the will for war," Mort told me. "Now they're looking for the way. And the press is just letting them improvise it, right out in the public arena."

In his anger, Mort didn't pay much attention to my return. He asked perfunctory questions about the trip and reimbursed my expenses, but it seemed as if he barely recalled the subject of my story.

There was a burgeoning mania in him that I see, now, as that of someone losing his grip on history. Mort had been formed by the LBJ and Nixon years. He saw journalism as the shield of democracy. I don't think he was prepared for how the press was unraveling. Reading the news, you might think Saddam was developing warheads in a bunker beneath a hospital in Baghdad. You might think Iraqi agents conspired with a 9/11 hijacker in Prague. You might think Bin Laden met with high-level Ba'athists in Khartoum.

We never recovered from the fissure of those months, when the press did such a miserable job of sifting fiction from its facts. Since then it's become common to meet people, on the left and the right, who categorically discount whatever the media reports. When asked why, they invoke the lead-up to Iraq, and there's nothing you can say.

Mort was lost in this new reality, or perhaps it would be better to call it a realm, an adjacent zone where fact and fiction mingle freely, and the effort to distinguish them is wasted. Mort's vision of journalism assumed a reader with a common understanding of facts, facts as solid things, the foundation of meaning. It seems ridiculous now that an entire industry could go so long believing people wanted facts, when in fact they crept, like me.

3.

A few days passed without word from Dr. Kriss, so I tried getting started on the story.

I'd begin with Zeke's stabbing and use him as a case study to dramatize the crisis of blood shortage, *the permanent drought*. Zeke's struggle for survival would punctuate the narrative beats of the piece, each of which I'd join to another aspect of the trial. Along the way, I'd paint my portrait of Dr. Eva Kriss one stroke at a time, until she came to preside over the whole. I felt the pressure of the story in my chest. I wished for a friend to tell about where I'd been, what I'd seen, and all it meant to me.

About a week after coming home, I arrived at the office to find an e-mail. The sight of Dr. Kriss's name in my inbox carried the thrill of a reunion.

> *Whitney,*
>
> *Please accept the attached report with sincerest gratitude for your hard work and kind attentions. You'll notice that Rubicon has redacted some sections, but those contain proprietary information and would be immaterial to your article anyway. I'll be happy to answer any questions you may have.*
>
> *I look forward to seeing the story.*
>
> *Yours,*
> *—Eva*

I brought my laptop to the Donut Shop, ready to write at last. To my horror, I found a sign taped to the door saying it would close at the end of the month.

"Rent hike," said the woman at the counter. "Five hundred percent. Someone said they're rezoning the area."

We introduced ourselves. For years we'd been all about the transaction, but that's often how it is in the convulsions of gentrification—at the very last moment you get to know what you're losing.

I bought a large coffee and coconut donut and opened my laptop. The document was titled *2001–2002 Annual Trial Report, Prepared for Inland Medical by Rubicon Technology.*

The report gave onto a massive appendix of dense clinical data. Anything deemed proprietary, most notably the actual contents of the solution, was redacted. But everything else was there for my analysis.

Our extensive trial has produced sufficient data to warrant bold assertions, said the report, which I heard in the voice of Dr. Kriss. *We have developed an artificial universal blood substitute. Its potential is perhaps unrivaled in the history of modern medicine.*

As I read the report, I'd make sure the citations lined up with the medical data in the appendix, but the nature of the data itself was a mystery. If something simply existed at the other end of the citation, I couldn't get any deeper. I needed help.

Back at the office, I knocked on Mort's door. He was watching Fox News, and even after muting the TV, kept glancing at it.

"Do we have anyone who could help analyze medical data?"

"How about Nate?"

Nathan Zimmer was the *Bystander*'s staff science writer. It's not that Nate wouldn't be helpful—on the contrary. But the story still felt like something that could be wrested from me, especially by a writer with that degree of expertise.

Mort watched the screen while I explained to him that I was sure Nate had better things to do.

"Alright," he said, "try one of the interns."

Donald Rumsfeld was addressing the press corps. Mort turned the sound back on.

"Sorry," he said, "I can't miss this."

The unpaid intern was sorting mail when I asked if he could help. He seemed pretty confident, or at least didn't voice any doubts, but when I laid out the appendix in front of him, he looked like he'd studied for the wrong exam.

"Think you're up for it?"

"Fake it till you make it, right?"

"You're not supposed to tell me that."

I began reviewing my own copy of the report, highlighting connections between the data and Dr. Kriss's assertions. Every now and then I'd check on the intern. He never looked up from the page, sometimes tapping his pencil on the margin, nodding.

After an hour, he said, "Is this, like, some kind of code?"

Passing my desk, Lane Porter noticed the intern, the pages intermixed.

"Can I help with something, Whitney?"

4.

Lane didn't waste time. On a corkboard he pinned each page of the report, numbered and highlighted into constitutive claims. Each claim referenced evidence in the appendix, and we set about cross-checking them, one by one. The challenge wasn't just that there were hundreds of claims, it was that each one derived from dozens of interconnected data points. Viewed individually, one point might not seem to substantiate the claim, but when properly contextualized, you could see how it fit snugly into the report's conclusions.

Afternoon slipped into evening and the staff started going home. Lane and I kept at it. Thus far the report was holding up. It wasn't easy to pass fact-check at the *Bystander*, and I found myself quietly rooting for Dr. Kriss.

"How sweet it is," said Lane, admiring row upon row of checked claims.

"What about this?" I asked, indicating a point in the appendix. "This was 0-600, but now it's 0-4."

"You've missed a transition." He underlined a phrase in my copy of the report. "It's moved onto a totally different data set here. See?"

"Right."

My eyes didn't seem to be fixing on the numbers anymore. Apparently sensing my fatigue, Lane suggested we call it a night.

"Yeah, you're probably right."

When I began filing things into my bag, he said, "You must be hungry."

I wished Lane understood who he was dealing with, but given we'd only made it partway through the fact-check and would be working together all week, I said, "I could eat."

"I know a place."

On the street, he hailed a cab. It had rained, and the asphalt bloomed with red brake lights, everything smelling of soaked garbage. I was tired and distracted and would've been fine with something from the Donut Shop, but Lane had plans.

The taxi dropped us at a tapas bar on the Lower East Side. There was a lineup out the door, but Lane cut to the front. It seemed he'd made a reservation. When? The hostess seated us at a small table strewn with plastic grapes. We flickered in candlelight.

Before we'd opened the menus, Lane ordered a jug of sangria and half an octopus.

"Trust me," he said, "everything here is super-fresh. Did you see the piece in the *Times*?"

"No."

I vaguely remembered what had been here before, a total dump a woman from *Artforum* took me to before she stopped returning my calls. I could map my memory of the place onto the contours of the tapas bar, and wondered if the same thing would happen to the Donut Shop.

"I think this place used to be a dive," I said.

"The *Times* says they're reclaiming this whole area."

"Who's they?"

He thought for a second then said, "I don't know, sorry."

The octopus arrived, charred and doused with lemon juice. At once I gulped down half my sangria and gnashed the wine-soaked cranberries. I wanted to talk about the story, but again, Lane had plans. He ordered most of the menu and began his interrogation.

"I'm so curious about how your mind developed," he said. "Your family's from LA, right?"

"Right, Los Angeles."

"What do your parents do?"

"My mother's retired," I said. "She taught chemistry at USC."

"And your father?"

"He passed away."

Lane frowned, communicating sympathy. The dishes came fast—veal sweetbreads, roast bone marrow, grilled beef tongue. He tucked his napkin into the collar of his shirt. A little loose with drink, I suddenly became ravenous, and when the food hit my stomach, I began to think I was being unfairly reserved. Lane had just spent a whole night helping with my story on top of his regular workload, and so I found myself telling him about my father. I'd been meditating on his death while preparing to profile Dr. Kriss, reminding myself to be on guard in case I started transfusing my own feelings into the story of her father's death, confusing the two.

Lane refilled my glass. "I have to confess, Whitney, I already knew about your dad."

"What do you mean?"

"Don't you remember you wrote about him, years ago?" he asked, scraping meat from a mussel. "It was in the *Seattle Post-Intelligencer*, your piece about the igloo."

"Oh, right."

I had to take a sip to hide my displeasure. I was sick of being interviewed.

"What about you?" I said. "What got you into the fact-check biz?"

"A talent for truth." He dabbed his beard with his bib. "It was more impressive before the Internet, but I was always the guy who'd intervene when he heard some spurious fact. My mom thinks I'll make a fortune on *Jeopardy!* one day. I've become pretty proud of the job over the years. Lies are on the march, like Mort says, and with public education not what it used to be, the citizenry can't be counted on to do this work itself. There's an urgency to the job I never felt before."

We were deep into our second jug. I plunged the ladle in and filtered out the fruit.

"To be honest," he said, "I've always wanted to do what you do."

"You mean write?"

"I sometimes try, but I can never find the right system. And then I meet people like you, and I realize just how far away I am. You were born to it, Whitney, to write the words that stick in all our minds. By comparison, I'm just a manual laborer with blisters on my hands."

I knew he was asking me to embolden him, to loan him all my self-esteem, but I had nothing to offer. I just said, "Writers work with their hands too."

I was pleasantly drunk when we emerged into the night. We had to get back to the fact-check early tomorrow, so I told Lane I was going home, but I planned to pop into my local for another drink or two. It felt almost dangerous to lie to him, but he didn't detect it. Thankfully, we were going in different directions.

He flagged a cab, and as it swerved to the curb, he said, "You take this one."

"Alright."

I pulled the door open as he came in for a hug. Before I could react, he'd kissed my cheek; I felt the impress of his beard.

"Okay," I said, and he stepped back, stuffing his hands deep in his pockets.

I glanced at his merry little eyes and ducked into the cab.

5.

At the *Bystander* the next morning, I didn't address the kiss. I was too hungover. I'd ended up drinking a whole bottle of wine at my local while watching the Lakers smash the Suns. In the middle of the night I woke on the couch with no idea how I'd gotten there. I crawled to bed, frightened by the gap in my memory. And so I arrived at the office in a terrible mood, my stomach somersaulting, and couldn't find the energy to say anything to Lane. I just plunged into the fact-check and minimized eye contact.

It wasn't the first time someone had developed an office crush on me, or made a ridiculous pass, and Lane's respect for me seemed so fanatical, I figured I could manage it. Over the next few days, I dressed with scrupulous conservatism, avoided personal subjects, and breezed past invitations. It was a passive strategy, to be sure, but after I missed that first opportunity to mention something, I felt passivity was best. I told myself anything more direct would make him think I'd been dwelling on it, and even that amount of interest could send the wrong message. Besides, I really needed his help.

Julia Rawls was listed as "Subject 12" in the report. It was uncanny to see her rendered into faceless medical evidence, but that was how Rubicon protected patient privacy. According to the report, a fourteen-year-old was taken to Ocean General Hospital with a partly severed breast. By receiving the solution, Subject 12 avoided terminal hemorrhage before successful reattachment surgery.

Subject 12 can be counted among the signature achievements of the trial, said the report, *an early confirmation that the solution will be viable for minors.*

Late one Thursday afternoon, with rain lashing the windows, I asked Lane to take a look at the contents of Sunshine Ray's CD, pointing him to the raw medical data pertaining to Subject 12. He winced at the photographs and began sniffing through the spreadsheets.

I turned back to the report, and worked for another little while until I heard him say, "That's a bit much."

This tiny utterance caused me to drop everything. The fact-check had been on a glide path through the report.

"What?"

"The record here's pretty thin," Lane said, waving the CD case. "Take a look."

He pushed his laptop across the table along with his copy of the report, and then stood behind me to indicate the relevant sections.

"All this," he said, sweeping his pen over a page of the appendix, "derives from this," and he pointed to the spreadsheet from Ray's CD. "And that, in turn, becomes this." He showed me the paragraph of the report concerning Subject 12. "Just a single test has snowballed into a whole set of conclusions."

"So?"

"It's like pointing to a single star and calling it a constellation."

I looked up at him and said, "I like that."

"Really?"

"Yeah."

"Thanks." Lane sat back down and tried another analogy. "Or like a single-source story. Everything derives from just one point, but you've stretched it until it seems, to the reader, to have resulted from a whole array of data. It's not unethical, exactly, but it's a stretch."

"What do you recommend?"

"I'd confirm whether the CD from—what's his name again?"

"Sunshine Ray."

"If the CD is a complete record of Subject 12, or only partial. In other words, is that section of the report really founded on just one test, or are we missing something? I'm no doctor, but it's odd that only one test would be run on the subject from December to February."

I said, "February?"

"That's what the report says."

He showed me the line in the report. But I pointed to Ray's data, which clearly stated that Jules had been discharged in December 2001, not February 2002. That's what I'd told her friends—December.

"Good catch," he said, "very nice."

"What do you think's going on?"

"Hard to say."

"Could there be a simple explanation?"

"There usually is." Lane sighed and stretched. "Today's been a long one. Want to grab a drink? There's a new place I read about in Brooklyn."

"Brooklyn?" I said. "No, I need to keep working."

"Okay." He opened up his notebook.

I could hear his pencil roughing the page and said, "You can go, you know."

"No, it's fine, I'll stay."

6.

I'd found my two-bedroom place in Hell's Kitchen in 1997. It cost $1,300 a month, so I planned to die there. Paperback books were stacked to the ceiling to cut the cost of heat, a massive Persian rug covered a perplexing purple stain on the hardwood, and I tried to keep a fresh bouquet of lilies on the coffee table, though they usually turned a dismal spotted brown and broke apart before I bothered replacing them.

That weekend, I awakened to find a scaffold had materialized outside my window. Men were stomping around in steel-toed boots and Wranglers. I caught one of their eyes. He smiled and nodded, and I kept the curtains closed all day.

It seemed like the entire neighborhood swarmed with construction that year, the sound of drilling ripping up the air. Wealthier renters were descending on the area with a very Hollywood-back-lot notion of what New York looked like, and all the landlords were racing to restore their buildings accordingly. My building was blessed with oriel windows. You could probably charge another thousand per month off them alone, but they were hideous with mold and the paint hung off like picked-over scabs. I worried that by the time the men were through with the restoration, I'd feel too squalid to live inside my own building.

My mission for the weekend was to determine whether Sunshine Ray's CD was a complete record of Jules's stay at Ocean General, and exactly when that stay ended, but I couldn't just call up Dr. Kriss and ask without burning my source. I'd promised not to screw Ray over. *Nothing can happen to Romeo or me.*

I was listening to the men take lunch on the other side of the curtain when I reached him. It sounded like he'd fumbled his cordless phone. All I heard was a bunch of wooden knocks and then, "Jesus, hello?"

"Mr. Rix?"

"Hello?"

"Hello?"

"Who's this?"

"It's Whitney Chase calling from the *Bystander.* Is this a good time to talk?"

"Is your line secure?"

"Secure?" I said. "I think so."

I heard him settle into a chair. "Have you gone through my files?"

"Yes, we—"

"Who's we?"

"One of our fact-checkers has been assisting me."

Through the receiver, I could hear the spark of a lighter, water bubbles rushing over glass. He exhaled and said, "So you saw."

"Yes."

"Pretty shoddy work, huh."

I admitted my fact-checker had concerns about the data.

"You wouldn't know it from outside," Ray said, "but Rubicon's a two-bit operation."

"And you're certain that these are all the tests they ran in December? You'd be willing to stand by that, on the record?"

"Absolutely. I can speak to that directly." He took another pull. "See, that's my work on the spreadsheets, my garbage work. Whenever I'd perform a panel test—basic metabolic, hematology, whatever—I entered it into the record. There just weren't any goddamn tests."

"Is it possible there were other records being kept?"

"I don't know how," Ray said, "or when. Eva fired two statisticians in late November, so by December everything was falling to me."

But then, Dr. Kriss had everyone divided into their own little silo, Ray said. No one knew what anyone else was up to. It was rare that a single technician saw a subject all the way from intake to discharge.

"No one but Eva knows the whole picture," he said. "Well, maybe Rainer."

I turned a page in my notebook. "You mentioned Rainer before. Austrian guy, is that right?"

"At first I thought he was her husband. He's not a doctor, that's for sure. Honestly, I couldn't tell you his official title, but he has the authority to go where he likes. He's the one who'd run tests on the subjects after discharge—well, the ones he could track down, anyway."

I remembered Dr. Kriss mentioning how difficult it was to stay in touch with subjects after they'd left the hospital.

"Did you ever see those tests?" I asked.

"Wasn't my job."

I circled Rainer's name in my notes.

There was another rip of bubbles, another delicious exhale.

"Is that a bong, Mr. Rix?"

He held the smoke in tight and said, "No."

"We've obtained Rubicon's report to Inland Medical," I said. "It includes Julia Rawls as one of its subjects. Do you remember Julia?"

"She went by Jules," he said. "Of course I remember her—the little one. You don't forget things like that."

I explained the discrepancy in the discharge dates.

"I discharged her myself," Ray said, his voice rising. "It's one of the last things I did at Rubicon."

"It wasn't February?"

"I'd quit by February. I was gone."

"I wish we could find her," I said. "I'd love to speak with her. I feel like she could settle some of these questions."

"Yeah," said Ray, and then he seemed to think twice. "Wait, what do you mean?"

"No one's seen her since her discharge, whenever it happened."

"I told you, it was December."

"Well, either way," I said, "she hasn't been seen by anyone on the south side since Common Dreams took her away."

There was a long silence, the dead hiss of the line.

"Mr. Rix?"

"That doesn't make sense," he said. "I saw her get in the truck. They were taking her right to the south side that morning."

"I don't know what to tell you."

"And no one's seen her? Really, no one?"

I paused, unsure of how to respond. "Well, there might've been one sighting, by one of her friends, but she isn't really sure. The girl in question appeared to have been wounded."

"Wounded how?"

Saying she seemed to be eating her own face felt too sensational. "To her mouth," I told him. "But that's just one version of events."

"Well figure it out. Christ, you're the journalist, aren't you?"

"I'm—"

"You're all the same," he said. "Doesn't matter if you're with the *Examiner* or the—what's your magazine?"

"The *Bystander*."

"You're all dazzled by flashy results, but don't have the patience or the stamina to actually follow it through."

"Mr. Rix—"

"What happened?" he said. "Can you answer me that?"

"I can't—"

"What happened, Whitney?"

He hung up.

7.

At the office on Monday morning, I received an e-mail:

> *Whitney,*
>
> *I've been on pins and needles waiting for your opinion of the report.*
>
> *—Eva*

After my conversation with Sunshine Ray, I'd spent a long time looking at the photo of Jules her friends had given me, and realized I didn't know enough about what happened to the subjects after discharge. I looked at the outline of my article, still sitting on my desk, and knew it was incomplete.

I called Dr. Kriss and offered congratulations for the report.

"As you can imagine, the response at Inland has been overwhelming," she said. "I think I short-circuited a few pacemakers. Now they're giving me the red carpet treatment. They're arranging a review article for me in the *Lancet*, so I'll have maximum credibility when we go public."

"Good for you."

"Speaking of articles," she said, "how's the big one?"

I glanced at the dead outline. I told her I was working on it.

"I talked to my Rubicon bosses recently," she said. "They're still pretty nervous about having our work come into the open, but I told them what a great job you're doing. I can't wait to see the results."

"You'll still have to wait a bit. My editor has a couple questions he wants answered first."

"Like what?"

"He's wondering if the piece would be stronger if I spoke with a subject," I said, "maybe something like a year after being in the trial. I don't know if that's something you could arrange?"

"Rubicon protects patient privacy like Fort Knox. I can't dispense personal information to whoever I like."

"I understand. Would you be able to ask them on my behalf?"

"I'll definitely try. It could be tricky, though. Not many of our subjects have a fixed address."

"But you follow them, right, to study long-term effects?"

"We do our absolute best, for sure, with the resources available. It isn't always easy."

I thanked her for trying and she said, "You know, Whitney, I don't mean to be difficult or anything, but I pushed to do this because I thought the piece would come out soon."

"I don't control when things go in the magazine."

"Yeah, I get that. But it's me who has to go to bat for you at Rubicon. For every inch of access they give you, I have to fight like crazy. I might've gone a different route if I'd known it would take so much time. Someone at *USA Today* was interested, but I turned them down. Now I'm wondering if that was the right decision."

There's nothing quite as stinging as the threat of having a story taken away from you.

"I can't answer that for you," I said.

"I guess it's something to think about. Anyway, is there anything else you need?"

"Who's Rainer?"

It was a knee-jerk response to *USA Today*, reckless. I had to bring myself under control. The emotional structure of an interview should never be apparent.

"Rainer who?" she said.

"I don't know his last name. He worked for Rubicon in Retreat."

"Right," she said. "Rainer was a technician."

"Not anymore?"

"No, not anymore."

"He would run tests on the subjects after discharge, is that right?"

"Who told you that?"

"I can't reveal my sources," I said. "But do I have that right?"

"Yes, Rainer had the unenviable task of tracking down our subjects— who, as you know, can be somewhat nomadic—and running tests to ensure everybody's safety."

"Who's responsible for that now?"

"Now? Lots of different people. But those tests are strictly proprietary, so I'm not sure it matters to your story."

"Can I ask if you were romantically involved?"

"What?"

"With Rainer," I said. "Did you have a relationship?"

"Who's feeding you this stuff? Jesus, no, we didn't. It's hurtful that some-one would say that. Just because I'm a woman, I have to be romantic with everyone I work with?"

When I didn't respond, Dr. Kriss mastered herself.

"Look, I have an idea," she said. "If your deadline isn't so tight after all, why don't you come to Arcade? Inland is hosting a tour of my lab for some investors next month. It won't be easy—I'm probably crazy even for suggest-ing it—but there's an outside chance I can persuade them to let you come along. Maybe I can use my new standing in the company to leverage an invitation."

"That would be great."

"Alright. Don't worry, I'm still committed to this. I'm just new to the process, and a little impatient."

"It's okay."

"I'm thinking of the first time we met," she said. "Do you remember?"

"Of course."

"I promised you a great story, didn't I?"

8.

The *Bystander* closed an issue that week. When Mort first green-lighted my story, I told him I'd help with little things on the culture file, so I set Dr. Kriss aside and circulated the office, offering captions and headlines and reworking copy.

Closing a magazine is always frantic. After the long lead times for features, and the indolent manufacture of essays, it all comes down to a few hours' crush. The writers have had weeks to move their words around, now they have five minutes. But if closing weren't chaotic, the issue wouldn't hit newsstands with the proper verve. A magazine has to bottle up that last-minute energy so it stays hot all month.

The War on Terror dominated the issue. Mort had tasked his political writers with dismantling the Bush Doctrine, from the neoconservative mandate abroad to the civil liberties violations at home.

One piece led to a serious argument at the office, and Lane Porter found himself in the middle. Richard Calvin, a writer with decades of experience covering the Middle East for the *New York Times*, had composed a story about the hunt for Osama bin Laden. It revealed embarrassing new details about Bin Laden's escape at Tora Bora in the mountains of Afghanistan, when he'd slipped beyond the military's reach into Pakistan's tribal area. The Calvin piece presented a devastating slapstick farce of American incompetence. We all loved it.

But it didn't make it past Lane's fact-check. He argued that the number of unnamed sources was simply too high to tolerate in such an incendiary story. A tense meeting between Lane, Calvin and Mort was convened, and after deliberating overnight, Mort pulled the piece from the issue.

"I agree with fact-check," he told his writer. "You don't have the story, Rich."

And so, all through closing, we dealt with Calvin's brooding. If you happened to stray off from the group, you'd suddenly find yourself in his hulking shadow, berated by his version of events.

"An attack on my integrity would be one thing," he said, "but a lot of good people risked their asses to get me this information, and now some little prick from a fashion rag"—he meant *Vanity Fair*—"wants to school me on the nature of facts. When the *New Yorker* runs the same story, Mort's going to look like a total asshole."

I felt bad for Lane. He was only doing his job, preserving the magazine from lawsuits it couldn't afford. But everyone respected Calvin's work as a foreign correspondent, especially in the aftermath of the Daniel Pearl tragedy, and no one except Mort stood up for Lane. The fact-checker just hunched there with his headphones, hiding behind his row of action figures, working through another story.

So I was impressed when he came out drinking with the rest of the staff after closing. Mort always took us to Englander's, a stodgy old pub that made us feel like real Fleet Street hacks. It was the only time you'd catch Mort out of the office. He'd drink exactly one pint of Guinness, regale us with stories from when editors wore green eyeshades, and then quietly go home to his wife, leaving the tab open.

The staff quickly divided up, with Mort, Calvin, and a few political writers in a red leather booth, the rest of us mingling at the bar. Even the 9/11 issue had resulted in a more festive closing party than this one. The writers in Mort's booth spoke low like conspirators, never laughing. They were intent on stopping Bush, and had worked themselves into believing the issue could help achieve it.

At the bar, I stuck close to Gordon Stone, the magazine's literary editor. He was originally from Atlanta but had been working at the *London Review of Books* when Mort poached him for the *Bystander*. Tonight he wore a jet-black suit and lavender tuxedo shoes, his feet dangling from his perch on the barstool.

"Why on earth have you gone into investigative journalism?" he asked, gently swirling Scotch. "You had the best job in the world. You could lounge in the most comfortable chair in your apartment and get paid to read a novel. Now you're out god knows where, digging into who knows what. It'll age you."

"Haven't you ever wanted to do something a little more serious?"

"Someone has to be the chocolatier. Anyway, it's a question of character. Journalists are a mean-spirited folk, haven't you noticed? Angry, tremendously angry. They spend their whole lives avenging some primal wound to their ego. Everything is subordinate to their vengeance, which they exact on the grandest possible scale. Heads must roll—yours, mine, anyone's. They don't think twice about collateral damage. Just take Mr. Calvin over there. You know, he has two sets of children on two different continents, locked up in finishing schools so they won't interfere with his vendettas."

"I'll be sure to tell him you said that."

"Don't you dare."

Lane sipped IPA at the end of the bar, watching the rest of us with a smile that painfully bunched the skin around his eyes. Every time my glance wandered his way, I could feel those eyes cling to me, so I stared at Gordon and nodded even when he wasn't talking. I resented how male desire becomes a center of gravity in a room, something you're forced to deal with, like a foundling on your doorstep.

Eventually, Lane put his glass down and started working his way toward me. I quickly told Gordon about his crush.

"The fact-checker?"

"Yes."

"But he's adorable," he said. "Why don't you throw him a bone?"

"You're out of your mind."

"I suppose he's more my type. I like little fat boys."

But Lane didn't make it. Mort had slipped out by now and everyone had gathered at the bar, including Richard Calvin. I'll never know exactly how it happened, but somehow—perhaps because his eyes were trained on me—Lane bumped into his nemesis. Beer flowed over the lip of Calvin's pint glass and dripped down his shirt, and the reporter, totally blasted, smashed the glass down on the floor. The pint exploded, shards flushed out in all directions.

"You prick," he said. He grabbed Lane's shirt. I think he got a handful of chest hair. "You know-nothing little prick. Come outside."

"No."

"Outside."

"I'm sorry about the story," Lane tried.

Now Calvin swung him around and pushed him toward the exit. Lane slipped on beer and broken glass. I reached out in time to steady him.

"Richard," I said, "cool it."

I found myself holding Lane about the shoulders. He cowered into me. When Calvin tried lunging at him again, I thrust myself between them. The bartender came around and told Calvin to get the hell out, and the reporter, with a furious glance at his colleagues, abandoned the pub.

I let go of Lane and he rushed to the bathroom. I don't know why I went after him—maybe because it didn't seem like anyone else would. I found him in the back hallway. It looked like he was hyperventilating. When I put my hands on him again, he was hot to the touch, his cotton shirt damp with sweat.

"You alright?"

He nodded, then smeared water from his eyes. "I'm crying."

"He's a big guy."

"Did you want me to fight him?"

Now I sensed the rage coursing through him, like a tensing of the veins.

"No," I said, "of course not."

"Really?"

To my relief, Gordon Stone came toward us. "That brute is lucky he didn't speckle my shoes," he said. "I'd have sent his coordinates to the Taliban."

9.

The issue hit newsstands to wide acclaim. I spotted it in people's hands all over the city, the pitch-black cover evoking Pentagon intelligence, secret interrogation sites, perpetual surveillance. Mort considered it one of the finest issues of his career. He thought it had a real chance to move the needle on public opinion. Just ride the subway, he'd say, and look at how many people are reading the *Bystander*.

One night, shortly before my trip to Colorado to cover the tour of Dr. Kriss's lab, I was lazing at home with a bottle of wine. I relished these evening hours, when the construction workers had gone home. It was almost rustic to hear traffic noise again.

My phone rang.

"Whitney?"

Roland was calling from Denver, where he was on leave and visiting friends before being redeployed to Turkey.

"The whole army's on the move," he told me. "We're pouring into the Persian Gulf, twenty-four-seven."

When he said this, it was as if I felt a rush of air thousands of feet above my building, a great migration over the bending earth. I pictured boots trampling the current issue of the magazine. In the end, did it matter how many people read it cover to cover?

"Is it about Iraq?" I said.

"Of course."

"We're going to war?"

"No question."

I asked if that made him nervous.

"It's Americans who should be nervous. You don't know the half, Whitney. If Saddam finds a way to get his WMDs—"

"You really think he wants WMDs?"

"Wants? There's a lot you don't know."

"Alright."

He said, "I have a chance to come through New York before shipping out."

"When?"

But I'd be in Arcade. I was a little drunk and would've loved to fuck, if he could somehow materialize in my apartment that very moment, and then dematerialize. But I had to tell him it was really too bad, I'd be on a reporting trip.

"Damn," he said, "missed connection. I feel like I owe you one."

"You don't."

Now he sounded like he wanted to get off the phone, so I quickly asked about Floella. "I think about her sometimes," I said, and ripped the cap off a pen with my teeth.

"Funny you should ask," said Roland. "I tried checking up on her while I'm here, but I think she's finally out of my life for good. No one in the Tomahawk has a clue where she's at. I stopped by the hospital, thinking maybe something had gone wrong, you know, but they told me she'd been discharged back in January."

"What do you think happened?"

"My guess? She probably took off for Vegas. That's where she belongs, anyway. But who gives a shit. I'm just glad I don't have to deal with her anymore."

When we said goodbye, I told Roland to look after himself.

He laughed and said, "Thanks, Whitney. And good luck, wherever you're headed."

It's difficult to reconstruct now, how easy everyone said it would be. That was the whole point of Iraq—high technology, precision strikes—but I've searched all over social media for Roland, and never found a trace.

10.

The day before my flight to Denver, I paid a last visit to the Donut Shop. I needed a coffee, bad. I'd had another spoiled sleep, this time waking on my Persian rug, freezing, no idea how I got there.

The place was packed. Tomorrow they'd close for good. There weren't any coconut donuts left and I couldn't get a seat. I didn't recognize these customers, but everyone seemed to know each other, and they were much more familiar with the staff than I'd ever been. Maybe they were the morning crowd.

I stood in the corner with my coffee and plain donut, eavesdropping.

"There's just no way to keep up selling donuts," someone offered.

"Not unless someone's going to pay five or six bucks each."

Everyone laughed and said dream on.

"I voted for the guy, but what the fuck."

"We got yuppies out the ass."

"Yuppies were twenty years ago. There's no name for these people."

"Schmucks."

It didn't escape me that I was one of the schmucks. My bona fides in the neighborhood went back only a couple years, and I had enough money that, should the mood somehow strike, I could afford a six-dollar donut.

Still, I felt like these customers were my people. We were all losing something, together. But if the history of New York is composed of scenes like that, then it will never be told, because there was nothing more to our love of the Donut Shop than that we'd sat in it, and time had passed for us there.

I stayed until the very last donut was sold, observing with a heavy heart the end of this totally crappy place.

THE MONEYMEN

1.

At the base of an ice-blue mountain, the sprawled chalet of the Club at Angel Fire reflected on a spring-fed lake, flat as hammered silver.

My flight had been late and I'd pushed the Jeep Cherokee to get to Arcade on time. After quickly checking into my hotel, a stuffy little room with a fire escape obscuring the window, I crammed my notebook in my bag and hurried to the club. Everyone would rendezvous there, and then Rubicon would take us to the lab.

Cocktails were being served in the Lookout Room, which gave a panoramic view of the mountains, cold rivers running from the peaks. A woman played Nat King Cole on a baby grand, and wait staff in tuxedos shook martinis and served champagne. My tongue tingled, but I asked for club soda with lime.

I counted twenty people in the room, many of them military officers in blue service uniforms. I wondered if they were from the nearby air force base. The only person I recognized was Baker Watt, the Rubicon middle manager.

He was dangling bright slips of salmon into his mouth and chatting with a woman with a helmet of gray hair and purple-tinted glasses. When I approached, Watt introduced me to the mayor of Arcade, Peggy Vance.

"Whitney's writing about Common Dreams," Watt said, and gave me a knowing wink.

"Good for you," said the mayor. "I think I've said to you before, Bake, they don't get enough recognition."

"What do you think of the program?" I asked, flipping open my notebook.

"There's no denying Arcade's got serious problems," she said. "Just last week, some tourists were assaulted in the Tomahawk."

"Really?" said Watt.

"You didn't see it in the *Ledger*? That's a relief, I thought everybody did. A mother and daughter made a wrong turn. It could happen to anyone. I hear they got out of their car, but I couldn't tell you why. Let's just say they both needed tetanus shots when all was said and done. If it weren't for one of those purple trucks, who knows what might've happened."

"I wouldn't take Alejandra up there even in an armored vehicle," Watt said, adding quickly, "That's my wife."

"Ninety percent of Tomahawk residents have engaged in criminal activity at some point in the last year," the mayor said.

"Really?" I said. "Ninety percent?"

"That's what our internal data indicates. For a long time, no one did anything about it. We let the wound fester, and we all share some blame for that. My administration's made the Tomahawk a top priority."

"The mayor campaigned on a policy of rejuvenation," Watt told me.

"It begins with initiatives like Common Dreams," said Vance. "But in ten years, I envision a whole neighborhood reclaimed and revitalized. The Tomahawk is actually one of Arcade's most historic districts. You can quote me on that. Its heritage is just waiting, right beneath the surface."

A waiter rang a bell, and everybody streamed from the Lookout Room to the drive outside, where a row of black limousines awaited. I saw Dr. Kriss with a few military men and someone I recognized as Kenneth Sample, the CEO of Rubicon. They got into one of the limos, I piled into another, and in one long caravan we crawled toward downtown Arcade.

Four men rode with me, three of them bunched together on the sofa along the side, sharing a bottle of wine. They introduced themselves as investors from Dallas and I let them know I was a journalist writing about Rubicon.

"If I were you," one of them said, "I wouldn't be writing about this company."

"No?"

"I'd be buying stock."

The Texans laughed and splashed some wine as the limo took a turn.

I said, "I take it you own a piece of Rubicon?"

"Kenny brought me in at first offering."

"Can I ask what you paid?"

"Well, darling, you can ask anything you like."

"What did you pay?"

The Texan kept his eyes on me as he tipped his head back, finished his glass, and exhaled with satisfaction. Then he broke into laughter.

In the corner opposite me, the fourth man gave a snort. The Texan noticed, the smile draining from his face. "There a problem over there?"

The man had lit a cigarette and was staring out the window.

"Hey, you."

The man turned to the Texan, blinking. "Yes?"

"There a problem?"

"How could there be a problem?"

Their eyes locked briefly, then the Texan muttered something and refilled his wine.

I slid over so I was facing the man in the corner. He was about my age, with gold-rimmed glasses and a closely tailored suit. He noticed me watching him, but kept his pale-gray eyes focused out the window, on the city scrolling backwards.

"Are you an investor as well?" I asked.

"I'd prefer not to speak to a journalist, thank you."

"Off the record?"

I thought I detected a French accent.

He glanced at the Texans, who were talking amongst themselves. One of them clamped a bottle between his knees and pulled out the cork with a jocund pop.

"I represent others' interests," said the man.

"Others such as?"

"That wouldn't be for me to say."

"In France?"

He just let the smoke drift from his nostrils.

"I sense you're not so keen on Rubicon," I tried.

The man reached into his pocket, removed some tinted lenses, and clipped them to his glasses.

2.

It was midafternoon when the limos parked outside a three-story brick building downtown. There was an old laundry service advertisement preserved on its side, and sunlight struck the windows, sending shapeless reflections to the sidewalk below.

At some point in the drive, our group had reduced by half. Mayor Vance and Baker Watt were gone. Only ten of us passed through the door and headed up to the lab.

In the front room, we were supplied with blue scrubs, caps, and masks. The Texans were pretty drunk by now and made a clownish show of getting dressed, while the Frenchman secured everything crisply, as if accustomed to the protocol.

Dr. Kriss entered her code on a keypad and we filed down a corridor, bright from the skylight, where through glass you could see rooms filled with cages. Most of the cages were empty, but in one of them I saw a rat's pink tail disappear between the bars.

I stuck close to Dr. Kriss, who hadn't acknowledged me yet, eavesdropping on her conversation with one of the military officers.

"Those were for pigs," she said, indicating some cages, "and those were for rabbits, back when we were still in the animal trial. Are you in the market for some cages?"

The officer laughed, and so did Dr. Kriss, but I thought I detected some anxiety in her voice.

Kenneth Sample, on the other hand, seemed loose, confident. The Rubicon CEO was a little over seventy, his wrists all bone where they shot from the scrubs, but as he guided the tour, he spoke with youthful enthusiasm. "This is, frankly speaking, one of the most advanced medical science labs in the world."

Dr. Kriss entered her code on another keypad and we moved into a room with a long laboratory bench, where some Rubicon technicians were at work. In a series of flasks, bits of pink-and-purple flesh were floating.

"I'll let Dr. Kriss explain what we're looking at," Sample said.

She cleared her throat, "Here we have a series of devices and tools to evaluate, ex vivo, the solution's long-term effects. We study everything from brains to hearts and lungs, kidneys, the urethra, everything."

The Texans hung toward the back, but the other, silent man drew close, inspecting the flasks.

"As you've read by now in our report," Sample said, "human trials are already successfully underway."

The man raised his hand and Sample said, "Yes, Maxime?"

"Dr. Kriss, you've gone from rats to humans in just over a year."

"That's right."

"How have you been able to secure the necessary approval in such a short time?"

"I can answer that," Sample said. "The trial was preceded by the requisite lab and animal tests, all performed by technicians using FDA-approved materials. Based on that success, it became the collective assessment that our product could be tested where no conventional solution was available."

"And where is that?"

Sample said, "Well, in other words, in situations where the subject would otherwise die."

"How is it determined who meets that standard?" asked Maxime.

"It's determined in situ," said Sample, "on a case-by-case basis, by trained professionals."

I studied Maxime closely, and though it was hard to gauge his reaction behind the surgical mask, he seemed satisfied. Sample smiled and asked if there were any more questions, then gave Dr. Kriss a little nod, prompting her to enter her code into yet another keypad. We headed into a small, cold room full of stainless steel refrigerators.

"In the blood bank of Rubicon Tech," Sample said, "this is the vault."

Dr. Kriss opened a fridge and retrieved a bag of the solution, and the group passed it around. One of the Texans jiggled it, holding it up to the light.

"Would you look at that," he marveled.

Maxime handed the sack along without looking.

"We believe that, almost immediately, Rubicon's artificial blood substitute will become the hospital standard," Sample said.

One of the officers asked if they manufactured it in this laboratory.

"No," he said, "Dr. Kriss oversees that process at a different site here in Arcade."

"This lab is strictly for research," she added. "The process of manufacture requires a more industrial environment."

Maxime raised his hand. "I have another question, if you don't mind."

"Christ, can't it wait?" said a Texan. "It's freezing in here."

"Please," Sample said, "go ahead."

"My associates have voiced concerns about the report," said Maxime.

I glanced at Dr. Kriss.

"What sort of concerns?" Sample asked.

"They would be considerably more comfortable if Rubicon would open up the raw data from the trial."

She was about to respond, but Sample said, "No, Eva, allow me."

The CEO glanced around the group, then cracked a smile. One of the Texans chuckled.

"Everything new is scary," Sample said. "That's the difficulty with such a major innovation, and it isn't helped by the fact that we need to play everything close to the vest. I have no doubt, Maxime, that your associates would be very happy to see absolutely everything, right down to the contents of the product and the process of its manufacture. That's impossible at this point, but in a very short time, everything we've developed here, and every step of the trial, will be a matter of historical record. We have a journalist for that."

To my surprise, Sample pointed at me, and I went hot in the cold air as all the men looked my way.

"Does that answer your question?" the CEO asked.

Maxime gave a gracious little bow and we exited the vault.

We got back into the limousines to return to the Club at Angel Fire. The Texans slumped on the sofa, the middle one asleep. The others poured themselves tumblers of Scotch and stared into them.

I did my best to interview Maxime, who sat across from me, jotting notes on a pad, a cigarette stuck to his lower lip.

"I'm interested in what you were asking," I said.

He looked out the window, then jotted something else on the pad.

"I've gone over the report as well," I went on. "Specifically, what do your associates think is missing?"

Maxime plucked the cigarette from his lips and ashed it in the armrest.

I drew breath for another question, but he cut me off. "I have no comment for you," he stressed. "I was sent here for one purpose only."

"What's that?"

He sighed, took a deep drag, and peered at me as the smoke seethed out. "In Paris," he said, "I will be called into a room, where I sit before some men and answer a simple question, yes or no, that's all."

"And what will be your answer?"

Maxime crossed his arms and closed his eyes, cigarette burning in his hand, and before the edge of flame met the filter, we'd arrived back at the club.

3.

Drinks were served on Wigwam Deck. It was nearing twilight. The line of mountains broke the violet sky. I saw Dr. Kriss talking to some of the military officers and couldn't snag her eye, but I did get an interview with Kenneth Sample, pinning him alone by the tigerwood rail.

"I took out a subscription to the *Bystander* when I heard about your interest in Rubicon," he said. "It's not always to my taste, and I think you've got a lot of things upside down, but I can tell you're serious, and that's what matters."

I asked about his working relationship with Dr. Kriss.

"Believe it or not," he told me, "I've had to go to war for Eva. A lot of influential people think she's too young. You might say there's some chauvinism in that. But Jeff Sloan brought me on board and told me to shoot for the moon—you can imagine what a thrill it is to hear the CEO of Inland Medical tell you that—and that's where Eva comes in. I spent a long time in Silicon Valley, Whitney, and my mantra is trust the youth, follow the youth, empower the youth. That's what I've done with Eva."

He said that when he first met Dr. Kriss, and she told him the story of her father, of the sense of mission his death instilled in her, he realized he had to do everything in his power to help her vision come true.

"The revolution is only beginning," he added. "Just wait. Medical science isn't the only industry in store for some disruption. Do you invest, Whitney?"

"No."

"Because I could name five companies you'd be crazy not to jump all over."

"Is Rubicon one of them?"

"Absolutely."

"Anything else?"

"Well, with all due respect, I wouldn't be pouring money into print magazines."

His smile was so wide it strained his forehead.

Sample said he had to move on to other guests, but I seized the chance to press him to lift the privacy provisions on a few of the subjects. I said I still needed to talk to someone at least a year after they'd participated in the trial.

I expected the CEO to cite Rubicon's endless protocol, but he said, "I don't see why not. I'll ask Eva to dig into her files for you."

Before heading off, he gave me his e-mail.

"Send me the story when it's ready," he said. "I'd love to see what a fine young writer can do with Eva Kriss."

I saw Dr. Kriss on a cell phone at the end of the deck, scanning the gathering as she talked, and that's how I finally caught her eye. I thought I perceived some distress as she came over.

"Everything alright?" I asked.

"Just a little chaos in Retreat. You wouldn't believe the lengths our competitors are willing to go to, or the depths. I'd fill you in, but right now I'm afraid of saying something libelous." She sighed, then leaned in close and told me, "I'm dying for a nap. Ken and these guys from Dallas play eighteen holes before lunch and eighteen after. My hands are on fire."

"What do you shoot?"

"Depends," she said. "I have to strike a balance. If I focus on the game and play well, I embarrass the men. If I just yap my way through it, I embarrass myself. It's a conundrum."

After a waiter brought her a glass of 7UP, Dr. Kriss gestured toward Kenneth Sample, who stood surrounded by officers.

"You talked to Ken?" she said.

"Yeah."

"What about?"

I told her he was open to granting permission for me to talk to one of the subjects. "He's going to ask you to dig into your files."

Dr. Kriss began by shaking her head, then broke into laughter. "God, he's good," she said. "Ken really knows how to work it."

"How so?"

She jerked her head, signaling me away from the guests, over to the rail. "I've been pestering Rubicon for permission ever since you asked me. They've given me no sense whatsoever that they intend to grant it. If I had to wager, I'd say I won't hear from Ken about this at all, and when you follow up, he'll say we hit some kind of snag with patient confidentiality—'It's out of our hands,' something like that. But here's the thing."

She checked again to make sure Sample was out of earshot.

"I've found a subject who's willing to go on the record with you."

"That's great news."

"There's only one downside."

"What?"

"He's in Mimico. That's California." Dr. Kriss sucked the soda straw.

I said the magazine wouldn't mind sending me.

"It's up to you," she said. "That's the best I can do, for the time being."

"I'll be there."

"Okay," she said, "then do me a favor? Despite what Ken told you, Rubicon won't be happy if they know I helped coax a subject to talk. So just be careful. If you don't have to, maybe don't mention how you got in touch with him, okay?"

"Sure."

Maxime passed by, trailing smoke, and we fell silent. He nodded at Dr. Kriss, and after he'd gone a little distance, she rolled her eyes and pretended to gag on a finger.

"Who is he, anyway?" I said.

"Ken invited him. I don't know any of these people, Whitney. They're moneymen, not scientists. To them, the solution is just a product. It could be Prozac, Viagra, some new breast implant, it doesn't matter."

"It didn't sound like your report persuaded him."

"The French are nowhere when you need them," she said with a playful smile.

"Do you think he's wrong to want your raw data?"

"It's not about right or wrong. The data is proprietary—I don't have a say in who sees it. If it were up to me, you know, science would be completely open, but that's not the world we live in."

We stared into the ravine under Wigwam Deck. The crowd was thinning, and Dr. Kriss said she still had a long night ahead of her, hopping from suite to suite at the Antlers.

"The military is very interested in the work we're doing," she said, "and Ken is trying to secure its funding. There's a lot of money headed in that direction right now."

I repeated what she'd said on the rooftop in Retreat: "War is good for medicine."

"That's the hope."

Once again I felt easy in Dr. Kriss's company, our arms touching as we leaned on the rail. But I had a job to do. I didn't know when I'd see her again.

"There's something I need to ask," I said, straightening up from the rail. "The *Bystander* has obtained portions of your data, and we have concerns about some claims in the report that seem like a stretch."

"Some what?"

"Certain gaps."

It was like the air hardened around us. I held my face firm, then she suddenly laughed, laughter without humor.

"I'll never understand journalists," she said. "How can you just throw up a wall between us like that?"

"My fact-checker and I—"

"Is he a doctor?"

"No."

"A scientist?"

"No, but the magazine covers medicine, and our fact-checking is world-class."

"How did you get the data?"

"I can't speak to that. It's our policy to protect sources."

She kept her voice low. "Whitney, I just went around my policy for you, and now you're the one citing protocol?"

"We found a discrepancy in the discharge dates."

"What on earth does that mean?"

I explained how, in the case of Subject 12, the report listed a period of observation considerably longer than what was recorded in the raw data.

"Do you realize what you're suggesting?" she said.

"Yes, I think so. Can you comment?"

She was repeatedly smoothing the front of her shirt. "You know, Ken warned me about doing this story with someone who's never covered medicine. He told me to give it to *USA Today*, but I said I'm sticking with you. I've liked you all along."

Sweat trickled from my armpits. I insisted it wasn't personal, but the magazine couldn't afford to ignore these discrepancies.

"There is no discrepancy." She cut the air with her hand. "There isn't. We have means of observation you don't know anything about." She laughed again. "Jesus, Whitney, you're mistaking the standard precautions of corporate medicine for—what did you call them?—'certain gaps.' Why don't you ask Purdue to open up its data, or Bristol-Myers Squibb? They'll all say the same thing. I know this is your first time covering a story like this, but come on, you can do better, don't you think?"

She glanced over my shoulder, seemed to catch someone's eye, then said she had to get back to work.

"Time to sell that stretched report you're talking about," she said, and actually elbowed me. "Let's connect about this later, okay? I'm sure I can walk you through whatever you think you're missing. Sound good?"

She searched my eyes until I felt so awkward I smiled and said, "Yeah. Of course."

I stayed by the railing for another few minutes, composing myself in the cool open air. I asked for a glass of wine. It helped a little. The last restful light was in the sky, and a few officers stood by the rail, pointing to the distant peaks, while one of the Texans peered through binoculars. Jets in formation flew from the nearby air force base, silver clusters gliding through the air until at once they curved in our direction and came rumbling over the valley.

4.

That night, I saw him again. When I rattled awake in my hotel room, he was hunched by the closet. The same frozen shape, the same faceless head, that I'd seen in my Retreat bungalow. I couldn't move. I tried calling out, but the words slurred off my tongue. The shape wouldn't go away and I couldn't end the dream. He was black within black, like a hole punched in the dark. I closed my eyes, tight, and was falling.

In the morning, I checked the window and doors—nothing. I sat on the edge of the bed, depleted, all the doubts about my fitness as a journalist crushing in. What if I botched the story, or lost it to *USA Today*, or Mort reassigned it to our science writer, after telling me what he'd told Richard Calvin—*You don't have the story?*

And so, no matter how raw I felt that morning, I knew I had to press forward. Before heading to Denver for my flight home, I decided to explore the Tomahawk to get more Colorado color in my notes.

Driving around in the Jeep Cherokee, I noticed all the changes since I'd been here in December. You could still see pup tents under tarps and the occasional black frame of a burned-down house, but in open fields, where I could've sworn houses had stood just months before, I saw signs—COMING SOON: AVALON HOMES—and spray-painted stakes driven into the earth where the digging would begin.

Three boys, very young, crouched together, checking out something on the sidewalk. Startled by the Jeep, they glanced at its tinted windows. One of their hands went to cover whatever they were looking at. It glinted in the sun as I turned the corner.

I kept replaying my last conversation with Dr. Kriss and seeking routes around my objections. With the possible exception of Maxime—and I didn't know what he'd tell his superiors in Paris—everyone had seemed satisfied by the trial's integrity, from major investors to the military. Maybe it had been premature of me to cast aspersions, relying only on Ray's CD. When billions were at stake, transparency had a limit.

That's why I had such high hopes for the Mimico trip. If someone whose life had been saved, someone like Floella or Zeke, would go on the record, a simple quote could answer everything. The proof was in the people.

As I bent the Jeep around another corner, I felt myself creep. Already in a recess of my head was the subject in Mimico, the subject I wanted for the story. It startled me to realize that I was pulling for Dr. Kriss. Like the moneymen, I was invested in her success. It felt as if the world around me were drawing something in from my imagination, like the shape from last night, and mixing it into the truth.

I decided to distract myself by visiting one of the encampments. Maybe someone had heard news of Floella or had another friend taken in by Common Dreams.

That's when I saw the boys again. I must've driven in a circle. They weren't crouching anymore, but standing shoulder to shoulder. One had his hands over his ears. Then another extended his arm, I saw the glint again, and my window exploded, glass blowing across the seat as I swerved up on the curb, my head slamming the roof before the Jeep met the pole.

5.

I roused in the back of the truck. They had me on a stretcher. Someone was tweezing glass from my cheek and the pain was blinding, one side of my face swollen and hot, as if boiled. I felt the plastic mask over my mouth and breathed deeply.

When I blinked awake again, eyelids sticking, I was in Ascension Hospital, and there was Dr. Kriss.

"Everything is going to be alright," she said, smiling.

I touched the throbbing side of my face. Dr. Kriss arranged the pillow behind me.

"You were lucky," she said, quickly checking my pupils with a flashlight. "It's not more than a minor concussion. The glass missed your eye. I stitched you up myself."

To this day, in a certain winter light, you can see the scars on my forehead and cheek.

"The bullet missed you," she said.

"Bullet?"

"Some kids shot at your window. I came off the golf course as soon as I heard."

I looked over my bruised arms in search of an IV.

"It's okay," she said, reading my mind. "You didn't need a transfusion. I suppose it would've created a conflict of interest if you'd been given the solution."

My smile was cut short by the pain in my cheek.

"Sorry," she said, and took one of my hands in hers. "Just relax, Whitney. You'll be out of here later today."

I asked about the Jeep. She said it was a write-off. I closed my eyes while she stroked my hand. Very few women had ever touched me like this. I felt safe, ready for sleep. Then I heard: "Animals."

It was Mayor Peggy Vance. Dr. Kriss told her to be quiet, but I was awake again. She came forward bearing a massive gift basket wrapped in pink foil and set it on my bedside table.

"Whitney," said the mayor, "I'm absolutely devastated."

"It's alright."

"I've got half the city's police force looking for these thugs. We've been counting on you to give Arcade a chance. I don't want this to be your lasting impression."

Dr. Kriss passed me a paper cup of water. Then, in my foggy way, I told the mayor the incident was unlikely to make it into the story. At best, it would warrant mention to illustrate conditions in the Tomahawk, but I wasn't writing a review of her city.

My assurances seemed to cheer her up. In fact, they caused her to lose interest.

"Good," she said. "That's good. Please, accept this with our compliments."

The mayor gestured to the gift basket, an assortment of goods from the merchants of Arcade: cranberry pistachio bark, buffalo sausage, an Antlers bath pillow.

"If you need anything else," she said.

"Thanks, Peggy," said Dr. Kriss, and the mayor left.

I thought Dr. Kriss would say something about our conversation on Wigwam Deck, but this was no longer about the story. She'd accepted me into her care, and so she sat with me, silently, consolingly, until I fell asleep.

6.

Everyone at the *Bystander* was impressed by the scabs that peppered my face.

"I heard you were in a firefight," said Nathan Zimmer, the science writer, on my first day back at the office. I didn't disabuse him of the idea. "What were you doing out there, anyway?"

I demurred. Now that I'd been shot at, there was a flurry of interest in what I was working on, but I kept the story to myself.

To my relief, I soon received an e-mail from Dr. Kriss, and not only was it solicitous, reminding me to stay the course of antibiotics she'd prescribed against infection, but it included contact details for the Mimico subject. His name was Pavel Firea. She added that west-side Mimico was about as hazardous as the Tomahawk, if not worse.

After what happened, she wrote, *I'll understand if you don't want to make the trip. Maybe ask someone else to go on your behalf?*

I wrote back that no, I was going. Then I booked a flight to Los Angeles and knocked on the door of Mort's office. He had two TVs on mute and was taking his red pencil to the proof of a story. Riveting stuff, he told me. The *Bystander*'s London correspondent had gained remarkable insight into the Iraq debate as it was playing out in Downing Street. Sources indicated that British intelligence was highly skeptical of any Iraq–Al Qaeda link, as well as Saddam's WMDs, but it seemed Prime Minister Blair was willing to accommodate Bush at any cost.

I remembered Dr. Kriss's remark about military funding. "Sounds like war," I said.

"They're going to walk all the way up to that line, but will they really step over?"

I handed him an envelope of receipts and asked him to authorize my expenses. Mort signed off, but not before inquiring into the status of the story. I told him it was still far from finished, and he seemed displeased.

"Is something wrong?" I asked.

"No," he quickly said. "It's just that we've invested about ten thousand into your reporting already."

"The story will be worth it."

"I know it will. More importantly, I hope it's worth it for you." He waved at my face.

"This is nothing."

"Would you be more comfortable if I assigned someone else to work with you?"

I immediately said no, and after a moment's contemplation Mort said alright.

"But if you could try to wrap it up with this California trip," he said, "it would really help us out. I'm trying to siphon as much as possible to foreign correspondents. I hope you understand."

"No problem," I said, though I felt oddly embarrassed as I left, as if he'd called me wasteful.

7.

At home in Lakers sweatpants on Saturday, I was eating cranberry pistachio bark and trying to read Bethany McLean's Enron reporting in *Fortune* while construction workers hammered on my building. They'd made an incredible amount of progress, so to speak, in a very short time. Already they'd removed the moldy wood, replaced the crumbling bricks, reframed the oriel windows. One of my neighbors, whom I'd never spoken to until the restoration started, informed me that the whole facade would be painted white. The news signaled a truly ambitious new era of building maintenance that shocked and frightened us both.

The phone rang. To my surprise, it was Lane Porter.

Other than a few curious remarks about my injuries, he'd been ignoring me, maybe something to do with the incident at Englander's. The office felt much more spacious without his pressing attentions.

"Whitney," he said over the phone, "sorry to bother you on the weekend, but I had some thoughts about the story."

"No problem," I said. "What's up?"

"Do you want to get together?"

"Can you tell me on the phone?"

"It would be easier to show you."

I checked my watch. I was leaving for California on Monday and thought I might as well get this over with. In fact I could use another lead like his tip about Sunshine Ray. When I'd come back from Arcade, I found my reporting a little patchy. I had the tape of the Kenneth Sample interview, but reviewing my notes about what I'd seen in the lab, as well as my talk with Dr. Kriss on Wigwam Deck, I found them oddly incomplete, like I hadn't written down as much I'd thought.

I asked Lane if he wanted to meet at the office, but he suggested I come to his apartment. "All my materials are here."

I didn't want to get dressed. "You're sure it's really worth it?" I asked, chomping off some bark.

"It's worth it."

With a hideous, confectionary appearance, all mint-green and red velvet details, Lane's building on the Upper East Side looked like it had undergone a restoration of its own. I buzzed and climbed to the fourth floor, a hint of sawdust in the air.

When Lane opened the door, he offered a low, rushed apology—his mother was here. I said I could come back another time, but he assured me she was just about to leave. We joined her in the living room. Louise Porter wore a baby-blue cardigan, khaki capris and wine-dark lipstick, and shared her son's soft features and orange hair.

"I've heard wonderful things about you," she said, glancing at Lane. "I've read all your articles."

"That's very gratifying."

"I read everything Lane sends me."

Lane offered me a beer and I accepted without thinking. I'd kept dry during the course of antibiotics.

I occupied an armchair while Lane and Louise sat on the white leather couch across from me. They were listening to that CD with brackets on the cover by Sigur Rós.

"Lane always plays new music for me," Louise said. "It's beautiful, glacial, don't you think?"

"Not really."

"No?"

"It's so formulaic." I sucked down half the beer. "Always these long buildups before the cinematic crescendo. I think band music is more or less bankrupt."

Lane and his mother exchanged a happy look, as if it was a benediction to have your taste maligned by a staff writer from the *Bystander*. I felt bad for being so blunt, but I was impatient to get on with our business.

To my dismay, however, Lane poured Louise another drink, passing me a second beer in the process, and she began telling stories about Lane as a boy, Lane as a teenager, Lane off to college. But I shouldn't call them stories. They were a steady stream of very specific, very inconsequential facts. I learned Lane was born on the same day Evel Knievel jumped nineteen cars, that he always liked his blueberries sour, that he'd considered Syracuse but chose

NYU—why?—because he could save money by eating at home; the cost of food was rising all the time. I soon began wondering how I'd ever shut her up and get out of there.

"Have you seen my son's herbs?"

"His what?"

"Herbs. His herb garden."

"Mom—"

"Come look."

Louise went over to the window. I dutifully followed and looked over her shoulder at the pots on the fire escape. The front of the building may have been restored, but the back, which Lane's apartment faced, remained slimy and dark. I wouldn't have wanted to put my weight on the rusted ledge of that fire escape.

"It's rare that a man can garden, don't you think?"

"I wouldn't know."

"Well, it is."

Meanwhile, that pointless Icelandic music kept playing and I kept drinking, so by the time she finally said, "I'll leave you two alone," I was halfway between drunk and hypnotized.

As soon as the door shut behind her, I said, "So, what's this all about?"

Lane collapsed on the couch with an exhausted groan. "Just give me a minute," he said, an arm flung over his face. "I'm a little worn out here. Thanks for being a good sport."

"Don't mention it."

"She just drops in like that."

Lane didn't look like he'd be getting up, so I went into the kitchen for another beer. When I turned around, he was in the doorway.

"I'm starving," he said. "Want something to eat?"

"I guess."

He began pulling pans from the shelves.

"It doesn't have to be a meal," I added.

"There's a recipe I've been meaning to try," he said, and plucked a *Times* clipping from where he'd stuck it to the fridge.

Over the next half hour, Lane was consumed by his cooking. He could barely make small talk, let alone articulate whatever thoughts he'd had about the story, as he trimmed the fat off duck legs and sliced up onions, carrots, and celery. Then he browned and seared the meat and cooked the vegetables in chicken broth.

"Try this," he said, offering a shred of duck on a steaming wooden spoon.

"No thanks."

He ate it himself, looking right into my eyes as he responded to the flavor with a moan.

All the while, I told him about my visit to the lab in Arcade, Dr. Kriss's reaction to my pushback on the report, and the upcoming Mimico interview.

"Would that help it pass fact-check," I asked, "if a subject who's a year out of the trial is all clear?"

To my annoyance, Lane wouldn't give me a clear yes or no. I suppose that's one advantage of the fact-checker—they can lord their veto power over you.

He disappeared into the living room, where he unfolded a table and arranged it with a single candle, a bottle of wine and two folding chairs. Jazz of the nondescript sort you choose when someone has scorned your taste in contemporary music was now coming through the speakers.

Then he leaned out into the fire escape and plucked a sprig of rosemary from his garden.

When I complimented the duck, Lane looked pleased, but he gave all the credit to the writer in the *Times*. He seemed familiar with the various styles of all the paper's food writers, while I never, ever read anything about food. But again, Lane had the almost nineteenth-century air of someone committed to knowing everything, albeit secondhand and filtered through various New York publications.

"I want to ask your advice," he said. "I've been thinking of pitching something to Mort."

"What's the idea?"

"It's about this new style of barbershop. Actually, it's more like an old style, but these young barbers are reclaiming that very classic barbershop look, you know, checkered floor, straight razors, a stag's head on the wall. It's a Brooklyn thing. You go into these places and you see a lot of young men in there, just hanging out, and it's very, I don't know, not metrosexual, exactly, but they're comfortable being groomed."

He searched my face for a reaction.

"Because one thing they're reviving—and this is what the piece would be about, mostly—is an old-time code of civility, something we're losing with technology and all that, just being in the moment, getting your hair cut, treating other men with respect. It's like a male kind of feminism, maybe."

I'd seen several of these places open up, and of course they're everywhere now, but I associated them more with the grotesque masculinity of hunting lodges and beer halls than with some moral rejuvenation.

"Maybe there's something there," I said, trying to be nice, "but you'd probably have to take a more critical view. I'm not sure Mort would run something that was enthusing about a bunch of Brooklynites trimming each other's beards."

"Oh, it wouldn't be like that."

I didn't mean to sound discouraging, but the idea was so boring, I didn't want to lend it my support even in the privacy of his apartment.

"It's hard to get anything into the *Bystander* these days," I added, "unless it's about the Middle East."

"You're probably right," he said with a bright, false smile.

By the time dinner was over and the dishes were soaking in the sink, night had fallen and I felt pretty drunk. We sat on the couch, its white leather sticking to my leg, while jazz drifted through the room, and I recall thinking to myself that I didn't really feel like working anymore. My whole reason for being here seemed long submerged.

Still, I asked, as he emptied the bottle into my glass, "What were these thoughts you had about the story?"

Lane set the bottle down, then shifted a little closer on the couch. He drew a deep breath and said, "No thoughts."

"No thoughts."

"Nothing." He was smiling. "I just wanted you to come over tonight."

In the instant of my confusion, he grabbed me by my biceps, butted his mouth into mine, and sucked. He made hot, almost panicked noises, and when he came up for air, he said, "I'm in love with you, Whitney," then climbed on top of me, his firm dick poking through his jeans.

"Get off—" I gasped. "Lane—"

Now he was pressing on his dick like he wanted to take it out and play with it.

I freed an arm and punched him in the padded ribs. He coughed and I wriggled off the couch. I touched my face where he'd grabbed it. Some of the scabs had opened and I was bleeding.

Lane stared up at me, confused, and it was the hypocrisy of his confusion that enraged me. How brutally harsh did you need to be to a man?

I'd later doubt the wisdom of all the things I shouted at him then. "You really think I find you attractive? How many signals have I sent you? How blind are you, actually?"

He sprawled on the couch, disheveled and squinting, as though he couldn't believe what he was hearing.

"I love you," he said, as if it couldn't be refuted.

As I pulled on my shoes, I said his feelings didn't matter, and in a moment of terrible change, something burned behind his eyes.

THE WEST

1.

"What happened that last year?"

I'm startled to attention. The girl from *Vice* and I are coming to the end of the interview, and I realize I've been answering automatically, reaching for the nearest canned phrase as I watch the fading daylight cut across a neighboring tower. I wonder if she sees how the question interests me, if she can sense the weight atop my story, muting it.

"What do you mean?"

She opens *The Complete Bystander* and says, "In the introduction, Gordon Stone writes about the magazine's unraveling."

"Right." I settle back in my chair.

"Can you talk a bit about that?"

"Everyone in the industry was dealing with the same thing at the same time," I tell her. "Ad revenues were declining and all the magazines were wondering how to reckon with digital. Should we give it all away? Can we make people pay? Do we publish original stories online and, if so, does that alter the nature of the stories? A magazine has to have a digital aesthetic almost as refined as its print aesthetic, and no one really knew what that meant. Anyway, I can't think of an editor less prepared to answer those questions than Mort."

Back then, the end of journalism seemed like the only conversation my colleagues wanted to have, but despite our apocalyptic visions, we had no clue what was really coming. We always pictured ourselves unemployed, not retrofitted into single-person, twenty-four-hour news franchises, each expected to dispense scoops all day and night and be funny online. I wonder if the *Vice* writer is funny online. She probably has to be.

"Mort was in denial?"

"I wouldn't say denial. He had the numbers crunched, he had a bird's-eye view of the revenue streams. It's more that he genuinely, wrongly thought it was all a kind of fad, that like the dot-com boom it wouldn't last, and any outlet invested in digital was doomed. He just couldn't see it. His idea of the future looked like the '90s. He was the sort of person who'd say the fate of print magazines was secure because no one was ever going to take a computer monitor into the bath."

"And what about you?"

"What about me?"

"In that last year," she says, "you seem to drop out of the magazine, and the next time anyone hears from you, you're out of the industry altogether. What happened?"

I can tell this is her big question—the one she's been saving for the end. I picture her with colleagues: "Once I have her comfortable, I'm going to find out why Whitney Chase stopped writing."

The truth amasses on my tongue.

I say, "Personal reasons."

2.

As soon as Mom opened the door, I knew she'd had an attack. She was using the quad cane and there were purple pockets stuffed beneath her eyes. She saw me notice too, because after leaning into a brief hug, she quickly turned and shuffled down the hall.

I'd landed in Los Angeles in late afternoon, and almost felt like a tourist as I crawled down the freeway in a rented Toyota Highlander, then edged Elysian Park on my way to Los Feliz. It was so different from my New York world, where everything was fronted hard by brick and glass, I sometimes couldn't believe I'd grown up here. When I parked, I saw the succulents reaching for the street, and pink flowers, like weeds, overgrowing the neighbor's fence.

In fact, things were getting more luscious, more ornamental, as Los Feliz attracted wealthier residents. Many of our neighbors' homes had been reno-vated, their grounds upturned and replanted, mismatching my memories. But my old house was still shabby, the lawn a scorched brown square. That wasn't because of her MS, that's just how Mom kept things.

I'd stay here for the night before driving up to Mimico for my interview with Pavel Firea, the trial subject. Before leaving New York, I'd called him, and he said he'd be happy to speak with me.

"You understand," he said in an accent I couldn't place, "I owe my life to the trial. A little interview is the least I can do."

"I like this," Mom said, and touched my shortened hair, "but my god, what happened to your face?"

I told her about the shooting in Arcade, and my concussion.

"You had a concussion?"

"It was minor. I had a good doctor."

"Your brain is your livelihood, Whitney." After inspecting the wounds and satisfying herself that I was healing, she said, "Colorado is just crazy. Is that your only bag? I made up the bed in the guest room."

I teased her that it was still my room, but she replied, factually, "All your things are in the basement now."

"I know."

Around the age of forty, Mom was diagnosed with multiple sclerosis, and even after all this time, it hurt that she didn't keep me apprised of her attacks. When I was on the brink of moving to New York, I remember offering to come back to Los Angeles instead. There's no cure for MS—it only gets worse—and I thought I should be near her. But she wouldn't hear of it. The way she spoke of Los Angeles, you'd think it was some fringe outpost where I'd never find work in media.

In truth, Mom preferred to be alone. If she needed anything, she called her friends. That's a part of her life I never puzzled out—the strength of her friendships. After dropping my bag in my room, I passed through the kitchen and once again marveled at the photos on the fridge, all of Mom and a group of women she called "the gang," an assortment of former USC colleagues, their sisters and sisters-in-law. The gang went hiking, saw movies, took trips to Arizona, where one of them owned a ranch. In the photos, Mom was always smiling, eyes bright, like a kid with something sweet. The photos seemed so out of place in that house, where she never turned on the lights, never made a joke, at least not while I was in it.

She sliced watermelon and poured Perrier and we sat in the shade in the backyard, its earth baked, cracked. As I perched there with my sunglasses, sipping through a straw, I recalled my uncle's girlfriend, the KTLA reporter. I'd finally grown into her image—I was her now. Little did I know I'd never publish a piece of journalism again.

"Mimico," Mom said. "I don't think I've ever heard of Mimico. What takes you there?"

I was excited to tell her about the story. She didn't mean to, but she'd always withheld approval from my cultural work. Nothing could really impress her about an essay on *Exile in Guyville* or a profile of P.T. Anderson. Yet, as I began, I could see her face harden. I found myself not even telling the story, exactly, but trying to prove to her that it was worth hearing out.

"What's it made of?" she asked.

"Plastic, basically."

"Plastic blood? I've heard we're still years away from that."

To my surprise, I sounded like Dr. Kriss. "You're not a medical doctor."

"You don't have to be a doctor to know the idea is ludicrous. If someone's going around transfusing plastic into people, they've got a serious problem."

"I've seen it myself."

Mom brought the glass to her lips and looked out over the yard. I pretended to scratch my nose as I fought the emotion turning to mucus in my throat.

She'd taught organic chemistry at USC before the MS forced her into retirement. Science, for Mom, was a way of shutting everything down. Only strictly, narrowly true things commanded her attention, and if you happened to wander near her field of expertise without ample learning, you came away from the encounter feeling demeaned, not enlightened. I couldn't help but question what the point was of her knowing so much, if it only dried out her imagination.

The sun dipped and went golden, shadows lengthening, and a mockingbird on a telephone pole cycled through the sounds of a car alarm. Time stood still in the backyard. If all else changes, I thought, every building restored and renovated, this jacaranda will still be here, throwing shade on the dead, dusty ground.

"It's good to be home," I said into a long silence.

"I'm going to lie down."

"Are you feeling alright?"

She laughed once, as if I could never understand, and started gathering the dishes.

"Leave those," I said. "I wish you'd tell me when you're not feeling well."

"Why?"

"I'd like to help."

"That's impossible."

Was that why she'd bristled at the story? There was no cure for her. Science can do a lot of things, not everything.

"I was planning to go into the village for groceries," I said. "I thought I'd make us dinner."

"Just look after yourself, Whitney." She saw me frowning and became, for an instant, very soft. She cupped my wounded cheek and said, "I'm fine, really. This is normal."

I followed her inside. She went into her bedroom and closed the door. I found some beer in the fridge and cleaning supplies under the sink, and for the next hour I scrubbed the bathroom, getting down into places where Mom couldn't crouch, while two or three bottles disappeared. Then I did the kitchen, and only stopped my unconscious cleaning when I reached the dents in the floor. They'd been made by the stretcher when they took Dad out, decades ago. This was where he fell after the heart attack. I never understood why Mom didn't get the floor refinished, how she could live with the feeling of the dents through the fabric of her socks. I took a calming breath, sprayed cleaner on the floor, then wiped the grime that had gathered in the dents. When I was done, it looked as if they'd wheeled him out yesterday.

3.

Mom kept napping, and now that I'd been drinking and thinking of Dad, the shade of the house felt morbid. I pictured her behind the bedroom door, waiting for me to go out, and why shouldn't I? I only had this one night in the city, and the Lakers were in the Western Conference Finals, with Game 4 versus Sacramento being played at Staples that night. I'd reconciled myself to missing it so I could spend time with her, but now I walked out to a nearby bar.

The game had started by the time I arrived, and everyone was nervous. The

Kings were leading in the series and had quickly asserted control of Game 4. I found a seat at the far end of the bar and ordered a burger and beer.

It was hard to watch. Mike Bibby of the Kings kept beating his man off the dribble. No one was adjusting to his penetration. The Lakers looked confused, disengaged. They weren't responding to the superior ball movement. After the first quarter the Kings led by twenty, and I heard some premature chatter about how the Lakers had had a good run, that it was almost impossible to three-peat.

At halftime, the Kings held a commanding lead. I considered going home, but despite the tension of the game I felt more relaxed just sitting here drinking, my gaze dumbly fixed on the TV, than brooding in the darkness of the house. Anyway, the Lakers kept making it interesting. They'd cut the lead down before slacking off and letting it grow again.

"What do you think?" asked the man beside me.

"I think it's not looking good."

He bobbed his head and sipped his Bud, peering at the TV so I could take a long look at him.

"They'll come back," he said, then switched his gaze to me.

He introduced himself as Hector. He was about my age, strikingly muscular in a fresh blue polo, with some light acne scars that gave him a distinguished air.

"I want the Lakers to win," he said. "It's good for the city, I like to see people happy. But to be honest with you, I'm a Clippers fan."

"Really?"

"Clipper Nation."

"Weird."

His laugh came with unexpected giddiness, charming me. When Kobe got to the hole, cutting the lead to six, he whooped and slapped the bar. Now that we were watching together, he loosened up, and I did too, urging on the purple and gold as they tried to mount a comeback, until the Kings hit another calm, deflating shot and silenced us.

And then it happened. With the Lakers down two and only ten seconds left, Kobe drove to the rim but couldn't get it to go. Shaq squeezed the rebound but couldn't put it back. It was totally bleak. But in an inexplicable stroke of luck, the ball was slapped out to Robert Horry, poised at the top of the three-point arc. Without thinking, he let it fly, the final buzzer sounding as the ball soared, and it went. Just like that, the Lakers won.

People hopped on tables, fists clenched and pumping, eyes rolling wildly, everybody making crazy sounds. Hector and I gripped each other's hands and were jumping up and down. The bartender poured tequila over a row of shot glasses. On TV, Jack Nicholson was flabbergasted.

Then we were in the street. Cars blared their horns and we cried out to them, as if cheering on guerrillas surging down from the hills.

Hector said, "I love it."

"Me too."

"Do you live around here, Whitney?"

He had a gap-toothed smile, and I kissed him. As I'd grown drunker, it occurred to me that it might be nice to get laid tonight, and what better time than after Robert Horry's shot, in the afterglow of victory?

But as soon as Hector touched me, hands strong on my hips, the stubble around wet lips, I thought of Lane's trapping weight, the hard little dick. I couldn't thrust it from my mind. I squirmed away in anger.

Hector backed off, showing both hands. "Okay," he said, "no problem."

"I'm sorry."

"No, it's okay."

He scratched the back of his head, shyly observing me out of the corner of his eye. My rage gave way to pity and I grew frustrated. Why couldn't I just enjoy this guy? I was thousands of miles away, he had nothing to do with Lane, Lane had nothing to do with my sex life.

But I'd hit a wall and just started down the block, weaving through the crowds.

4.

Mom was awake when I got home, watching the news in the living room with peppered cucumber slices and a glass of Perrier.

She said, "What's happening out there?"

"The Lakers won."

She turned her attention back to the TV. The anchor was reporting on the terrorist threats that might strike on Memorial Day. The FBI said they'd been tipped off by Afghan detainees about a plan to use scuba divers to sabotage atomic power stations. We were meant to stay alert for unattended packages, we were meant to report suspicious-looking people.

Mom seemed so small in the blue TV light, and so exhausted. In an excess of tenderness, I crawled onto the couch and took her in my arms.

"Don't make me spill," she said, and held her cup away.

But I pressed closer, breathing her in. I became large and proud, like I was capable of this intimacy even if she wasn't. I was big enough to hold her like this, big enough for both of us.

Mom said, "You smell like your father."

I was rocking her back and forth, lost in my love, but released her when she said, "He had a drinking problem too."

5.

In the morning, over coffee and green-onion omelets, we said goodbye. Mom had looked up Mimico on the map, which annoyed me, as if she didn't quite believe what I'd told her yesterday and had to check it for herself. The traffic was fine on the highway north, she said. Then we leaned into a hug and I got in the Highlander.

On the road, I tried to think of other things, reviewing what I knew of Pavel Firea. Dr. Kriss had shared with me the raw data from his stay at Legacy General, the hospital in Mimico. Even at a glance, I could tell it was more comprehensive than what I'd found on Sunshine Ray's CD, a good sign.

In April 2001, Common Dreams had responded to Pavel, who'd called 911, saying he'd been shot in a home invasion. The data stated that Pavel was kept under observation for about sixty days, the same number listed for Jules in the report, though not on Ray's CD. The goal of my interview was to determine whether there were any discrepancies between this data and Pavel's version of events.

Mimico was an abomination of urban planning. In its very center, five highways converged and shot out in different directions, carving up the city. As a result, the map never cohered. It seemed like a loose affiliation of unrelated districts, each contained by another annihilating slab of highway.

I checked into a motel before driving to Pavel's house through what must've been the least green city in America. The air had the texture of exhaust. On the west side, where Pavel lived, the roads were like endless stretches of bone-white desert sand. Only by cowering under highways could you find any shade, which is where I saw the tents, sheets of cardboard, and shopping carts filled with rags that told me I was in a Rubicon trial area. The houses were all boarded up and bleached by sun, convenient backgrounds for campaign signs, cardinal red with white letters: REELECT MAYOR JOCK FISH.

Pavel's house was in an especially bizarre location, among a row of homes perched high on a slope above a four-lane arterial thoroughfare. Turning off that road was frightening—it felt like slowing down would cause a fifty-car pileup—but I maneuvered the Highlander over to the gravel at the base of the slope and parked. Then it was a matter of climbing the switchback path to the house on foot. Halfway up, I paused and squinted across the street, the oils of my skin beginning to cook. A guardrail ran along the other side of the road, beyond which everything plunged into a canyon.

Of these houses on the slope, Pavel's looked like the only one currently occupied. The others had plywood sheets on the windows and doors, but Pavel's house reminded me of Tori's grandma's place in Retreat, everything welded and caged.

He answered the door in a smudged tank top and cutoff jeans. Balding on top, he was hairy all over, coarse black sheathing his legs and shooting from his shoulders. All the features of his face were clustered in the middle: a small, broken-looking nose and crumpled lips, purple like liver.

"Do you think my car will be safe?" I asked, looking down to where I'd parked.

"We'll keep an eye on it," he said with that accent, maybe eastern European, "but no promises, okay?"

I couldn't believe the heat inside. Pavel didn't have any AC and he inexplicably kept the windows closed. The air burned my throat. It didn't help that he chain-smoked.

"This is my good time of day," he said, sort of joking. "After my first pills wear off, before the next ones kick in."

With a pronounced limp, he led me to the kitchen. I took out the recorder and he leaned in to it when he spoke. The first thing he wanted to tell me about was the shooting.

"That one right there," he said, and pointed to a window above the fridge. "I guess the old bars were rusted through, so they pried them off the frame and broke in while I was watching TV. Fucking idiots thought there was a safe in here, like I must be rich because I own the place." He opened the fridge, cracked a Coors Banquet, and said, "Want one?"

"No thanks."

When he broke it to them that there was nothing in the house, he thought he'd be executed. His only chance was escape. In one athletic gesture, "the last quick move I'll ever make," he threw a bottle at the gunman and yanked the front door open.

"That's when they clipped me. Three shots, two passed through. I curled up right there in the doorway while they ran out the back. I barely had time to call the ambulance before everything went dark. Check it out."

In the wall by the front door, Pavel indicated two bullet holes, and when he kicked the doormat aside, I saw a dark stain on the floor. I asked if he would mind showing me the scars, but he said no, they were in an embarrassing spot.

We settled on the white plastic lawn chairs he kept in the living room. Amber pill bottles were scattered on the table between us. Pavel made space for my recorder and then swallowed a few different meds, washing them down with beer. He lit another cigarette and switched on a fan so the smoke crawled up the staircase. A diluted vinegar smell was coming from my armpits.

I asked why he continued living here after the shooting, when all the other houses were abandoned.

"That's just what they'd like."

I told him he didn't need to lean in to the recorder.

"Sorry."

"Who's they?" I asked.

"Real estate. If this whole row of houses gets condemned, there'll be a development here in a couple months, I promise you. See, if you can build a little higher, you'll get a beautiful view of the canyon, and the noise from the road up there is like nothing. They're going to make mansions here one day, but they'll have to buy me out first."

Transcribing the interview later, I heard the little gasp I made when an ember from Pavel's cigarette dropped on his tank top and burned a tiny hole. He just swept it to the floor.

"I want to ask about your experience in the trial," I said. "What do you recall of your time at Legacy General?"

"I remember liking everybody," Pavel told me with a shrug. "Some of that's painkillers, but you have to understand: I thought I was a goner, I'm surprised I woke up at all. So I love those people, forever. They really cared. People from around here don't carry much weight in Mimico, but you'd never know it from the way the doctors treated me."

"And how did you feel when you found out about the trial?"

Pavel lit another cigarette, and with it burning in his lips, he slapped his forearm with two fingers, smiling, and said, "White blood."

"Yes."

"I thought it was pretty damn wild, plastic running through my veins. I'm like a medical miracle."

"Did they explain to you the idea of informed consent?"

"Yeah, but how I see it, they didn't have a choice, it was the only way to save my life. I'm grateful they made the decision. But then, I'm grateful an ambulance came at all. That wasn't exactly common here, before the purple trucks. You know, I feel bad for all those people, all over the country, bleeding to death while we sit here right now."

"Did Dr. Kriss talk to you about that?" I said, remembering her speech about the permanent drought.

"Who's Dr. Kriss?"

"She invented the solution."

"No shit? No, I never met any Dr. Kriss. But the doctors at the hospital said how many people die from blood loss, it's like hundreds every day, and how they're going to change all that."

I asked how long he'd stayed at Legacy General.

"I think it came to fifty-eight days," Pavel said. "Believe me, everybody was nice, but by the end I wanted to get the hell out of there. All I could think about was getting back home. The Common Dreams people said they'd secured the house for me, but by the time they got here, all my shit was gone. At least I didn't have any squatters."

"And have you had to check in at the hospital?"

"They send a guy around to check on me."

I took this to be the *means of observation* Dr. Kriss had mentioned in Arcade.

"Is his name Rainer?"

Pavel shrugged. "Could be."

As I jotted down some notes, he said, "So this is really going in a magazine?"

"Yes."

"Will you send me a copy?"

"Sure, I can do that."

"I want—" Pavel paused, his gaze zoning out on the array of pill bottles. "Quote me on this."

"Alright."

I had the pen ready, but he seemed engulfed, the next wave of medication washing over him. I pictured the pills in his belly, breaking down in beer. Later, I had to replay his words a few times just to make them out: "I want to thank the doctor," he said. "I want to say thank you for saving my life."

Now his eyes looked bleary, his chin dropped closer to his chest. I began gathering my things.

"Perhaps this would be a good place to stop," I said. "Thanks for taking the time, Mr. Firea."

"You'll come back? I have more I want to say."

"I will, yeah."

"Good," he said, "yes."

I left him drowsing in the lawn chair, but not before taking the cigarette from his fingers and extinguishing it in an empty can.

I entered back into the blistering heat and struggled down the switchback to the road, cars zooming by and flashing in the sun. To my relief, the Highlander hadn't been broken into, but on the driver's side, across the door and window, someone had spray-painted the yellow outline of an enormous cock and balls.

6.

I took the Highlander to a car wash, but the penis paint had dried and they said I'd have to leave the car overnight for them to blast it off. I had no other way to navigate Mimico's knotted overpasses, so I just had to drive the thing, facing forward with deadly intent as people leered from car windows to heckle me, as if I'd chosen the dick design as a custom decal.

By the following afternoon, when I arrived at Mayor Fish's rally, I'd almost forgotten about the graffiti until the unamused looks of people standing around the parking lot reminded me. To a cop surveying the penis, all I had to say was "I parked it on the west side," and he gave a comprehending nod.

Tents had been erected on the lawn outside the courthouse, an imposing neoclassical building flanked by palm trees with Ionic columns and a dome painted gold. I framed the building in the middle of my vision, and two overpasses, one on either side, ran toward a vanishing point somewhere behind it. From this distance, the sound of traffic was almost soothing, like a water feature.

In the square shade of the tents, food had been set out—a pyramid of hamburgers, a bucket of macaroni salad, and cantaloupe cubes all reaching the same temperature—and it looked like they'd bused in some people from the west side for a meal. The homeless had been given bright-red XL T-shirts that said REELECT MAYOR JOCK FISH, making them easy to supervise as they hurriedly ate off paper plates.

Waiting for the mayor to appear, I reflected on the Pavel Firea interview. He'd called that morning to arrange our follow-up.

"Sorry I dozed off," he said, and I heard him pull from a cigarette. "You can come by tomorrow, same time."

It was such a spare, solitary existence, alone on that slope in a medicated daze, no pictures on the walls, no postcards on the fridge. My goal for tomorrow's interview was to dig deeper into his private life. He could turn out to be one of my story's key threads.

A small crowd had gathered around the stage by the time Mayor Fish arrived. He wore a blue suit and red tie, impressively cool-looking in the heat, his hairline weirdly low, like a ballcap's brim. He had a lockjawed smile and reddish hairs on the back of his hands. The sheriff stood beside him, observing us from behind reflective shades.

The theme of the mayor's speech was law and order.

"Four years ago, I stood right here and read the crime statistics," he said. "They were shocking—so shocking, people asked why anyone in their right mind would run for mayor in Mimico. My administration inherited the worst crime epidemic in our city's history. But I don't need to tell you that. You know it already. You feel it each morning as you drive through the west side, hoping to God there's no gridlock so you won't have to slow down. And you feel it each night when you bolt your doors three, four different ways, praying your family will be safe."

But those four years had seen remarkable gains, said Fish, gains previously unimaginable. In close partnership with Sheriff Doyle, and in tandem with a variety of creative charitable initiatives, his administration had overseen a 50 percent reduction in violent crime. Were it not for the situation on the west side, which remained city hall's top priority, that number would be even higher.

"Now I'm asking you to let me finish the job," he said. "If reelected, I promise a complete revitalization of our most troubled urban communities. It is our collective goal to make Mimico, all of Mimico, safe for families and open for business. Vote for me, and vote for a 21st-century Mimico."

The applause was tepid but not cruelly so. Driving around the city, I hadn't seen signs for any political opponents. It seemed that Fish's reelection was a matter of course. He was just going through the motions, and the crowd did the same. They were here for hamburgers.

As the mayor came offstage, I tried approaching him, but a handler intercepted me. I told her I was a journalist, but she hadn't heard of the *Bystander* and wouldn't grant me an interview. He stood just a few feet away, talking into a tape recorder held by a man about his age, though heavier, with sweat soaking through his shirt in shapeless patches.

I introduced myself to the journalist when he came away from the interview. His name was Tim Braun, a reporter with the *Mimico Messenger*.

"The *Bystander*," he said. "Seems like there's a glossy new mag out of New York every couple months."

Braun assembled a burger, two patties and a bolt of mustard.

I asked if his beat was city hall.

"City hall, crime, high school sports, and I filed my first piece on ballroom dancing just last week." He laid into the burger, mustard dotting the corners of his mouth. "I'm not sure what it's like in New York, but advertisers have been leaving the *Messenger* in droves. At this point, I'm doing the work of four or five reporters on my own. Thankfully, some real estate ads are starting to trickle in, which is a relief. Advertising is our only lifeline."

"I get the sense Fish's reelection is a lock."

"Fish is our man," he said. "He received a totally unanimous endorsement from the *Messenger*'s editorial board, the first time that's happened for any candidate in thirty-odd years."

"What makes him so appealing?"

"We're sick to death of writing about rapes and robberies. Mimico's never going to be Palo Alto, but why can't it be a nice place to own a home, build a business, start a family?"

Braun didn't seem to mind me picking his brain while he ate, but as he finished, sucking the grease off his fingers, he said, "You've come all the way from New York to cover Jock's election?"

I didn't want to tip him off about Common Dreams and Rubicon, so I just said I was writing about the west side.

"Let me get this straight." He dabbed his lips with a paper napkin. "Your magazine sends you out here to write about Mimico, and you've chosen to focus on the west side?"

"More or less."

He scoffed. "If it bleeds, it leads, right?"

"Well, that's not strictly accurate."

"I hope you'll find it in your heart to write something positive about the hardworking people here."

"Are the people of the west side not hardworking?"

Now he peered at me, like he was seeing through my face into some ulterior motive. "What's your name again?"

"Whitney Chase."

He balled up the napkin, strangely put it in his breast pocket, and said, "Nice meeting you."

The sun set beyond the courthouse, the dome a dazzling gold, and the overpass concrete blushed faint rose. I hung around just long enough to see Mayor Fish leave. With a salute to the remaining supporters, he and Sheriff Doyle got into the backseat of a black Escalade, all smiles as Tim Braun piled in after them.

7.

The next afternoon, I set out for Pavel's in the vandalized Highlander. A strange film had accrued in the Mimico sky, giving the city a soiled yellow cast. The sun was a flat disk of painful white heat, and even in the seclusion of the car's AC, I could sense it, like the weight of the ocean around a submarine.

I hoped to catch Pavel in the caesura between medications, but as soon as I merged onto the road to his house, I encountered a lava flow of brake lights. Traffic both ways was jammed. I slumped in my seat, easing the car forward a few hopeless feet at a time. The heat came off the hoods in waves, and out of the overpass shade emerged the west-siders. In dusty flip-flops, skin burned to blisters, they carried squeegees and buckets and bottles of water for sale. I shook my head as they passed.

I tried calling Pavel to let him know I was running late but got a busy signal. Meanwhile, I was stuck with the guy in the car beside me. He was packed into the cab of a landscaping truck, the cargo bed piled with rakes and mowers all covered in blades of grass. I'd accidentally made eye contact and he'd looked from the penis to me with a horny grin. I stared forward but could feel him watching, finding a way to keep himself perfectly framed in my wing mirror.

Finally, we curved onto the last stretch before Pavel's house. That's when I saw a black pillar of smoke rising high and unfurling, lime green at the edges in this uncanny light. The sight gave me a vague, sick feeling as I sized up the distance between the car and the source. After another moment I pulled over to the side of the road and got out. An acrid smell stung my nostrils. I crunched along the road's rocky shoulder, eyes fixed high on the smoke, and began running when I knew I was right.

Up on the slope, three homes were on fire, the middle one Pavel's. Orange flames ripped through wood and spewed from windows. Walls collapsed in a burning whirl, crackling white at the core. Firefighters blasted water into the house beside Pavel's, subduing the flames, the structure now buried in a blue smoke that piled in the air. Water ran down the slope, red hoses writhing like snakes in the dust.

I was stopped at the yellow tape by a cop.

"No entry."

"I'm a journalist."

"Who with?"

"The *Messenger*."

To my surprise, she let me through. I stood by one of the fire trucks, where I could listen to the radio and watch the scene on the slope. Pavel's house burned so purely, the flame was almost clear in the daylight. You could hear the wood of the house crack and snap. The firefighters' beam of water vanished in the flame and the smoke turned gray.

When they'd finally beaten down enough of it, a firefighter took his ax to Pavel's door while another began prying the bars off the windows, smoke disgorging from every hole and flowing smoothly up the roof. The men pushed through the wreckage into the house, flames still gnawing at the walls.

I heard over the radio: "DOS."

Paramedics bolted from a white ambulance. I watched them hustle the stretcher up the switchback path. They couldn't get too close, smoke still pluming out, but a firefighter emerged from the house with something in his arms.

It was black, gnarled like a root, but you could see the naked toes dangling. He laid the body on the stretcher and the paramedics brought it down the hill.

I approached the body—it was what you had to do—and saw the head, cooked and faceless, baring its teeth. Then they zipped the bag and the ambulance surged away.

I don't know how long I stood there before Tim Braun, the *Messenger* reporter, came along the shoulder of the road on a scooter in a sparkling gold helmet. There wasn't anywhere to hide, so I had to watch him converse with the cop, who gestured in my direction. He came stalking over.

"So you're writing for the *Messenger* now."

I didn't answer. It was too strange just looking at the thick pink flesh of his face.

"Anyway, you owe me one," he said. "I told her you were with us."

Braun shielded his eyes and peered up the slope. The houses smoldered and fell.

"I knew I'd be too late," he said. "These things go up like tinderboxes, happens all the time."

I was thinking of Pavel's cigarette burning in his lips as he drowsed off on pills.

"Another daily drama on the west side," Braun said. "I guess you got what you came for, huh."

"I knew him."

Braun's eyes flickered. "Who?"

I gestured toward the house.

"Is he okay?"

I shook my head.

"I'm sorry," he said. "I didn't realize."

I coughed and he offered me a bottle of water. There was a strange taste in my mouth that I tried washing out, but even after I'd swirled and spat, it lingered.

"Hey," he said, "I need to ask a few questions around here, but it shouldn't take long. You want to get a drink or something? I know a few good spots. You buy me a round and we'll call it even, okay?"

I thought I'd inhaled human remains.

Braun shouted something after me as I set off down the road, hacking up whatever I could and spitting on the rocks. At one point I looked up and saw the people in the gridlock watching me, but I just kept spitting and spitting, it wouldn't come out.

THE TAPES

1.

Upon landing at LaGuardia, I had a message from Dr. Kriss. I called her back at the baggage carousel.

"I heard," she said. "It's awful, I'm so sorry."

I told her I'd seen the body.

"Between this and the shooting," she said, "you've been through so much, too much. Are you alright?"

I wanted to say there are things you can't unsee. But I remembered telling her about Quinn's mutilation, how she'd taken it as a hint of my inability to write a story like this. I still feared her cutting me loose and going with *USA Today* or something.

"I'm fine," I said.

"How did it happen?"

The only explanation I could offer was that, when I'd seen him, the medication had knocked him out with a lit cigarette in his hand. "It's horrible to imagine," I said, "but he might've set himself on fire."

Dr. Kriss let out a long, defeated sigh. "Christ. When I heard about the fire, it just took the wind out of my sails. We got some really good news this week, but it doesn't matter anymore."

"What was it?"

"Remember I told you we were courting a military contract?"

"You got it?"

"You'll be able to read all about it in *Medical Businessweek*. Everyone at Inland is celebrating. They're expecting a bump in stock price in the wake of the news."

Once again I felt the panic of losing my exclusive.

"Does that mean they'll make an announcement about the solution?" I asked.

"Not necessarily. People don't need to know exactly what we're working on, not yet. But you have everything you need to start writing, right?"

"I think so, yeah."

My suitcase flopped onto the carousel, end over end.

"I only ask because I'd understand if you had to take some time after, you know. And we won't be able to hold off the public's curiosity much longer. But don't worry—now that they're reconciled to your story coming out, I think my bosses see another big stock boost from the publicity."

"What about you?" I said, hauling the case off the track. "You're a major shareholder, after all."

"It's incredible to think what I'll be able to do," she said. "Imagine just one share of Rubicon applied to a place like west-side Mimico."

Turning from the carousel, I saw Annette, the woman I'd gone for drinks with once. She was seated on a bench eating an airport salad, half a hard-boiled egg on the plastic tines. I said goodbye to Dr. Kriss.

I considered just walking past. Annette hadn't seen me yet, and she'd evaded all my invitations. Why impose myself, humiliate myself? The call with Dr. Kriss, that was something—not friendship, but not far off. Real events played out in time and we connected through them. By comparison, Annette was just a face in the city, an allure blurring by.

Perhaps it was the intensity of the last few days that emboldened me to walk right up and say hello. As I might've predicted, her eyes sparkled and widened as she greeted me, like a special effect. She gulped the egg with mock embarrassment, then got up and embraced me with one arm, the lid of the salad box swinging in her hand.

"What are you doing here?" I said.

"Waiting for my sister. She's coming in from Omaha. How about you?"

I told her I'd been on a reporting trip in California.

"That's exciting," she said. "What's the scoop?"

"I can't really talk about it."

The appearance of delight rippled through her.

"I like that. Top secret, very sexy."

"Not really."

"I can't wait to see the results. We're long overdue, aren't we? We should really get together. I'll be busy entertaining my sister for the next little while, but drinks sometime soon?"

I glanced at my suitcase, which I'd set between us, then looked up and said, "I don't think so."

A line I'd never seen before appeared between her brows. "Sorry?"

"Well," I laughed, "you don't really mean it, do you? You've said the same thing a few times now, and when I follow up, you always make some excuse. Even now, you sort of tucked an excuse right into the invitation. Call me crazy, but if I invited you out in a week or so, wouldn't you say you're still busy with your sister, or if she's gone, that you're still tired from hosting her? And then more weeks would pass, and nothing."

Annette was considering me seriously, her fork upright in the salad's drizzled hunk of cucumber.

"I'm not trying to make you feel bad," I added.

"You're not," she said. "It's true, what you're saying. You're not imagining things."

It felt like a breakthrough, the first glimmer of intimacy.

"Then why?" I implored. "Why is it like this all the time?"

"I don't know," she said, giving me a look of such contempt that I felt it in my eyes a long time after. "It's just something in you, something—I don't know—blank."

"Blank?" I said, a harsh laugh escaping.

"Look, you asked, okay? I don't want to be saying any of this. I mean, you're funny, and interesting, and devoted to your work. But you're not right with people—you're always holding something back."

Only men had ever said something similar—that wall they hit with me—and I felt about to well up in front of this woman I'd really tried opening myself to, someone I would've, after getting closer, told anything, or almost anything.

"Just because I don't gush," I said, "or blurt out every last stupid thing that's on my mind?"

"That superior attitude doesn't serve you at all."

I sounded desperate. "All I mean is—"

"You might think you're smarter than other people, Whitney, but you're not."

"I'm sorry, really, what I meant—"

"You're missing something, that's what I'm saying, and it gives me the fucking creeps."

"Annette!"

A woman came stomping across the floor, arms outstretched. Annette exclaimed, went to greet her sister, and I was out the doors and running for a cab.

2.

I didn't want to face the blank page. I was at the *Bystander* office, looking over my research, but Annette's words kept cutting through my focus. I felt restless, strangely desirous of getting back in the air, off to some new location, transported out of myself.

The temptation for a journalist is to research forever. There's always something else to learn, and it's easy to worry that the very thing you don't know will prove the most important. But the truth is, you'll never get the whole story, there is no end, you only have the story you're going to tell. That's what I had, buried somewhere in the notes on my desk, if I could just focus long enough to find it.

First I had to string everything together on a strong through line. A magazine piece needs a spine, at once hard and flexible, so the reader never feels lost, never asks why they're taking all this time to read it. But the wealth of material was overwhelming, far more than I'd ever amassed for an article. Annette's voice in my head said I couldn't do it justice. Trying to capture real human suffering, I was bound to hit that wall.

The fucking creeps—

I set about cutting down the notes, trying to sort out which details the reader needed. Once I'd determined what to include, I began creating an outline, beat by beat. It took hours to produce this mess of points, with notes cramped in the margins, arrows connecting ideas, whole swaths X'd out, and as I worked, fully formed sentences kept emerging from nothing in my mind, and I preserved them on a separate sheet.

When at last I got to the end, I looked up to find most of the staff had gone home. There was silence at the *Bystander*. I realized with gratitude that Annette's voice had faded.

3.

I'd been dreading seeing Lane Porter. The thought of that night at his apartment still filled me with revulsion. Would he find a way to normalize relations, or would he keep coming on? There's nothing worse than a man who's learned persistence.

But that week was a reprieve. He didn't show up. A colleague told me he was on vacation, another said his mother was ill. I had lunch with Gordon Stone, and he said something about Lane's mother as well, though he sort of merged the stories, saying the two of them had taken a trip together.

"Where to?"

"Somewhere between coasts."

We were eating at one of Gordon's preferred spots, an Italian restaurant that served me one large ravioli stuffed with goose liver. I missed the Donut Shop. We'd had to pass it on our way here, and it was already a ghastly boutique called Full Throttle that sold motorcycle-themed clothing.

"Has anyone told you about Mort's little explosion?" Gordon asked.

"No, what happened?"

"The details remain obscure," he said, slicing grilled branzino. "All we know for sure is that one of the investors marched into Mort's office, demanding changes to a story."

"Which investor?"

"I can't keep them straight, I'm sorry. I'd never actually seen one before. You know, I always pictured them dressed up like robber barons, but the man was in sneakers and jeans. Well, he was terrifically upset, and Mort didn't react gracefully to his so-called editorial suggestions. We were all frozen in our seats as we listened to the shouts, like muted bombs in the room next door. Then the investor stormed out of the office, Mort calling after him, 'Don't ever come in like that again, you son of a bitch!' Or was it 'bastard'? None of us had ever seen him so angry. He was volcanic."

I broke the bread and mopped up the brown butter that had been spooned over the pasta.

"Any idea what set the investor off?"

"It's too byzantine for summary," Gordon said, "but Ben's been reporting on some of the new lobbyists that have been appearing in Washington since the attacks. He indulged, a little too freely in my view, in that sort of paranoid conjecture about Halliburton and Iraqi oil fields and so forth. Clearly the investor's got skin in the game somewhere."

"Do you think he'll pull out his money?"

"I suppose it depends on whether he's idealistic about the fourth estate. Most of these millionaire sorts rather enjoy the idea of bankrolling journalism, as long as it's vanquishing their enemies. Once the lens gets turned on them, they suddenly have a very different philosophy. Regardless, the check has been cashed, so we're safe until the end of the year. But I must admit, Mort has looked a tad remorseful."

When Gordon and I got back to the *Bystander*, Mort was out on the floor with all the other writers. Some were grouped around a table and some hung back, watching over cubicle walls.

The intern saw me and called, "She's here."

"Whitney." Mort motioned for me to hurry over.

I heard, "Don't get too close, Whitney."

In the middle of the table was a package. It had been delivered while Gordon and I were at lunch. In uneven lettering, it was addressed to me, care of the *Bystander* but marked CONFIDENTIAL, with about a dozen stamps and no return address. The whole thing was wrapped around and around with Scotch tape.

"Were you expecting this?" Mort said.

"No."

"What could it be?" someone asked, and someone answered, "Anthrax, obviously."

"I have friends at NBC," Nate Zimmer said. "They're all on Cipro."

"Alright, alright," Mort said. "What do you want to do, Whitney?"

I looked around at my colleagues. They all held the War on Terror in contempt, but in the presence of this package, they were freaked.

"I mean, I'd just open it," I said, and someone groaned. "But I don't want to be responsible for infecting anyone with biochemical weapons. Is there someone we can call?"

"I'd rather not have the FBI in here today," Mort said.

Everybody muttered agreement.

"Well," I said, "I guess to hell with it, then."

The intern said, "Do you want me to open it, Mr. Brewer?"

Mort looked at him a moment, but said, "No, probably not. Alright, everyone, get back."

He stood with me. The writers clustered near the exit.

"I didn't think I'd go out like this," he said.

"Nice knowing you, Mort."

"It's been fair-to-good."

I tore off the tape, dug my nails into the paper, and ripped. The package broke open and a set of videotapes spilled over the table. Mort and I stood there a moment, waiting for them to explode.

"You feel okay?" he asked. "Nausea?"

"No."

"Lymph glands normal?"

I touched my throat and said, "I think so."

"All clear," he called. "Just some cassettes."

Most of the staff went back to their desks, but a few came over to look.

"What's on them?" asked the intern.

"How would I know?" I said.

Mort gave me a pat on the back as I gathered them up. "One day we'll be terrorized," he said, "and then we'll know we're really in the conversation."

4.

The streetlight that usually burned through my window was dim, the scaffolding covered with a hunter-green cloth that shaded the glare. The restoration was almost complete. I kept expecting to come home to find the facade painted white. Then people would glance to the upper windows and think how brilliant it must be to live in New York in a pristine white apartment building. They'd start making inquiries, they'd be willing to pay almost anything.

I poured a glass of red and sat on the floor in front of the TV, the tapes in a stack beside me. They were numbered one through five but otherwise bore no labels. When I pushed #1 into the VCR, the screen went blue and then a picture wobbled into focus.

It was a shot of someone's basement, a washer and dryer and a row of fishing rods. The camera zoomed in to frame a stool set on the concrete floor. In the lower-right corner of the screen was a date: 05/02/02.

A man came out from behind the camera. It was Sunshine Ray. He wore a neon-green T-shirt that said *Hecho en Florida*, the color too harsh for the lens and sort of washing out at the edges. Ray sat and adjusted himself on the stool, but he'd done a poor job of framing and the upper half of the shot was filled with the stained ceiling, his face at the bottom. Somewhere off camera, a dog barked twice.

"Hi, Whitney." He waved. "If you're watching this, understand that what I'm about to show you is actually important, important enough to entrust this footage to the US Postal Service. And it means that, knock wood, noth-ing's happened to me and Romeo."

Ever since we'd spoken, Ray explained, he'd been angry at me. It wasn't personal; he knew I was only doing my job. "It's the job that pisses me off," he said. "You want the more thrilling story—Rubicon's medical miracle—so I realized, unless I did something crazy, you were going to run with it. I'd have to give you a better angle."

Now he rose and left the frame. Through the faint buzz of the tape, I heard a fridge door open and close, dogs barking in the background, and when he returned, he held two bags of white blood. He jiggled the solution for the camera.

"You're probably wondering how I got my hands on these, so maybe now's a good time to start taking notes."

As if watching a self-help tape, I obediently took up my pad.

Yesterday, Ray said, he and Romeo went hunting for Common Dreams. They located the purple truck roaming by the Glades—I pictured Gwen and Vince—and for a long time they stalked it through the south side, waiting for their chance. When the truck wandered onto a burned-down block, Ray and Romeo pulled ski masks over their heads. They each carried a snub-nosed .38.

Romeo lay down in the middle of the street while Ray hid behind the last standing wall of a burned-down house. The truck rolled to a stop just a few feet from the body. One of the paramedics hustled over to Romeo, who suddenly rolled over, pointing the gun.

"She threw her hands in front of her face and dropped to her knees," Ray said, visibly fond of the memory. "Meanwhile, the guy had gone to open the back and I swooped in behind him, yelling all kinds of wacko stuff. He figured we were junkies or something. He kept saying there wasn't anything I could use back there, that they were on our side. Romeo told them to stand against the side of the truck, legs spread, and kept his gun on them while I swiped the bags."

Now I recognized the significance of the date in the corner of the screen, *05/02/02*. The day before, I'd stood on Wigwam Deck, and Dr. Kriss had alluded to some kind of incident in Retreat.

You wouldn't believe the lengths our competitors are willing to go to.

Sunshine Ray removed the camera from the stand and the shot swept across the basement floor. I saw the dogs. There were three in a pen—two charcoal, one apricot—the sort of stray mutts that prowled the streets of Retreat. Romeo was leaning into the pen, pouring food into their bowls.

"We're going to find out what really happens when you transfuse living creatures," Ray narrated. "Romeo and I rounded up some subjects from the local wildlife here. I explained the solution to them in detail. It's hard to tell how much they understand, you know, but they wag their tails and that's good enough for me. Better than informed consent by Rubicon standards, right? Here, Romeo, put this on the tripod."

He passed the camera to Romeo, who zoomed way in on Ray's mouth before pulling back. Then the camera was screwed onto the tripod, framing the pen.

Ray had pulled on blue plastic gloves. He squatted down with the dogs, whose tails swished around him as they munched the food. He said he'd named them Rumsfeld, Cheney and Bush—"All the gang, right here."

"This is Rumsfeld," he said as Romeo passed him a syringe.

Face buried in the bowl, the charcoal mutt didn't even notice as Ray injected the sedative.

He passed the syringe back to Romeo, who handed him another.

"This is Cheney." He injected the second dog. "And Bush is for control," he said, petting the apricot mutt. "So this lucky guy won't be given the solution. Rumsfeld and Cheney will get a transfusion and then we'll compare the results. It won't be perfect, but even just me and Romeo in our goddamn basement will be more professional than Rubicon."

Ray was raking through the control dog's fur.

"Alright," he said, "I think that's it. Cut, Romeo."

The picture blinked, and now the camera framed a table and an IV stand. Romeo held Rumsfeld in his arms. The sedative had kicked in. He laid the mutt on the table. Ray came into the shot in a white lab coat, carrying an electric razor. Romeo exposed the dog's neck and Ray shaved off a patch of fur, exposing white flesh. Ray pinched some skin and punctured it with a needle, and over the next few minutes I watched as he drained some blood. Then he hooked a bag of the solution onto the stand and transfused it into the dog.

"We'll know almost instantly if he can handle it," said Ray, his voice bouncing off the concrete walls. "The solution makes matching unnecessary, so there shouldn't be any agglutination, at least in theory."

The solution flowed into the sleeping dog. I don't know what I expected— for him to rouse, wolflike, and lunge for throats—but after the transfusion was complete, the vital signs were normal.

"I think we can proceed," Ray said, and Romeo brought Cheney over.

When both dogs had been transfused, Ray turned to the camera.

"And now we wait," he said, and the tape shuddered to black.

5.

I stayed up all night watching tapes #2 and #3. The footage was almost heartwarming.

"Off they go," said Sunshine Ray, and Romeo set the dogs loose in the backyard. The trio galloped over dark-green grass, the camera clumsily seeking them as they pounced, collided, and rolled. Cut to the kitchen, where Romeo doled out rib bones and the dogs held them in their grins, tails erect as they trotted proudly across the tiled floor. Then it was back to the chase, the Florida sun flowing over their coats, before all three got tired at once and there was a long scene of them lazing in the living room, the strains of "Blue Hawaii" on a stereo, eyes fluttering shut.

Once I heard the workers outside, I realized it was morning. I went to bed for a few hours, then felt compelled to go in to the *Bystander* after lunch. My reporting was meant to be over, and any day now I expected Mort to call me into his office and ask for a draft. I had to show him at least part of something. I told myself I'd work on the story's cornerstones—the biography of Dr. Kriss, the trial in Retreat, the investors' tour in Arcade, the Pavel Firea interview—things that wouldn't be altered by Ray and his dogs no matter what the final tapes revealed.

The story in its final form, in stark *Bystander* sentences, seemed near to my fingertips, just waiting to meet the keys. But when I got to my desk, I saw a sheet of paper.

CLOSE ENCOUNTER, read the headline. *Whitney Chase, Special to the* Seattle Post-Intelligencer.

It was an article from 1994, printed off the Internet. Certain names were circled in red, certain lines were underscored.

I snatched the page and looked around. Mort was in his office, massaging his temples. Gordon Stone was reading the *Times Literary Supplement*. It seemed impossible that no one, in this room of professional observers, had noticed the page, but nobody was paying attention. I folded it up and walked over to Gordon's desk.

"Is Lane back from vacation?"

"I haven't seen him," Gordon said, folding the *TLS*. "Why, are you finally coming around on your furry little admirer?"

"Just a fact-check thing," I muttered, and turned away.

"I was only kidding, Whitney."

I tried settling down to work, but every time the elevator stopped at our floor, my eyes shot to the doors.

I stayed at the *Bystander* until some of my colleagues started going home, then headed straight for my local. The first beer vanished in replenishing gulps. Now, in the darkness and coolness of the bar, I unfolded the article, smoothed it on the table, and read.

As soon as it premiered, my editor at the *P-I* started pushing everyone to watch *The X-Files*. Along with grunge and the local comics scene, the show's filming up in Vancouver confirmed his vision of the Pacific Northwest as the epicenter of '90s weird. The editor himself was square, not part of that world at all, but like many members of Seattle's professional class, he liked the idea of being surrounded by eccentrics. They were an ambience, a feature of his lifestyle, accessible through CDs and network programming. He pinned up one of those I WANT TO BELIEVE posters in his office.

When he heard that a group of amateur ufologists met regularly in Yakima, he sent me down to cover a meeting. In particular, he said, he hoped I'd find someone who claimed to have been abducted by aliens. But the story he had in mind wouldn't be sarcastic, he stressed. He wasn't interested in another lampoon of tinfoil cranks who'd seen a meteor shower and claimed they'd traveled to Zeta Reticuli. No, he told me, peering at his poster, take it seriously, write it straight, write it like you almost believe it.

The problem was that the Yakima meeting was impossible to take seriously. It was held in the basement of a bingo hall, just a half dozen middle-aged men and some of their wives, bored out of their minds. None of the men had been abducted, though a few said they'd seen UFOs. In fact they saw them often, they said, it was just a fact of life near Mount Rainier. Had they ever made contact? No. Were they trying? Not really. The men seemed to enjoy withholding information. I felt they were competing for who could be most mysterious. Then the questions turned on me: What was my agenda? Did I fully understand the danger of what I was writing about? By the time the meeting adjourned, I had virtually nothing of use in my notes.

But on the drive back to Seattle, the story started to creep. Soon a man emerged, a composite figure. I identified him as Craig Sweeney—*he requested that we use a pseudonym*—a logger from Union Gap. He'd been the star of the meeting, the other men treating him with an almost holy respect. Sweeney claimed to have been abducted one night in the late '80s. Coming home from a fishing trip on the Columbia River, Sweeney found himself drowsing at the wheel and pulled off the highway for a nap. That's when he saw a blue light, *like a torch above the trees.* He approached it, the most beautiful thing he'd ever seen, then felt wind rushing through the pines, so powerful he felt his skin might rip away.

He awakened. Standing over him were short, hairless creatures with domed foreheads and tiny black eyes. For three days and three nights, Sweeney was held in what he described as a benevolent captivity. But when he was set back on the forest floor, totally naked, only scraps of memory remained—the cold blue heat of the light, the stampeding wind, and the aliens' glittering eyes.

"What gives Craig such credibility," I quoted one of the ufologists as saying, *"is that he's just a regular guy. He doesn't want the fame, he just wants to share his story, let people know this stuff is really out there."*

That's why I used a pseudonym, I explained. In Sweeney's words, *"I've seen how guys like me get treated. People think they're looney tunes."*

In the article on the table before me, everything about Sweeney was underlined.

My editor had loved the piece, it was exactly what he'd sent me out to find, but even at the time it turned out to be more trouble than it was worth. A few of the ufologists contacted the editor, saying Sweeney didn't exist and the article had clearly been planted—but by whom, and why? Their conspiratorial zeal undermined their complaint. My editor didn't believe them.

For several years afterward, I received mail from all over the world, asking for Sweeney's contact information. People needed to get in touch, they'd had a similar experience—the light, the eyes, were the same. It was one of my most unwieldy fabrications. But it died down eventually. I'd written that story—all my *P-I* stories—at a time when things really could disappear. The Internet existed, but it wasn't like it is today—a dragging weight, an inescapable record—and so even when I crept, I didn't write with the fear that, years later, my words would crush and destroy me. I thought they'd exist as radio transmissions exist, beaming into space, vanishing into nowhere.

By now I was sedated by beer and could think more clearly about what message Lane, and of course it was Lane, was trying to send. If he simply wanted me fired, he could've gone straight to Mort, so why the printout on my desk? It was like he wanted me to tremble at how he could expose me.

I shredded the article into tiny white squares. The waiter swept them into his hand.

"Love letter?"

"My secret admirer."

"Poor bastard." He tossed the paper in my empty glass. "Another round?"

I pretended to think.

"Yes."

6.

I was drunk, but I don't remember noticing anything unusual when I got home.

I cracked a Miller and decided to watch the rest of Ray's tapes, hoping to calmly zone out on dogs dashing through a coastal afternoon. But tape #4 opened on a carpeted staircase, the camera bouncing as Ray hurried to the basement. I could see his feet taking the stairs two at a time, and then realized that the strange tone on the tape, pure and sustained, like feedback, wasn't some defect, it was the wail of an animal.

"It's about three-thirty a.m.," Ray narrated, "and we've been—" He almost slipped. "Christ, we've been woken up by that sound, can you hear it?"

Now he was in the basement, the wail penetrated my eardrum, and the camera fell out of focus as it adjusted to the light of the overhead bulbs. When it zeroed in again, I saw Romeo at the table, restraining one of the charcoal mutts.

"Hold on," Ray said.

He set the camera on the tripod but didn't zoom in on the table. Romeo and the dog were just a silhouette.

I checked the date. The animals had been under observation for twenty-two days.

Ray hurriedly prepared a sedative and injected the dog. Then he picked up the camera and we glided toward the table.

"It's Rumsfeld," he said, and focused on the dog's front legs. The fur was gnawed away or stuck with blood to exposed flesh, glistening like raw chicken. "He did this to himself."

The dog was already drowsing, but his breathing was still rapid, with a small, pained squeak at every exhalation.

"Show the mouth," Ray told Romeo, who pulled back the dog's black lips.

Blood jetted onto the table. The teeth were being pushed out at the roots by some strange pink growth splitting open the gums.

Ray's gloved hand prodded the pink. "It's solid. Feels almost rubbery."

The camera swooped away and showed Cheney. He was licking his front legs but otherwise looked normal. In the corner of the basement, Bush sat watching his fellow subjects.

Then the shot cut to two days later, and I didn't know what I was seeing anymore.

On the table was a heap of fur. The dog was still alive, panting, but he must've been tranquilized almost to death. His jaw was broken open, over-flowing with a shapeless mass of pink. The stuff had ruptured the skin along his ribs and braided with the tendons of his legs. Bulbs of pink protruded from his asshole.

Cheney was sedated too, and looked just as Rumsfeld had two days before, his teeth cracked, pink breaking through the gums.

"It shows first in the mouth and lips"—Ray gulped—"maybe—because the flesh replenishes fastest there—"

The voice behind the camera spoke: "We have to kill them."

I'd never heard Romeo speak.

Ray said, "We have to see it to the end."

"This is the end."

The camera cut to black.

7.

I paced around the apartment, a pattern dancing, strung together like lanterns on a wire, behind my eyes—Quinn's shadow that night at the barbecue, the way he gnashed the meat, Zeke on the day of his discharge, his lip chewed and bleeding. I'd thought it was just a nervous tic.

It shows first in the mouth and lips.

"I thought I saw her," Carmen had said, and her friends told me it was just a junkie, it couldn't be Jules.

Like she was eating her face.

I didn't think about Lane. Pink globs intruded when my mind veered from Floella to Quinn to Jules to Zeke. When at last I went to sleep, I slipped into a dream of sitting in Pavel's house in Mimico. The front door was open and I could see cars on the road below. In my lap, yellow flames began to catch. I couldn't get up, I tried brushing them off, but they gathered on my wrists and leapt to my chest. I heard the air around me crackle and still I couldn't stand. The door was right there, cars rushing by, and I spread the fire over myself until it screamed.

I awakened. He was there.

It was him, the shape I'd seen in my Retreat bungalow, in my Arcade hotel, the figure of my half dreams. He was frozen at the foot of the bed. I knew he wasn't real, because this time I could see his face. It caught streetlight and floated in the dark. It was Pavel Firea, unmistakably—Pavel's clustered features, his broken-looking nose and crumpled lips.

Unlike the times I'd seen him before, I could move. I felt fury toward the ghost, how he'd crept into the waking world, and in one thoughtless motion I lunged for him. But my hands met something solid, a real man, warm to the touch, and he wasn't a dream as he stumbled back with a yelp of surprise and fell against the dresser.

The lamp toppled and I got to my feet, clutching the sheet, as he scrambled out of my room.

I slammed the bedroom door and pressed it shut. I don't know how long I leaned against it, barely breathing as I listened to the apartment. The space seemed to expand for miles in every direction. There was silence, as if I really was still sleeping, and only the fallen lamp exposed the truth. It had happened.

8.

It was after dawn when the cops arrived. I'd made coffee and watched the sky pale. Rain had fallen at some point in the night, and it was soothing to hear the morning traffic glide over wet asphalt.

I poured coffee for the officers and they took notes. After I told them what had happened, they asked for a physical description of the intruder. I sketched Pavel's features, but added that I'd been dreaming of someone I once knew, a dead man, before waking up.

The officers exchanged glances.

"I understand," said one. "But you'd recognize this creep if you saw him again?"

"I think so."

"Invasions like this are getting more common," he said, peering out my window at the scaffolding. "A really committed perv will climb a few stories, easy."

"This is pretty good stuff," said the other officer, swirling his mug. "Can I get a refill?"

"Scaffolding is like monkey bars to them. I've seen a guy swing on these bars like a fucking orangutan."

"He's not kidding. You notice anything missing?"

"No."

"Then you're lucky. But you've checked, you know, panty drawers and all that?"

I dutifully went to the bedroom but didn't notice anything. I righted the lamp and smoothed the sheets.

The officer flipped his notebook shut. "Well, you gave us a solid description. I don't want to make any promises, but you never know. In the meantime, you'd better get locks on these windows. How's your landlord?"

"Average, I guess."

"Then it's probably a stretch to expect enhanced security. But he should know every time there's construction like this, you get a little crime wave in the building."

"Still, we encourage renovations," said the other. "Quality-of-life measures— a nice new facade brings crime down, long-term."

The cops agreed with each other: "Long-term, crime is going down all over the place."

"Local crime."

"Terrorism's a whole other thing."

"That's way up."

"You don't know the half, Whitney, and you don't want to know."

It was only when they'd dusted for fingerprints and left, and I lay down on my couch, facing the TV, that I came to think the ghost might've been in the apartment before I'd even come home. I don't know where he would've hidden, in the closet maybe, peering through the slats, but I knew he'd observed me as I'd watched Ray's experiments and paced around, horrified, and he must've grasped the importance of what I was watching, what I was thinking. I understood all this because my eyes fell to the floor and I saw he'd taken the tapes.

THE SKULL

1.

"I think that's everything."

The girl from *Vice* closes *The Complete Bystander*. As soon as she stops recording, she becomes relaxed, as if we're friends. She has to rush back to Brooklyn and change before heading for drinks with her boss, she says— holding on to this job is exhausting. Do I have plans for tonight?

When I say no, she starts asking for my opinion on various TV shows. I tell her I haven't seen any of those.

"How do you spend your free time?"

"I read. Sometimes I watch sports."

She slings her bag over a shoulder, waiting for some elaboration. When it doesn't come, she says, "I'll send you a link when the story's up. It shouldn't take more than a couple weeks."

"Will I get a call from fact-check?"

"Probably not."

I offer my hand and thank her for the interview. "It's very gratifying to know someone is still so passionate about the *Bystander*."

"You know," she says, lingering just inside my office door, "I can't help but feel like I haven't gotten everything. You promise you're not working on a memoir or something?"

"Who would read something like that?"

"I would."

"I assure you, I'm not."

She shakes her head and says, "It's hard to believe you'd just walk away like that."

"Why?"

"Someone of your talent. It just seems like a waste." When I don't immediately reply, she adds, "Sorry, but it does."

"I remember feeling like you," I say. "I couldn't understand anyone who didn't think writing for magazines was the most important thing in the world."

"Exactly," she says, excited, as if I'm leading her toward some key revelation.

"That feeling goes away."

At last she leaves. The sun has fallen, a cold blue light pressed against my office window. My colleagues have quit for the day, but I like to be overworked. There are things I can do before I go home.

I begin combing through a press release that's been submitted for my analysis by some Midwestern agricultural concern. They're trying to get ahead of reports of toxic runoff from their pig farms in Nebraska. Blood-rimmed fingernails clicking on the keys, I offer notes, e-mail it back. Tomorrow, the corporation will disseminate the release to the wire services and I'll watch the words I've inserted, like germs under a microscope, multiply in newspapers all across America.

This is how I make the news today.

·

On my walk home, I take a detour and pass by Lane Porter's old apartment building. The *Vice* interview has brought the story to my tongue, so while I'd usually avoid this block, I'm attracted to the landmark, as if to confer with someone else who knows.

Lane's building still has its green-and-red detailing. Back then, I'd thought it was the height of tastelessness, but now it looks like a minor architectural masterpiece beside the deadly conservative restorations on the rest of the block.

What would my old colleagues think, I wonder, if one of them ran into me outside this building? Would they even recognize me? The last time I saw any of them was at Mort Brewer's memorial, almost ten years ago. Mort retired after the *Bystander* folded, then died of a heart attack in his sleep, a death to envy.

At the memorial, I sat with Gordon Stone. All along our row I saw the old *Bystander* team: Ross Briggs, Nathan Zimmer, Richard Calvin, names the *Vice* writer associates with some golden age of the American magazine. I felt we were distinguished from the other attendees, we'd shared in something near to the dead man's heart, but I also remember feeling almost unwelcome. The *Bystander*'s demise was when people started smelling earth on Mort, and I felt like we'd failed him. We were responsible for the beginning of the end that had brought us together that day.

But more than anything, as I listened to eulogies from Bob Silvers, Harold Evans, and Lewis Lapham, I was relieved. No one ever believed in me like Mort had, yet I was glad to see him go, just as I'd be glad to see Lane's building torn down. Mort was the last one I ever told about the story.

2.

Once I saw the tapes had been stolen, I called Sunshine Ray. He didn't answer. I left a message, then tried to sleep, daylight framing the closed curtains. But I kept shuddering awake, as if the ghost were there again. It couldn't be Pavel, of course, but someone had followed me, someone had stolen the tapes, and he could only be from Rubicon.

Who'd sent him? I thought of Kenneth Sample, the CEO. His job was to protect the product Rubicon was selling to investors, the military— to me.

Everything we've developed here, Sample had said at the lab in Arcade, *and every step of the trial, will be a matter of historical record.*

When they first met, he told me, he'd vowed to protect Eva's vision. Was that why he'd sent the ghost—to make sure I wouldn't spoil her rise into medical stardom? That would explain why, each time I'd seen the apparition, I'd lost a chunk of my reporting— the recording of Zeke thrashing in the bed, my notes on the Wigwam Deck confrontation—things Rubicon wouldn't want on the record. He'd crept into my bedroom and stolen the story.

I slipped into a shallow sleep, but when I awakened, all the sheets kicked off, I realized that something about my Sample theory didn't add up. He had the money, yes, and Rubicon had the reach, but how would he have a clue what my notebooks contained?

On a hunch, I dug out the number for Baker Watt's office in Arcade. When he picked up, I asked him how things were going.

"The trial's nearly wrapped," he said. "They're discharging the last subjects from Ascension on Friday."

"And then what?"

"And then my contract's up. I'll be sorry to say goodbye to Rubicon. Once you're part of something like this, everything else seems trivial."

"I understand what you mean."

"But my Rubicon stock means I can afford to wait a while for the next opportunity. So what's this all about?"

I told him I was calling with a bit of a strange question.

"That's okay," he said. "Shoot."

"I got started on this story after we met," I said. "You remember?"

"Of course."

"I'm curious, looking back—why did you want me to meet Dr. Kriss?"

Watt paused and said, "I'm not sure I follow."

"I mean, you said you wanted to help me understand the trial."

"Yeah, that's what you wanted, right?"

"Right. But why Dr. Kriss? Why not someone else at Rubicon—Kenneth Sample, for instance? Wouldn't he know more about the overall operation? Doesn't he control it?"

There was a long silence.

"Hello?" I said.

"Are you recording this?"

"No."

"Let me call you back," he said, and hung up.

I spent a few minutes cleaning off the soot the cops had left on the window frame when dusting for prints. Then the phone rang. When I answered, I could tell Watt had switched to a cell phone and was outdoors.

"Sorry," he said, "I don't mean to seem evasive. It's just, you understand, I'm a couple weeks away from the end of the contract, and I don't want to be heard speaking personally about anyone at the company."

"I understand."

I repeated my question—why Dr. Kriss?

"I can always tell where the brains are," he said, a phrase I recalled from our first encounter.

"And why not Kenneth Sample?"

"Can this be off the record?"

"Alright."

"And you abide by that sort of thing, right? When I say off the record, that's binding?"

"Yes."

"Okay, well, the thing is, it's always been pretty clear to me that Ken doesn't really understand the trial. You've met him, right? He came out of retirement for this. He might be a legend in certain corporate circles, but he doesn't have the mental agility anymore, if you catch my drift." Watt paused. "Maybe he was in California too long. But I don't want to get personal. It's just that—off the record—from day one, whenever I had a question about anything, nobody but Dr. Kriss could answer. In my opinion, it's ridiculous that she isn't the most highly compensated person in the company. She oversees everything—three simultaneous trials, plus the product's manufacture, plus the reports—it's staggering."

I said yes, she was very industrious.

"It's gotten to the point that, when I need anything from Ken's office, they send me straight to Dr. Kriss. All the company itself seems to handle is payroll and drumming up investment. So when you came along wondering about the trial, the science, it seemed only natural to put you in touch with Dr. Kriss. I wanted Rubicon to put its best foot forward, and that's her."

"Did you have to clear the interview with Sample's office?" I was remembering that, from the very beginning, Dr. Kriss had made it sound as if Rubicon was against my reporting.

"Rubicon was fine with it," Watt said. "They left the decision up to her. But you turned out pretty good friends, huh?"

"Yeah," I said, "in a way."

"As close as a journalist can ever get, I suppose. Anyway, look, I probably shouldn't say more. Is there anything else?"

"I think that's it."

He must've detected some change in my voice. "So what do you think," he said with affected playfulness, "should I cash out my Rubicon stock now, or wait until your story comes out and juices it?"

"I really can't answer that."

He hung on the line for a second, then said, cautiously, "But there's no time like the present, is there?"

"Is that a general question?"

"Sure."

"Then no," I said, "there isn't."

When I hung up, my mind strained to lift the weight of the fact: only one person could've sent the ghost.

I went to the bathroom, flushed my face with ice-cold water, and watched the droplets rain into the sink.

I'd botched the story. It had all played out in front of me and I'd let it pass, unobserved. For the first time, I felt like I wanted to drop it, walk away, ask Mort to put me back on the culture file. How could I move it forward now? Every path seemed closed, every move anticipated. If I asked Dr. Kriss to produce another subject, she'd have an answer: contracts behind contracts, people protecting privacy, the black box of protocol. She'd insist she'd already gone above and beyond to secure Pavel's permission. Then she'd threaten to take her story to *USA Today*. And why not? Let her go. Billions are at stake for them, I told myself, and everyone who could corroborate the story has died or disappeared.

And then, in my terror, I felt the subjects. There was Jules, who'd vanished on a Florida night, and Floella, who'd slipped between the cracks in Colorado, and Pavel, who'd burned on a slope in California. I felt them inside me, wanting out. But how? The more I focused on the subjects, each in turn, the more fluid they became, diluted by doubt. I couldn't decide what was real. The truth was flowing through my head, a runoff into nowhere.

It stopped at Zeke. The bike thief, the subject in Retreat—he was solid. His blood had soaked my pants, he'd received the solution right in front of me, I'd observed him every step of the way. If I could somehow find him again, maybe the truth would follow.

I lay in bed that night, a knife on the table beside me, and knew I wasn't going back to the culture file. I was going back to Retreat.

3.

Before heading into the office the next morning, I booked my flight to Tampa. I had to pay for it myself, which wasn't ideal, I didn't have much saved, but surely Mort would find the money later if I managed to nail down the new dimensions of the story.

But when I arrived at the office, all thoughts of Florida voided at the sight of another printout from the *Seattle Post-Intelligencer*. It sat on my keyboard, defaced with red lines. They looked like they'd been scratched in with fingernails.

Lane Porter was at his desk, arrayed behind his action figures. As we locked eyes, the rage was like vomit surging up my throat. I couldn't open my mouth.

"Whitney?"

I turned to see Mort standing at his office door.

"Can I have a word with you?"

I glanced at Lane. He'd turned back to his monitor. I stuffed the pages in my pocket and felt my colleagues watch as I crossed the floor.

"Take a seat," Mort said, and shut the door behind me.

The TVs were off. For the first time in months, I had his undivided attention.

"We've got a problem."

I always knew this day would come.

"Mort—"

"I'm forecasting lean times," he said. "This is really embarrassing, but I'm asking if I can withhold your next paycheck."

I'd so expected certain words, I hardly heard the ones he'd spoken.

"My paycheck?"

"I'm only asking writers who've had research money directed their way recently. I'm trying to bank a little capital. There's going to be a gap that needs bridging soon."

"I see."

"It's your right to say no," he stressed. "I'm not demanding this as your boss, I'm asking as a friend. If you believe in this thing of ours, then I really need a favor."

I was so relieved not to hear him say "Seattle" that I was only too eager to grant the request. "Yes, of course."

"Thank you, Whitney. You have no idea what this means. I promise to make it up to you at the soonest opportunity."

"I'm sure you will, Mort."

"How's the story coming?"

It didn't seem like the right time to mention that I needed to go back to Florida. Instead, I said I'd encountered some difficulties structuring the material.

"Well," he said, "considering you won't be spending too many nights at the opera in the next little while, now's a good time to really sink your teeth in."

"I agree."

"I can't wait to read it. Let's see something soon, okay?"

When I emerged from Mort's office, I saw Lane heading for the elevator. Gordon Stone observed me as I dashed across the room to join him. I waited until we were alone in the elevator before pulling out the pages.

"What are you doing, Lane?"

He laughed in my face.

"Just because I didn't want to fuck you—"

The doors opened to people waiting.

Lane breezed past them into the lobby. I pursued him onto the street. I said I wanted an answer.

"This isn't personal," he said, continuing to walk. "It's about the facts. I checked your pieces, all the way back to the *P-I*. Do you know how many contain fabrications?"

"Okay, okay," I said, trying to placate him enough to keep his voice from rising.

"I've compiled a complete dossier," Lane said, and now he stopped and peered at me. "You don't deserve any of this, Whitney. You don't deserve to be who you are."

I took the printout and tore it in two, but Lane only smiled.

"You have twenty-four hours," said the fact-checker. "Either you come clean or I hand everything over to Mort."

4.

I bought a bottle of Hennessy and hurried home. The trees along the avenue rattled in a sweaty breeze, black clouds mixing in the sky. Rain began to fall, first as hot, heavy drops, then as one gray blanket in a sideways wind.

I ducked into the entrance of my building. When I got upstairs, I felt the eyes of the ghost.

I grabbed a knife and stalked around, searching every hiding place, finding nothing. Still I could feel the heat of his body, somewhere. I cracked the gold cap of the Hennessy. After the first glass, I didn't feel so observed. I had another, then sat at the window with my knife.

I considered what it would be like to confess to Mort. I'd knock on my editor's office door and tell him there was something he needed to know.

At first he'd worry it was about the money, but I'd watch his eyes harden as he absorbed what I was saying. I'd made unclean his spotless magazine. I'd defected, no better than the men on his TV, selling a war that shouldn't exist. Only absolute transparency would secure the *Bystander*'s survival. He'd have to expose me. In a matter of days my name would become like Janet Cooke's, a case to study in J-school ethics class, a story to strengthen the bonds of the journalistic fraternity.

I'd almost halved the bottle but wasn't drunk enough. I needed something hard and sharp to lance this fear. I poured another glass. There came the low growl of distant thunder. Would it be easier just to flee? If it was all coming out anyway, why stay in the city, the site of disgrace? Empty my bank account and in twenty-four hours I could be on the other side of the world.

I looked around the apartment and wondered what I'd miss, but all I had was my connection to the *Bystander*. There weren't any lovers, any friends, there were only some preferred restaurants, the route I took home, the place I liked to sit at the back of the movie theater, my local bar.

In one vertiginous flash, like a dream you fall into that spits you right back up, I thought of ending this. I looked out the window. I could climb onto the scaffolding, drop right off, right now.

I reeled back, poured one more glass, and dialed Lane's number.

"Hello?"

"There must be some way we can work this out."

"I don't think so."

"Please," I said, "let me see you, so we can talk."

There was a pause, and the distance over the phone seemed close, like my lips were on the rim of his ear.

He told me to come over.

5.

I only realized how drunk I was when I sat down on the subway. The car jolted and I burped a sour gas that would've burned blue. My eyes clamped shut and purple dots swirled in the dark. I nodded off, nearly missing my stop, but awakened feeling strangely sharp.

Rain smacked me in the face as I emerged from the station, the downpour swooping in the streetlights, the sky churning orange. Nobody was out. I hustled along the sidewalk, leaping over pools and jumping back as a bus sent a wall of water lurching over the curb.

"You're soaked," Lane said when he opened the door.

"Got anything to drink?"

"Some wine."

"That's fine."

As he made for the kitchen, I saw that his shoulders and back were wet. The window in the living room was open, the rain loud as it drummed the rusted fire escape where he kept his herb garden.

Lane handed me the glass and we stood dumbly for a second.

I said, "I'm going to talk to Mort tomorrow morning."

"Talk? You mean confess."

"Yes."

I think he was surprised. "That's good."

"But I want you to show me what you found."

"Come on—you already know."

He was about to turn away when I grabbed his arm. "No, I don't."

Lane looked at my hand. I released him.

"I really don't," I said. "It all happened so long ago. I want to know what I'm confessing to."

"You're sure?"

"Please. Do this one thing for me."

We sat on the white leather couch, just as we had on the night he'd climbed onto me. Lane pulled out a red file folder and began laying the contents on the table. Each article looked like the Rubicon report after we'd fact-checked it together, Post-it Notes overlapping up the margins like scales on a snake, each sentence underlined in blue or red—blue for fact, red for fiction. There was always at least one red mark, sometimes a gash across a whole section, sometimes just a little nick. He'd found more than I'd expected, including actual honest mistakes that now appeared to be part of my grand deception.

"Nothing from the *Bystander*?" I said.

"No."

I suppose I could be proud of that. After I moved to New York and began writing on culture, the creep had hidden itself from me, plaguing me with doubts about my work, what secrets it contained. But now I'd been fact-checked entirely. My stories for Mort had been real.

"Some stuff I could check over the phone or with LexisNexis," Lane said, "just minor variations woven into the texture of the piece." It felt like he was rehearsing his eventual interview with the *Columbia Journalism Review*. "But at a certain point I needed boots on the ground, so I took my vacation and went to Seattle. I spent a week in the basement of the Hall of Vital Records and crisscrossing the city looking for the people in your stories. How did you get this stuff in the *P-I* in the first place?"

Staying calm as I tried to figure out what to do, I told him what I could. "It's a part of me, just what I do, unless I fight against it."

"Didn't anyone check your reporting?"

I told him that if I actually noticed I'd invented a detail, I'd add it to my notes and camouflage it by surrounding it with other true but irrelevant things I'd dredge up from my memory.

"Anyway, they trusted me," I said. "I'd sometimes get corrections and the occasional letter to the editor, but these were just frivolous stories, things you'd find stylish and amusing and then forget directly after. Everyone preferred them this way. The creep made life more interesting."

"The creep?"

I don't think I'd ever said the word out loud before.

"That's what I call it," I said, looking at my lap.

Lane took notes as I talked. There was a certain grace to him now, legs crossed, the end of the pen to his lips as he peered at me, nodding seriously before jotting something down.

"You're a fascinating case, Whitney. I always knew I was too honest, too factual, to be a writer. The game is rigged against guys like me. But now this—you—fell right into my lap."

He had a true story all his own. I was something he could pitch.

"Look at this." He pulled out the article about the ufologists in Yakima and Craig Sweeney, my alien abductee. "It's really amazing what you did here—the creep. But these guys don't forget. You know what I did?"

"No, what did you do?"

"I drove all the way to Yakima and met with as many people from the meeting as I could. They were happy to share. To them, it's like it happened yesterday. A few still had the article, clipped out and laminated in these crazy scrapbooks. You know, they've built this whole theory around why you wrote that. It's all part of a massive misinformation campaign, Pentagon propaganda, that sort of thing."

As he marveled at his own handiwork, how he'd skinned me to the bone, Lane had grown excited, and I experienced something I hadn't felt in years, not since Keith showed me the tape, my naked body, his cock driving in. My spirit fled away and away until there was only this trapped feeling, breath squeezing out of me, no heartbeat, only skull.

It spoke: "Lane, look at me."

He turned, and when I leaned into the kiss, I felt the bristles of his beard, the dry contact of lips. At once he gripped me by the back of my neck, his fingers pushing in, his tongue in my mouth like a fish in a hole.

We disengaged. His little eyes were dreamy, sweat dotting his forehead. He roughly stroked my hair, as if he'd never petted something soft before.

"This is wrong," he said. "It won't change anything."

"You're the only one I've told that to. You're the only one who understands."

He looked at me then, trying to study me deeply, to perceive me totally, to bring all his powers of observation to bear upon my face, when there was no face. My rage had burned the flesh away.

I went for another kiss. Lane held me off.

"No," he said, "like this."

He turned away and fiddled with his fly, glancing at me over his shoulder. When he swung back, I saw he'd pulled his pants down partway and had his dick out. It was fat and red, nested in orange hair. He choked it, scowling at me.

"You like it."

I nodded.

"Say it."

"I like it."

His dick squished as he pumped it. He put a hand on his balls and started rolling them between his fingers. I watched the oozing purple head.

"Open your mouth."

My jawbone dropped. He looked into my mouth. When I glanced down, he was jerking it hard and come started sputtering out, falling like a web on the hairs.

Not zipping up, not making a sound, he reclined on the couch. I could smell the come. His belly heaved, dick shrinking, scrotum contracting.

He said, "Good girl."

Then he grasped me by the cheekbones and kissed the cold plate of my forehead.

We lay there a long time, Lane not meeting my eyes. Then I heard thunder and noticed him looking to the open window. Suddenly he stood and stuffed his dick back in.

"What is it?"

"My plants."

Lane gulped the wine in my glass, swirled it around his mouth, and went over to the window.

"I was about to bring them in when you knocked—the rain's so heavy."

He leaned out the window and began dragging in the terra-cotta pots.

I looked at the cushion—his ass had left some moisture—then back at the pages on the table. All the alcohol surged into the skull.

"Can you help me with this?" he said.

He hugged a heavy pot, rain dripping from his hair. I went over and helped him set it on the floor with the others.

Then he leaned out into the pouring rain, way out, reaching for the pot at the farthest corner of the fire escape. I put my hand on his back.

When I dare to remember this moment, I know I wasn't overcome, or seeing red, or crazy. In fact it all happened in a clearing of my rage—a gesture so minor, merely a shifting of my weight, a tiny incline as if taking interest, and I felt a shock shoot through his back as he lurched forward with a cry smothered by rain.

I saw his hand swipe for the rusted bar and miss. I heard a pot break below, nothing more.

The rain obscured the window like drapes. I looked down to the alleyway. There was smashed terra-cotta touched by a yellow square of light, the soil running to mud.

All at once the clearing closed, my drunk overtook me, and it felt like I might tumble after him. I stumbled back inside.

Call the police.

I looked at the dossier unpacked on the table. How could I explain it?

I gathered the pages into the folder, along with the notes Lane had taken, and searched for any other evidence of my presence. I recalled how the cops had moved through my apartment, hunting for signs of the ghost. I took my wineglass to the kitchen, then rinsed and dried it and used a towel to place it with the others at the back of the cupboard. I'd been in the apartment before. If they found prints or hairs, I could answer that, but I had no choice but to trust the storm was washing the body, all the fibers, all the cells.

The body—was it true? I staggered back to the window, looked down at a shapeless stain on the darkness.

I snatched some paper towel and used it to open the door. It automatically locked behind me. I put the towel in my pocket and seemed to float down the stairs, hugging the dossier, anticipating ambush at every echoing step.

There was no one. I pushed through the front doors into the rain.

6.

The white-legged spider fiddled with its web. I wavered on the edge of consciousness, a cold surface to my cheek. The thought that it was the floor of a jail cell startled me awake and I bonked my head on porcelain. I'd fallen asleep behind my toilet, where the spider had strung itself up, the web beaded with the juiced husks of fruit flies. I heard the voices of men on the scaffolding. It was already late in the morning.

Grains of cognac-brown vomit were splattered in the toilet bowl. In a fit of forensic paranoia, I scrubbed them off, as if the police would sample the puke and match it to the wine in the bottle at Lane's apartment, or in his stomach. I had to be smart, I had to think of these things.

In the shower, massaging shampoo into my scalp, I struggled to replay the night. I seemed to peer through a keyhole at the moment of the fall. You barely touched him, I thought. I looked at my hands. Lane is a big man, he'd once crushed you with his weight, remember? These hands couldn't move him like that. He'd leaned out, gravity pulled him down, I could see it.

When I left the bathroom, naked and dripping, I thought of the dossier. But it wasn't on the kitchen counter, it wasn't on the coffee table. I looked at my window—I knew the ghost had come. But the window was locked. In the bedroom, I saw the folder on the floor.

I made coffee and nibbled at a blueberry muffin. I had diarrhea. My entire body longed to escape into bed, buried under covers, but I had to go in to the *Bystander*, recapture the Whitney Chase of yesterday.

The dossier was a problem. I couldn't bring it with me and couldn't leave it here. Ideally, I'd watch it burn, but I couldn't start a fire. Sitting on the floor, I began ripping the folder's contents to shreds, page by page. I stuffed the paper bits into a plastic bag and mixed them up. I went back to the toilet for a while.

Then I walked all the way to the office with the plastic bag open in my purse, and at every other garbage can grabbed a random handful and threw it in. Last night's storm was evaporating in white molecules and there were a lot of NYPD on the streets, or at least I noticed them more. Cops with assault rifles posed on the corners, observing everything.

I pictured the paper scraps that had snowed over Manhattan when the Towers fell, and told myself that the city would absorb mine too.

7.

It was past lunch by the time I arrived in Chelsea. For a few minutes I lingered by the elevator downstairs, letting the AC freeze my sweat. It's hard to draw a true self-portrait, to consciously embody how you appear to others when you're not paying attention, and I worried about seeming like a caricature, not in fact myself.

We'd closed the summer double issue and a lot of people were on holiday, but I still should've noticed the silence. I was so concerned with putting one foot in front of the other, I just walked straight to my desk, oblivious to the chill.

There was nothing on my desk. The absence reassured me. I reminded myself that, had there not been an accident last night, I'd be confessing to Mort right now. In that alternate timeline, word of my downfall was already circulating among my colleagues, fanning out to the distant reaches of the profession.

Someone came up quietly behind me and I turned, I thought, a little too suddenly.

"Whitney," said Gordon, and he glanced about, "have you heard?"

"No, what?"

"Something's happened to Lane. He's gone."

"Gone?"

"I mean, he's dead," Gordon said. "He's gone."

Last night took on a stark factuality it had resisted all morning, as if the fall had had a chance not to be real until Gordon put it in words.

My hands went to my mouth. "What happened?"

"He fell, or something. I'm sorry, I'm not really sure."

"Whitney?" We both looked at Mort with a start. "Want to come to my office for a minute?"

Mort pulled the chair out for me and waited until I'd sat before settling into his spot behind the desk. As opposed to the usual lamplight, he had the overhead fluorescents on, and he looked awful, his skin all sore with eczema, soggy bruised bags hanging from his eyes.

I said, "Gordon told me."

"It's terrible, terrible."

"He fell?"

"It wasn't the fall that killed him, probably more like a hemorrhage. I'm not sure how much you really want to know."

I shook my head.

"The police are at his apartment as we speak," Mort said. "We'll have more information later today."

I saw a gloved hand reaching for the wineglass, a brilliant eye detecting residue on the rim.

"I know you worked closely with him," Mort continued. "Did you notice anything? I mean, was he acting strangely?"

"No," I said, "not really. Why, do you think—"

"It's a possibility. It's something they have to consider."

"I guess they'll consider everything."

"Yeah."

I zoned out on the papers covering Mort's desk, concentrating on the story of Lane's suicide, but it didn't creep.

"I didn't know him all that well," I said. "It was pretty professional between us."

"All the same, no one will mind if you want to take a few days off."

"Thanks."

"Christ." Mort dug his fingers into his eyes with an ancient fatigue I'd never seen in him before. "I feel like taking one myself." He shook it off and added, "I've written down the number of a counseling service, if you'd like to talk to someone."

"Alright."

"And you know my door is always open."

"Will you let me know what the police tell you?"

"Sure thing."

As soon as I left his office, I fixed on Lane's desk. It was just as he'd left it, the action figures flexing in a row. I wondered if he'd made copies of the dossier, if they were right there in the drawer. I guess I was staring at the desk a long time, because when I finally looked away, Gordon Stone gave me a sympathetic smile.

I sat at my computer, unable to make a decision. If the police had discovered I'd been at the apartment, then every second I spent at the *Bystander* was a second I should be escaping. But I couldn't take my eyes off Lane's desk. The longer I sat there, the more convinced I became that the dossier was still alive, waiting, like a snake coiled up in the drawer.

Maybe an hour passed before I glanced at the window of Mort's office and saw he was on the phone. I thought I could read his lips: "Hello, officer. Yes. Really? I see. You're sure?"

His eyes flicked up and he was looking at me.

"She's here right now. I understand. I'll do my best."

And sure enough, he came across the office floor. Whatever mask I'd been maintaining slipped off and I stared at him, unblinking.

"What is it?" I said before he'd even gotten close.

Gordon hovered nearby.

"I just got off the phone with the police."

"What did they say?"

"They're ruling it an accident."

Gordon muttered, "Poor bastard."

"I'm a little relieved," Mort said. "The idea that I could have someone on my staff, you know, as desperate as that, and not notice."

"How do you fall from a window?" Gordon said.

Mort built the story in our minds, word by word. "It was during the storm. He was bringing his plants in from the fire escape. They say he must've leaned pretty far out, lost his balance. There was nothing solid to grip. He'd been drinking."

"Jesus," Gordon said.

"He lay there a long time before anyone noticed," Mort said. "It was already morning. This city sometimes."

8.

The police had confirmed my version of events—*an accident*—and I should've felt some relief. But when I went to bed that night, I kept thinking about Lane's desk. It took a long time to fall into a sleep that only really deepened toward dawn. I dreamt of the desk, or more like I thought of it while sleeping.

The pounding on my door awakened me. I pulled on a T-shirt and jeans and approached the peephole. It was my building manager. When I opened the door, he licked his fingers and whisked a sheet from a stack.

"Just a heads-up they'll be painting next week," he said, and jabbed a finger at some text. "If you have any of these conditions, make sure to close your windows. And get one of those masks, if you need it."

"Thanks," I said, and realized the hall was strangely bright. The sun wasn't supposed to have tracked over the skylight by now. "What time is it?"

The manager had already turned to the door across the hall. "Eleven thirty."

I hurried to the bedroom, furious. How could I oversleep when I should be in the middle of everything, fully alert, exerting control?

And just as in my most devastating fantasy, Lane's desk was cleared when I got to the *Bystander*. I went straight for it, I couldn't help myself—the action figures gone, the surface wiped clean. The drawers were all pulled out, empty.

"I'm surprised to see you," Gordon said, walking over with a takeout cappuccino.

"Why? What do you mean?"

"I thought you'd take a few days. I know there was no love lost there, so to speak, but still."

"You're wrong," I said. "I liked Lane."

"Well, that was my point." He slurped the foam and licked it off his upper lip.

"Right," I said. "I guess I might take some time, eventually. But right now it just feels better to be here, you know—stay focused on something."

Gordon set his cappuccino on the desk. "Lane's mother came and cleaned it out," he said. "It was a bit of a scene."

"She came here?"

He pointed to Mort's office, and at that very moment Mort was pointing back at me, and I saw Lane's mother, Louise, crane her neck to squint through the window. Mort motioned for me to join them.

Scrunched-up Kleenex covered his desk and he looked totally depleted. Louise sat hugging a cardboard box, nostrils red, a tissue clenched in her veiny fist. Balancing the box on her lap, she opened her arms wide to me. I glanced at Mort as I leaned down for the hug. He'd taken the opportunity to rest his eyes.

"I'm glad I got to see you," she said. "You were his favorite."

"He was great at his job," I lamely replied.

"She's right," Mort added. "He was really first-rate."

"He would've been a writer one day," she said. "He had a lot of ambition. He didn't like to show it off, but in a few years he would've been one of your best."

Mort smiled and said, "I'm sure you're right."

Louise dabbed her nose with Kleenex, then tossed it on the table and yanked another from the box.

"Oh, Whitney, he adored you. Just look."

She rummaged through the cardboard box and withdrew a folder: WHITNEY. I watched in horror, unable to stop her, as she began unpacking marked-up articles from the *Seattle Post-Intelligencer* and laying them on Mort's desk.

"He studied all your work," she said. "Look, some of these are ten years old." She held up a sheet for my inspection.

"You see? He underlined his favorite passages."

I caught Louise's wet little eyes. The confession swelled up to my mouth, and when I made to speak, I didn't know what would come off my tongue.

"I'm glad you mentioned these," I said, picking up the page she'd laid closest to Mort's hand. "I was going to ask you about them, but wasn't sure it's appropriate. I enlisted him to help me put together a book proposal."

"Really?" Mort said. "What kind of book?"

"Sort of a *Selected Essays*," I said, my hands casually gathering up the pages from the desk. "I'd asked him to read over some of the older work and suggest revisions."

"Even your stuff from the *P-I*?" Mort asked.

"Typical Lane," I said. "Overzealous. He thought there was good stuff there. I couldn't convince him otherwise."

I held the papers at my side, out of sight, as if she might forget, but Louise reached out for them, exposing the ball of Kleenex in her palm. I laughed awkwardly and looked down at the pages. They felt glued to my hand.

"I know it's strange to ask," I said, "but would it be alright if I held on to these for a while?"

She kept her hands outstretched and I had to relinquish the pages. Louise straightened them and put them back in the folder.

"I don't know," she said.

"Please, it would mean the world to me."

"I don't know what to say."

"Whitney," Mort said, "maybe this isn't a good time—"

"No," said Louise, "it's okay."

I braced.

"I'd like them back," she said.

"As soon as I'm finished."

"It's a part of him."

"I know."

She handed me the folder. Tears overcame me as I held the copies close, the overhead light refracting in my eyes like white knives.

"Oh, poor girl." She pulled me in for another hug.

"I'm sorry," I said, my face buried in the perfumed crook of her neck. "I'm sorry."

9.

As soon as I got home, I opened the folder and emptied out the pages.

The destruction became so mindless that when I neared the end, I almost didn't notice the pages changing from my articles to materials about Dr. Kriss. I guess Lane started the file before the subject of his investigations shifted.

There was a copy of the Rubicon report, a printout of the forum post where he'd learned about Sunshine Ray, and a few pages of notes I'd never seen. One in particular caught my eye.

A. Kriss, it read, *777 Dowling Ave., Everett, WA.*

Nothing in the notes suggested where he'd gotten the address, but it occurred to me it could be Dr. Kriss's mother, or some other relative.

Then the shredding was over. Soon I'd go and spread these scraps through the city too, but first I poured a glass of wine and crawled out on the scaffolding.

The sun cast a soft yellow glow as it set behind the sky's humid skin. I'll never forget the peace that came over me then, watching light stretch across the pavement, touch the tips of trees, catch the folds of skirts.

As I gazed down at the shadows slicing the light, a chilling breeze brought thoughts of Lane, but I thrust them away.

"You never had a choice," I said aloud. "You had to give yourself a chance."

Now find the story, tell the story, make it count for something.

THE HOUSES

1.

I called the office and told Mort I'd take that leave after all, that I needed time to stabilize before I could finish the piece. He was a little surprised that I wouldn't be attending the funeral, but I said I couldn't face Louise again—it had been too hard the first time. He understood, and said he hoped I'd have something for him soon.

I caught my flight to Tampa and drove down the Gulf coast in a blue Ford Focus. The tropical heat was beginning to feel like my true element, and I hurled myself into the task at hand. I was in Retreat to find Zeke, check on Sunshine Ray, and expose Dr. Kriss.

This time, I decided to stay in a motel about a half hour outside the city. I wanted to avoid crossing paths with anyone from Rubicon. I wasn't sure where in the country Dr. Kriss currently was, but now I'd put it together that every time I saw or spoke with her, the ghost had a way of finding me.

As I drove through the south side, I noticed how Mayor Klausmeyer's Retreat 2010 plan had accelerated. For one thing, I didn't see many stray dogs. My notes from just months before contained packs sprinting along the roadside, but now they appeared, when at all, as eyes glinting in the deep shade, like a species on the edge of extinction.

The Glades was finished, about fifteen identical properties on the site. Each house boasted a hideous mélange of cascading gables, multistory windows, enormous columned porticoes. It seemed impossible that anyone would want to live here, but in fact the houses were already occupied. Men hosed down SUVs, toys were scattered on lawns, a Tampa Bay Buccaneers flag flew above the door of a garage. The place where we'd found Zeke bleeding was paved over. You'd never know things like that had happened here, that a whole community had been spread across this land.

A few blocks from the Glades, I came upon another, even larger expanse being upturned by backhoes, the red clay exposed. A massive sign said COMING SOON: BOUGAINVILLEA RAVINE. A similar sign for the Glades had been just a board on stilts, but this one came with bougainvillea shrubs planted around an ornamental pond, the whole apparatus plugged into a generator.

I parked the car and went into the showroom in an air-conditioned trailer. A woman got up from behind the desk and we shook hands. I told her I was visiting from out of state, only looking.

I examined the model for the development. They were actually digging a ravine, alongside which the houses would be built. It wasn't entirely clear, but I was pretty sure that Tori's grandma's place used to stand where the ravine would empty into a reservoir. On the wall above the model, you could track the progress of the construction. There was a photo of Mayor Klausmeyer in a yellow hard hat at the ground-breaking.

"The Glades went up in a hurry," I observed.

The saleswoman responded with that strange corporate pride adopted by employees on the bottom. "The Ravine is going to make the Glades look quaint," she said. "Not to be disrespectful. They were first, after all, pioneers. But from a landscape-architectural perspective, the Glades was a missed opportunity. They just leveled the ground and hammered things together. There's no sense of wilderness, no dynamism."

"No ravine."

"No ravine, you got it."

I asked if she remembered the people who used to live around here.

"Around here? I don't think anyone lived around here."

"There were houses," I said, "and encampments."

"I was probably still in Orlando," she told me, "but my impression is no one's lived here for a long, long time."

"It was only a few months ago."

She frowned and reached for a promotional brochure, and pointed out the *Historical Overview* paragraph. It talked about the Tocobaga and the Calusa. There was an illustration of Native Americans sitting cross-legged on a beach, seagulls alighting on their fingertips.

2.

I drove out from the Ravine in concentric circles, trying to spot Zeke's leather jacket, but couldn't find traces of the camps. Soon I was on the southernmost edge. Was this even Retreat anymore? About to turn back, I suddenly saw a boy cut across the road on a BMX. It was painted black, Zeke's handiwork.

The boy stood on the pedals, T-shirt billowing. When he made a turn, I followed. He cast a glance over his shoulder. I tried not to get too close, but didn't want him zipping out of sight. He stole another look at me and pedaled faster, wrenching the frame side to side.

After a couple minutes, he looked back one last time then veered off the road and sped across a swampy field. I braked and watched black mud flicking off his back wheel. He was making for the trees, and that's when I saw a dim blue spot in the brush.

The men heard me coming. I'd set the tape recorder running in my bag and, later, listened to the loud squishing as I struggled to cross the muddy field to the tents. When I finally pushed through the trees, mud splashed across my shins, I found the boy sitting with two older men around a grimy Igloo cooler. Jars of piss stood by a tree, blackflies zooming through the air. One landed on the back of my neck and chomped. If I'd been told, months ago, that the living conditions of the south-siders would worsen, I wouldn't have believed it.

They were two middle-aged men, the boy maybe sixteen, all fly-eaten, exhausted. The larger man wouldn't even look at me. He held a bag of hot dog buns and just kept chewing.

The other guy, in a sweat-stained Gators cap, said, "You followed him?"

I said yes, and introduced myself as a journalist from the *Bystander.*

"You from Miami?" asked the Gators man.

"No, New York."

The big one snorted.

"I'm sorry if I alarmed you," I said, "but I have some questions that I think you can answer."

I asked if they used to live in the camps north of here, near where the Glades now stood.

"I've lived in the south side my whole life, miss."

"I'm looking for someone who used to live there," I said. "His name's Zeke. I think he sold you that bike, do you remember? He used to wear all leather, then one day he got taken away in one of the purple trucks."

The big guy shook his head slowly.

The Gators man said, "You with them, the purple trucks?"

"No."

He stood. I took a step back and mud clamped the heel of my shoe.

"I thought we told you to go away," he said. "I thought we said we don't know nothing about him."

"I'm not with Rubicon, I'm—"

"We know who you are."

"But the bike—"

"Forget the bike."

"Lady, I'd go," the kid blurted.

The big guy laughed, half-chewed bun stuck to his teeth. "Lady, I'd go," he mimicked.

The boy put his hands over his ears.

"Alright," I said, "I'm sorry."

"Lady, I'd go." The man kept laughing, dough spewing from his mouth.

When I turned to leave, my foot came cleanly out of the shoe and I had to bend down to pry it from the muck. I hobbled across the field with one bare foot, not looking back.

I cleaned off the mud, took some notes, and kept driving around. Someone from Rubicon had come looking for Zeke before me, and then what? Where was everybody?

It was late in the day, the heat tyrannical, and I couldn't find any more tents. I remember feeling as if the south-siders had withdrawn to a deeper seclusion or had fled the county altogether. I crept, picturing their camps thronging with stray dogs, and the image had the impossible glow of the afterlife.

I was about to head back to the motel when I passed the Glades one last time. Landscapers covered the development, shearing hedges, whacking weeds, hosing turf. They looked like a prison detail in their orange jumpsuits, GLADES stenciled in black on the back. I braked hard when I recognized Tori, one of Jules's friends, pushing a mower on a lawn.

I stood on the sidewalk, clouds of exhaust wafting over me, and called Tori's name until she noticed.

"It's Whitney," I said, "remember me?"

"Sure."

She'd almost sweated through the jumpsuit, which was made of thick polyester. I offered a bottle of water from my bag and she drained it.

"I was thinking about your grandma earlier," I said. "I noticed her house is where they're building Bougainvillea Ravine."

"She took the money and moved to Orlando," Tori said. "Her sister lives there."

"Where are you staying?"

"I've got a room in Manatee, like a half hour south."

"Do you miss living here?"

Tori shrugged. "Things change. I'm not complaining. I can take the bus from Manatee, and there's jobs here now. Before—well, you saw it, there was just a big pile of nothing, and nobody doing anything."

I said, "My Lakers won the chip."

Tori smiled ruefully. "Yeah, well, they do that. Anyway, nice talking to you."

"Wait a sec."

"I don't want my supervisor seeing us."

"I understand," I said, and explained I was looking for Zeke but no one would talk to me.

"I'm surprised you found anyone from the old south side at all," she said. "Everybody scattered—they really cleaned this place up. But I still see some old faces in Manatee and on the bus."

"Could you ask around for me?" I said. "I'm kind of desperate."

I glanced at the window of the house and saw a woman watching us. Tori followed my eyes.

"Shit."

"I can pay for your time," I rushed, "and if I find Zeke, maybe I'll know what happened to Jules."

"Yeah, yeah," Tori said. "Okay, I'll try."

"Here."

I slipped her my business card, and without another word Tori hurried across the lawn and began yanking the starter rope. The woman in the house had disappeared, the curtain swaying in the window.

3.

Early the next morning, I was in bed at the motel, organizing my notes, when my cell phone rang. I hoped it was Tori reporting back about Zeke.

"Hi, Whitney."

It was Dr. Kriss.

I tried not to sound any different as I greeted her, but hearing her voice made me realize how much had changed since we'd last seen each other.

The reception in the room was spotty, so I opened the door to the little balcony and nearly planted my foot on a dead anole. Ants flowed over the lizard's body, a brown trail leading over the edge.

Dr. Kriss said, "Are you in New York?"

"No, I'm on vacation, actually."

"Whereabouts?"

For some reason, the first lie that occurred to me involved the ranch in Arizona where Mom vacationed with her friends.

"Sounds nice," said Dr. Kriss. "It's pretty early in Arizona, isn't it?"

"I'm still on New York time."

"Makes sense. Does that mean you finished the story?"

I found it reassuring that she didn't still have a ghost reading over my shoulder, that she didn't know anything about my progress.

"I've shown a draft to my editor," I said.

"Is that so?"

"Yes."

It almost looked as if the anole were still alive, the ants animating its body, twisting the tail around.

"Any idea when you might be publishing?"

I told her the December/January double issue was within reach.

"I'd love to have a look," she said.

"The *Bystander* will contact you for comment before it goes to press."

"They call it fact-check, right?"

"Right."

"So I'll get a call from your fact-checker?"

Finally the tail broke off and I watched it float along on the current of ants. I said yes, she would.

"How about you?" I said. "How's the trial?"

"We've wrapped up Retreat and Mimico. Soon we'll be done here in Arcade." I recalled Baker Watt saying they'd discharge the last subjects there on Friday. "Then it's just a matter of submitting all our data to Inland."

I offered my congratulations, but I guess something wavered in my tone, because she said, "Are you okay?"

"Why?"

"You just sound a little, I'm not sure—distracted?"

Now the ants were working on the head.

I said, "Actually, there's something I've been meaning to ask."

"What is it?" said Dr. Kriss, and in the following second of silence I saw the dogs in Ray's experiments, pink growths pushing out their eyes.

"Well, like I mentioned, my editor read a draft."

"Yes."

"He wants to know if I can see where you manufacture the solution. It's in Arcade, right? He thinks it would be good to have more details about exactly what's in it, you know, and how it's made."

Dr. Kriss sighed impatiently and said, "I've told you a dozen times, I'd love to just open everything up for you, but it's impossible. Rubicon will never allow it. The solution is private property, it's that simple."

"I'm not asking to publish the contents of the solution, I'm only asking—"

"You're only asking for access I can't give you, so I guess we're at a stalemate, aren't we? You won't publish without information it's impossible to provide. Honestly, Whitney, I thought we'd be done with this weeks ago. What's stopping me from taking the story to *USA Today*? They've been hounding me, I keep putting them off—"

"What is stopping you, Dr. Kriss?"

She paused. "Is there something you want to say?"

It was satisfying to see the ants finally dismantle the head, how it was borne along the line, held aloft.

"Eva," I said, "where's Floella? Where's Jules?"

The doctor ended the call.

4.

Sunshine Ray's number went to an automated message telling me it was no longer in service, so I drove to his house on Snowy Egret Place. There were cars parked everywhere in his neighborhood, but all the homes seemed reticent, withdrawn, as if people were hiding inside. I'd flipped through the *Retreat Examiner* over lunch and read an article about the booming property values. I supposed this was a city getting richer by the minute: silence, distance, vultures turning in the sky.

A FOR SALE sign was nailed into Ray's yard. I walked around the manicured lawn and tried peering between curtains, but everything was dark. The sign listed the number of a real estate agent named Mixy Munzenrieder. I called and told her I was passing through on my way to Tampa but had a few minutes and would love to take a look at the property.

I waited in the Focus until she arrived. The agent emerged from a Mazda, incredibly tall in high heels that caused her to walk as if descending stairs. She wore pink lipstick and had her hair dyed a brown that shaded into orange, nearly matching her tan. I think Mixy was younger than me, but her look seemed influenced by Florida retirees and their jewelers.

"You've got a great eye," she told me, unlocking the front door. "This is one of my absolute favorites, a classic example of late-modern Retreat architecture."

The house was empty and clean. As Mixy gave me the tour, I recognized settings from the tapes: the backyard where the dogs had played, the kitchen where Romeo fed them bones. Every surface had been scrubbed, the carpets had been vacuumed to the walls, and someone had plugged air fresheners into the outlets, the air sweet with synthetic vanilla.

"The single-depth floor plan is how you know it's authentic," Mixy said, "and I just adore these jalousies."

"Who were the previous owners?"

"Young professionals," she said, still opening and closing the slats.

"Did they hire you?"

"Yes. Well, technically, I'm employed by their holding company."

"So you've never met them?"

"No, why?"

"Just wondering."

I asked if I could see the basement, and as we went downstairs, Mixy said, "What brings you to Retreat?"

"Business. But my husband and I are considering a vacation home somewhere on the coast."

"What do you do?"

"Medical technology."

"If you bought here, you'd be making a secure investment. These old houses are much sturdier than what they're building now, in terms of hurricanes. I wouldn't be worried."

We were down in the cool of the basement, just a concrete floor and bare white walls. The only distinguishing feature was the water stain on the ceiling. From the outlet where the washer and dryer had stood, an air freshener made a little gasp.

I stood where Ray had set up the tripod to frame the transfusions. I applied the image onto the space: sedated dogs, the white blood flowing. But nothing came. I don't know what I expected, some echo or residue, some clue.

"Do you have any questions?" Mixy said.

I turned abruptly. "I don't think it's quite right for us. Thanks, though."

I headed upstairs, Mixy hurrying after me. "Is something wrong?"

"No."

"Here." She pressed a business card that doubled as a fridge magnet into my hand. "Just think about it. Even if it's only an investment—"

"I don't think so," I said, and was out the door, crossing the lawn.

When I pulled away in the Focus, I saw Mixy in the doorway. She was looking in at the house as if to see whatever I'd seen.

5.

I headed for Salty's Marina. In our very first interview Ray told me he and Romeo would sail to Mexico once they'd fixed up *Funny Valentine*. I didn't know where Mixy had gotten the idea of "young professionals," but it made sense they'd leave before commissioning someone to sell the house, then siphon the money through a holding company. But still, whenever I told myself Ray had calculated the danger and made plans to leave, something felt wrong. Ray had once told me he'd been leaned on by Rubicon; the technician named Rainer had paid him a visit. If Rubicon knew about the tapes, they'd come for him again.

I found the marina gate locked. I glanced around. A seagull made an irate squawk, the boats lightly knocked on the dock. I stuffed my notebook in the back pocket of my jeans, planted a foot in the chain-link fence, and hoisted myself over.

I was pretty sure I had the right place. I remembered walking down these same wooden planks, turning at the yellow boathouse, and seeing Romeo dabbing kebabs with lime juice.

I made the turn. *Funny Valentine* was moored. A black tarp was pulled over the deck, covered in sun-baked bird shit. Crouching down, I could see silver insulation on the cabin windows. Compared with its neighbors, the boat was filthy, a dark-green grime caked around the hull.

I crept with Ray and Romeo in the dark of the cabin, plastic bags over their heads, black with ants—

"What are you doing?"

The voice was so close, I nearly jumped into the water. The man looked sort of like security, sort of like a civilian, his black collared shirt tucked into blue jeans, eyes hidden behind Oakleys on a rubber strap. He was of a supreme bland whiteness, with a double chin and jowls covered by thin blond fuzz— neither shaven nor unshaven—that made his age indistinct.

Then I saw the utility belt, the gun in its leather holster. He seemed ready to draw as he approached me slowly over the planks.

"I was looking for my friends," I said, trying to stay light. "Do you know them, Ray and Romeo?"

"No."

"It's their boat." I pointed. "*Funny Valentine.*"

The man stopped coming toward me. I watched his hand.

"Who are you?" he said. I told him I was a journalist and he smiled, teeth butter yellow. "You're with the media?"

"That's right."

A seagull swooped by, pelting the tarp.

He said, "Who do you work for?"

"The *Bystander.*"

"Never heard of it."

"It's a magazine in New York."

He withdrew a cell phone from a Velcro pouch then pulled the antenna out, flipped the phone open, and dialed.

I said, "What are you doing?"

He drummed his fingers on the leather of the holster.

"Yeah," he said into the phone, "I got a woman here, a journalist. Yeah, exactly."

I wondered if this man was Rainer. He didn't sound Austrian.

"Who are you talking to?" I said.

He held a finger up.

They could have me arrested for trespassing, I thought, or worse—whatever they'd done to Ray and Romeo.

I waited until the man was angled away, still talking on the phone, so the gun was on the other side of his body. Then I drew one deep breath and broke into a sprint.

"Hey!"

I turned at the boathouse and went zigzagging up the dock, as if evading an alligator. I fixed my eyes on the gate. At any moment there could be darkness, permanence.

"Stop!"

He managed to boot the sole of my shoe and I went down hard on the dock, the planks shredding my pants. He tumbled onto me, a mass of sweat breathing heavy, and flipped me over onto my back.

He'd dropped the gun, its barrel nosing between planks, but my arms were pinned. He saw where the gun had landed and slammed me against the dock, my skull knocking off the wood. I tried to kick him in the dick but got him in the gut. He released me with a weird burp and, wheezing, went crawling toward the weapon. I clambered to my feet and got there first.

Suddenly armed, I didn't know what to do. I'd never held a gun before and now I was supposed to hold it for real. I couldn't bring myself to put a finger on the trigger. I pointed it at him, afraid it might go off.

His Oakleys had fallen and he squinted up at me, the sun too much for his colorless eyes. He sneezed.

I said, "Don't move."

I kept looking down at the gun, everything out of focus around it.

"Get in the water," I said.

"What?"

I glanced around. No one was watching.

"The water—get in."

"No way."

I thrust the gun at him and it worked. He perched on the edge of the dock, looked down, and said, "Jesus Christ."

"Do it."

He lowered himself down between boats and treaded water. His shirt ballooned around him and he scowled at me, bobbing on a swirling surface.

I backed away, the gun aimed in his direction until I reached the gate. Then I sent it spinning like a Frisbee and it landed in Salty's Marina with a gulp.

6.

The next morning, I tweezed the splinters from my leg. I thought I'd only suffered cuts when I fell on the dock, but overnight the pain had intensified, as if something were bursting from within, and I realized there were dozens of wooden teeth embedded in my skin.

Seated on the edge of the tub, I had to bite down on my leather sunglasses case while I burrowed deep, extracted each red splinter, and doused the spot with peroxide. By the time I'd pried out all the shards, I was drenched in sweat and exhausted. The housekeeper didn't say a word when I handed her a heap of bloody towels.

I went down to the kidney-shaped pool and soaked my numb, swollen leg, blood still leaking out in dark threads that briefly floated before dissolving. As I swooshed it, water rushing between my toes, Tori called. She'd asked around and learned that Zeke had stayed at the House of Brothers, an Evangelical men's refuge in Manatee. She could take me there if I gave her a ride home after work.

"You said you're paying, right?"

"Absolutely."

"Meet me at the Glades at six."

When I picked her up, the tang of freshly cut grass and her onion-sweet sweat filled the Focus. I cranked the AC, trying to put her on ice.

On the road to Manatee, she said, "Mind if I change?"

"Go ahead."

Tori squirmed out of her jumpsuit, sort of bucking against the seat belt, and pulled on the clothes she'd packed: rhinestone-studded jeans and a Miami Heat shirt that said WHITE HOT.

"I have to be at Bougainvillea Ravine tomorrow morning," she said, "six-o-fucking-clock."

"You work there too?"

"Landscaping four days a week at the Glades, then two days of construction at the Ravine."

"Which do you prefer?"

"The Glades, hands down. It's stressful, the way they watch you. But the plants are peaceful. The Ravine is just a shitshow. I mean, they have us down in that pit, like literally trying to hold walls of earth from falling so they can install the slope protection. A couple weeks ago, this guy had his legs crushed in a landslide. If he'd turned the other way, he would've been buried feet-up."

"I can drop you at home," I said. "You don't have to come with me."

"You said if you found Zeke, it might help you figure out what happened to Jules."

"Yeah."

"Then I'm coming. What's the pay, anyway?"

I wasn't really sure what was fair, but when I offered her a hundred bucks, she took it like she was ripping me off.

Entering Manatee from the north, I began to feel a little like I used to in south-side Retreat. Behind Spanish moss you could see the tents, and scorch marks sometimes defaced abandoned homes. I almost expected to find a purple truck patrolling the area.

"You know that show *Cops*?" Tori said.

"Sure."

"They shoot like 50 percent of *Cops* in Manatee."

The House of Brothers was a two-story family home on the northeast edge of the city, oddly situated among derelict warehouses, with a railway track running behind it. Tori told me Zeke went to stay here a couple weeks after I'd seen him discharged. It was his last known location, she said, the best she could do.

I limped to the front door, my leg bandaged and tight, and Tori stood behind me as I knocked. A man appeared behind the screen. He wore a wooden cross and an apron smeared with black paint. In his automatic smile I saw a glinting gold incisor.

I told him I was a journalist and he was surprisingly eager, as if we'd made an appointment weeks ago. His name was Lourdes, and this was his house.

"I'd invite you in," he said, closing the screen door behind him, "but I respect the privacy of the brothers."

"That's alright. Is there somewhere we can talk?"

Lourdes brought out a two-liter bottle of Coke and some cups, and took us to the backyard. To either side it was all concrete and dust, but this was a verdant patch, inspiring Tori to ask about his lawn-care program. We sat on plastic chairs and I set the recorder on the table between us. Throughout our conversation, a freight train eased its way along the nearby track, and on the tape it sometimes became difficult to discern Lourdes's words from the wheels of the train grinding down the rail.

Lourdes had taken off the apron and I saw tattoos of barbed wire across his arms and shoulders. He sported a strangely retro haircut, long in the back but parted in the middle, and had the fixed, unblinking eyes of the converted. He tapped his cigarette in the plastic tray and some of the ash bounced onto the recorder.

Tori sat beside me, smoking quietly and sipping Coke, as I asked him to tell me about the House of Brothers.

He'd established it in '92, he said, after serving twelve years on a manslaughter charge. At the age of eighteen, "a messed-up little junkie," he'd gotten into a gunfight with a hotel manager during an armed robbery. He thought he'd missed everything, but in fact he hit the guy, who'd bled to death on the office floor. When Lourdes heard on the news that the manager was dead, he turned himself in.

I adjusted in my chair uneasily, my leg still throbbing.

"In prison I got clean," he said, "and when I was released, all I wanted was to give back to my fellow man, to help him along the path, so he wouldn't suffer like I had, or inflict so much suffering. I worked seven days a week to make a payment on this beautiful house, and a few years later we became a registered charity. We usually have anywhere between ten and twenty brothers staying here, and it's been that way for almost a decade."

"What about now?"

"We're at maximum capacity right now. Twenty-two, a new record."

I looked at the little house. It seemed impossible.

"A lot of brothers are coming down the coast, looking for new beginnings, a place of retreat."

"Actually," I said, "that brings me to why I'm here. I'm seeking information about a particular resident of yours. His name is Zeke. He came down from Retreat a few months ago. You'd remember him, all leather, kind of paranoid."

As I spoke, Lourdes let the cigarette burn without inhaling. Then he put his hands together as if in prayer and stared down at his lap. "Lord Jesus," he muttered. When he looked back up, his eyes were wet, arrestingly bright. "I knew it was you," he said, gazing at me as though I'd understand. "I knew someone would come for him."

"So he stayed here?"

"He died here."

I glanced at Tori, but like a good journalist in her own right, she remained impassive.

"What happened?" I asked.

Lourdes said, "I'm sorry, Whitney, Zeke took his own life. We loved him, we took care of him, but there was nothing we could do."

Suddenly he got up from the table and hurried into the house. I thought he was going to get some tissues.

Tori exhaled in relief and said, "You do this all the time?"

"Not like this."

Lourdes came back out and placed a roll of Fujifilm beside the recorder. Now he spoke very meekly, as though the presence of the film made him ashamed.

"I found him in the upstairs bathroom. It was unspeakable, unspeakable." He shook his head. "When I found him like that, I knew I'd answer for him one day, so I took these pictures. I've never had them developed. I didn't think I could face it, I'm sorry."

"It's alright."

"Take it," he said. "Put it in your pocket."

I took the roll off the table. Lourdes relaxed and lit another cigarette.

"What happened next?" I said. "Did you call the police?"

"We don't break laws here, but we're very cautious about bringing police into the house."

"So what did you do?"

"I didn't have to do anything," Lourdes said. "A paramedic arrived."

"Did you call him?"

"Not me, but somebody did. The medic, he wrapped the body, then came in with a couple other people and took him down to the ambulance."

"Was the ambulance purple?"

Lourdes nodded. "A couple days later, I found out a charity from Retreat had been looking for Zeke, asking about him all over Manatee. We protect our own here at the house, but when one of the brothers found out he was dead, he called them. I guess there was some money involved. It was their ambulance."

"Common Dreams."

"Right, yeah."

The back door swung open and a man came out with a watering can. He nodded to us, lit a cigarette, and topped up the can with a garden hose. Then he gently poured the water around the roots of a pink oleander.

"Could you describe the medic?" I said.

"White guy about my height, going bald. It's hard, my memory's not so good for faces. I like to draw them to remember. I didn't draw him."

"What about his name?"

"I'm not sure."

"Was it Rainer?"

"I don't know. Maybe I never knew."

I asked if I could see where Zeke had stayed. Tori watched me take notes as Lourdes went inside to check with the brothers. When he came out, he said it was okay but asked that Tori stay outside. She walked over to the gardener, who was plucking weeds from the flower bed. He lit her cigarette.

Inside, the House of Brothers sweltered with men. They cramped the kitchen table, overflowed the sofas. In the bedrooms they murmured prayers, hands joined, shoulders slick with sweat. On the wall by the staircase was an enormous mural. Dozens of faces were drawn in black paint, two-dimensional and egg-shaped, and no two were the same. Lourdes told me that every time another man stayed at the House of Brothers, he added his face to the mural. That's what he'd been doing when he answered the door in his apron. It took him a moment to find Zeke, but I recognized the clenched underbite, the clairvoyant eyes.

In the upstairs bathroom, a brother was mopping the floor. He stood aside so I could see the tub.

"That's where I found him," Lourdes said.

I took notes on the tub: shallow, plastic, with mint-green tiles on the wall.

I asked the man with the mop if he'd known Zeke. He shook his head.

"No one here today was in the house with him," Lourdes told me. "We've been having to turn the beds over. But here, I can show you where he slept."

Three bunk beds were packed into a bedroom about the size of what I'd had as a child. Five men glanced up as I stood in the doorway.

"Zeke wasn't the easiest brother," Lourdes said. "I think he'd gotten into some trouble in Retreat."

"That's true," I said.

"But I love them all."

"We love you too," said one of the brothers.

Lourdes massaged his neck. The brothers looked up at him, faces simplified.

"I'm not sure Zeke ever let Jesus into his heart," Lourdes said, "but he surely believed that Satan walked the earth."

7.

It was after nine when Tori took me to an all-night drugstore that did one-hour photo. I ordered two copies of everything on the Fujifilm roll and, when I handed it over, asked the clerk if she had to look at the photos to develop them.

She glanced between Tori and me and said, "I don't have to."

"Then don't."

I bought us Wendy's and we sat at a picnic table by the road. I'd picked up some bandages at the drugstore, and while Tori unpacked the food, I changed the dressings on my leg. It still felt like there was wood in there, like termites in the bone.

Tori peeled her burger open, put the pickles to the side, and gradually scraped the cheese off with the fries as she ate them. Once she'd finished all these cheese-fries, she slapped the pickles back on and ate the burger. I protected my sandwich as a truck blazed by, kicking up dust.

Tori wanted to know how I'd gotten started and what the job normally entailed. I explained a bit about USC, my early work at the *P-I*, and an average month at the *Bystander*.

"Do you have to go to school for it?"

"Not necessarily," I said. "It's more common now than it was before, but there's no real training for journalism."

"Criminal record?"

"Also not a problem. If you like telling stories, that's the most important thing—the only thing, really."

She said, "I think there are a lot of stories here in Manatee."

"Is there a newspaper?"

She shrugged.

I wrote out my e-mail and reminded her she had my number. "If you're interested, stay in touch. I can give you advice on how to get started."

Tori thanked me with some embarrassment, as if I couldn't mean it.

"Seriously," I said. "Don't be afraid to ask, just reach out."

She balled up her garbage. The hour was almost over.

"So you found Zeke," she said at last.

"Yeah."

"What does that mean for Jules?"

"It means she's dead."

"It was the people in the truck."

"Yeah."

I saw she was gripping the edge of the picnic table, driving half moons in the wood with her nails.

"People like us," she said, "they think we're just, I don't know, only physical."

I nodded.

"They take us away, they put us wherever they want—"

Her rage gave in to hard, dry sobs. I came around to her side of the table, unsure of what to do. My conscious thought was to pat her lightly—"It's okay," I tried. It didn't help. I slid closer, our bodies touched. Then it felt like my hands were acting on their own, remembering lost gestures, as I gently cupped her head. It tilted easily to my shoulder.

I don't know how long we sat like that, pulses identical, before the parking lot lights shuddered on, insects thronging to the glow.

8.

On my way back to the motel, I passed through Retreat one last time. The houses of the Glades were shining, the south side all subdued, and Bougainvillea Ravine awaited tomorrow's excavation. I imagined ashes beneath foundations, teeth loose in the garden, fragments of skull in the seashell walks. Jules, Zeke, all the doctored numbers in the report—no one will ever find them, I thought. Time is bearing them away. But the tapes in my recorder, the notes in my book, the photos in my purse—the story could be told.

Back in my room, I sat at the desk, nothing but the lamp switched on. Beyond the open window, the sound of cicadas fizzled out like sparks. I opened the envelope, withdrew the photos. I can still recall how the world dropped away and everything in the image went sharp.

Can you bear witness to a photograph? I knew exactly how that bathroom felt, hot and close, condensation clinging to the tile, and I fell into the scene, seeing Zeke through Lourdes's eyes.

He was naked in the tub, legs splayed, penis slumped on the inner thigh. A chunk of his lip was chewed away, exposing teeth in a kind of sneer. Blood from his opened left arm had spilled over his torso and pooled in the tub.

I'd never seen a wound like this, never imagined one. At the edge of the photo I saw the blade he'd used to make an incision on the wrist. Then he must've dug his fingers deep in the wound, blood pulsing out, and pinched what looked like plastic straws, a hideous pink.

They were his veins, made stiff, and it appeared that Zeke had stripped them from his arm, plastic bursting up through the skin like a cable from the ground, all the way past the elbow. His arm hung open in two jagged flaps. The hard white bone caught camera flash. His fist still clutched bent plastic.

THE HOLES

1.

Before my flight to Denver, I shipped everything—tapes, notes, photographs—care of Gordon Stone at the *Bystander*. I called him at the office and told him to sign for the package and leave it on my desk.

"Roger."

"I'm heading into a sort of dicey situation," I said. "I'll try to check in when I can, but I might not be able to call every day. Do me a favor?"

"Of course."

"If I'm incommunicado more than forty-eight hours, start the search here." I gave him the name of the hotel I'd booked in Arcade.

Gordon laughed. "You sound like something out of Le Carré."

I pictured him at the office with a copy of the *New York Review of Books*, liking and disliking.

"For the love of god," he said, "be safe, Whitney, no story is worth it."

I thanked him for everything and hung up. Gordon's a brilliant man, I thought, and he has exquisite taste, but he doesn't know the half.

I was relieved to get through security, onto the plane, into the air. I felt able to think clearly for the first time since seeing the photos.

In certain very limited respects, what Dr. Kriss had concocted really could be called a medical breakthrough. Unlike the abortive blood substitutes I'd read about, the solution didn't fail in a matter of hours or even days. For a few weeks, at least, the subjects were stable, more than enough time to impress a journalist on a deadline. But once that period elapsed, the solution appeared to—I don't know what—settle or coalesce or congeal. It began in the mouth, where tissue regenerates fastest. Having lost all feeling in the lips, the subjects chewed them away. Zeke had sensed it coming, the hardening of his bloodstream. I wondered what would've happened if he hadn't killed himself, but my mind refused to overlay the image of Ray's dogs on a person.

I thought about Pavel. Only he'd survived, living for over a year after the transfusion before his house burned down. But he was dead too. There were so many holes in my story.

My eyelids fell and I snorted awake as the plane began its final descent. We slipped through steely clouds, and farmland stretched in patches of rust and emerald. I was back in Colorado to uncover Dr. Kriss's trade secrets, what hid behind the contracts. Now that she knew she wasn't controlling the story anymore, she must feel as I had when the *P-I* articles began appearing on my desk. That's why I would've been fine to stay in a holding pattern over Denver for the rest of the day. I didn't want to feel this solid bounce, this charge down the runway before the engines relaxed. As we trundled to the terminal, I dreaded stepping out from airport security. If Dr. Kriss felt that way, I knew, she'd kill me if she could.

2.

Considering what happened last time, the insurance was steep when I rented the Jeep, but it wasn't long before I was on the road out of Denver. I stopped at an outdoors store called Alpine Sports and bought a small pair of binoculars, some cargo khakis, a pea-green vest, and a ball cap with autumnal-forest camouflage. The man at the counter asked what I was planning to do and I told him I was going birding near Arcade.

"They'll be glad to have you down there," he said. "Seems like all the tourists are staying away this year, with the fires and all."

"Fires?"

He made sure to ring me up and swipe my card before saying, "You haven't read about them? The Hayman Fire was right around where you're headed. Largest forest fire in state history, if you can believe it. Felt like it was everywhere. They've contained that one, more or less, but the forest is still burning all over the place. If you end up camping, you'd better obey the no-burn policy and watch for wildlife. There's an exodus in progress and they don't care who's in the way."

I was looking at the receipt that had unspooled from the machine. With my paycheck withheld and the first of September approaching, my savings were all but gone.

"How are your lungs?" he said.

"Fine."

"Keep it that way." He tossed a respirator mask in my bag, no charge.

3.

I saw scorched miles on the road to Arcade. Some trees still stood, trunks black and thin like spent matchsticks, while in places the ground had burned to bare soil and looked like stretches of beach, the earth a fine ash gray. Deer clustered in odd spots, unsure of where to cross.

Arcade was hazy, smoke hanging low and white like mist, the sky a faded orange. Before checking into the hotel, I took a ride around the Tomahawk. The entire neighborhood had been rebranded. On antiquated iron streetlights, banners said THE HISTORIC TOMAHAWK DISTRICT in a rustic hunter-green font, with an illustration of pioneers in covered wagons overlaid with a half-dissolved image of a Ute warrior. They'd removed layers of asphalt to expose patches of original brick paving, and there were fiberglass sculptures of wildlife—deer, elk, mountain lion—spray-painted bronze and erected on street corners beside benches with extra armrests in the middle.

The sun turned neon red, setting in the smoke, the mountains reduced to simple purple shapes. The horizon looked like computer animation. I felt as disoriented as I had in Retreat, unable to recall where Roland and I had found Floella's Chevrolet or where I'd crashed after the shooting.

I did find the Avalon Homes, which were only being advertised during my visit in May. I parked and practiced using my new binoculars to study the grounds. Setting aside a few regional touches—stone chimneys, shuttered windows, quartz in the garden—the houses could've been the Glades. I saw a fox slink from the pines behind them, an orange glint, then panic in the open air. It broke for the road, where just a few weeks earlier it would've found forest.

It's like this everywhere, I thought, the land upturned from Retreat to Mimico. A house probably already stood where Pavel's place had ignited, suctioning up the vista. Soon there would be nothing but Avalon Homes, nothing for the people who'd been here and who, like the fox, had become nomadic and trackless, or burned.

4.

First thing the next morning, I went to the Buy Low Co. for dried fruit, bottled water, and disposable cameras. It felt as if an unusual number of people were in there, also stocking up on water and nonperishables. I had to settle for a bunch of off-brand stuff.

A woman in line ahead of me, her cart filled with toilet paper, glanced at the scant items in my basket and said, "You know they just announced evacuations in the mountains."

"That's awful," I said. "Do you have friends up there?"

"I wish. Well, I don't wish, not today. But I usually wish. I think those are the most beautiful homes in the world."

She began stacking the toilet paper at the cash.

"The wind could change anytime," she warned me. "That's what they said in the *Ledger*."

At Ascension Hospital, I parked and sat in the back of the Jeep, observing the ambulance bay through the tinted rear window. The morning had been surprisingly fresh, but now that the sun had fully risen, it suffused the smoke and choked the day. Yet even through the haze, across the parking lot I could see the purple truck of Common Dreams, A RUBICON TECH INITIATIVE. I kept the binoculars trained.

It was Friday. Baker Watt had said the trial was ending, and my hope was that, if Dr. Kriss hadn't discharged the final subjects yet, today was her last chance. But the truck just sat there. At one point a shadow flickered over me, and I saw the parking inspector lean over the hood of the Jeep. He didn't notice me as he checked the ticket on the dash and moved on. The next few hours were broken only by the medevac helicopter as it lowered to the landing pad on the roof of the hospital before taking flight again. Airlifts, I assumed, from the burn areas.

It was about noon when a woman finally entered the ambulance bay in the purple polo of Common Dreams. She swung the back door of the truck open and began emptying out surgical masks, intubation kits, defibrillators. No bags of white blood.

The binoculars were sharp. I could see the kanji tattooed on her nape and the dandruff in the part of her hair, which she wore short and bleached and gelled back. I wondered if this was the paramedic who'd picked the glass from my cheek when I crashed, and considered approaching her. I'd brought along copies of the Zeke photos. I could confront her with them. But the paramedic wasn't important, she was just cleaning out the truck. I had to stay patient.

When she'd finished the job, I saw her greet someone. Focusing the binoculars, I realized that I was looking at the back of a head. It wasn't Dr. Kriss.

"Turn around," I said.

As the man talked to the paramedic, she beamed, as if he was being more and more complimentary, and when he presented her with a small bottle of sparkling wine, she put her hands to her pruning chin. I could read her lips.

"Thank you," she was saying.

"Turn around."

"Thank you."

He wrangled her into a hug, looked out toward the lot, and I had a perfect view. Crumpled lips, purple as liver, a broken-looking nose—I cried out so loudly I could've given myself away.

It was him, Pavel Firea, the man from the house above the highway, the ghost in my room, observing me, mingling with my dreams—alive.

Then whose body had I seen taken from the house, charred black? I tried remembering my Mimico notes, which I'd shipped back to New York. Pavel was real, or he'd been real at some point. I'd been in his house, someone's body was in there. What if that was the corpse of the real Pavel, dead before I even got to Mimico? Or maybe another subject from the trial, another failed test? I thought of Zeke in the tub. The burning house was another part of the fiction they'd been elaborating around me since I met Dr. Kriss.

We're going to make a great story together.

I wanted to get out of the Jeep, go running at the man. I had to will myself into one last act of restraint.

I sat cross-legged, jotted some notes, and watched them pop the little bottle. The man wore slim blue jeans and a red collared shirt, unbuttoned at the top to expose a white T and a tuft of black hair. As Pavel, he'd seemed appropriately impoverished and overmedicated, but now he was robust, his chest toughly rounding out the shirt, eyes alert.

I kept the binoculars on him, as if to see behind those eyes. I wondered if this was Rainer, the technician, if he knew where the bodies were buried, or scattered, or dumped. But he just stood there, inscrutable, sipping sparkling wine in the smoky light.

It was after one when he said farewell to the woman and got in the purple truck. The reverse lights flashed, and I clambered into the driver's seat and started up the Jeep. I waited until he'd sailed by, then pulled out of the lot.

Even in low visibility, it wasn't hard to follow that conspicuous ambulance. I tried staying within its blind spots, accelerating into a tailgate position whenever he made a turn then easing back and sticking to the wing. In just a few minutes we were on the outskirts of Arcade, where he veered off the road and bounced into a Burger King.

Neck craned, I kept my eyes fixed on the truck until he'd turned into the drive-thru, then had to bury my foot on the brake when I looked back at the road to find a Honda's red brake lights flaring before me. The Jeep slumped to a stop just inches from the Honda's bumper, the seat belt seized below my ribs. Horns blaring all around, I muscled out of the lane and into a turn, then looped around the block. But when I passed the Burger King, the truck was still in the drive-thru.

Again I turned and made a lap, more slowly this time, so as not to pattern my movements. But when I glided by, I didn't see the truck at all. I checked the exit of the drive-thru to see if he might be coming out. A white SUV emerged. I stopped at the light. The truck wasn't up ahead. Had he gone back to Ascension?

I was about to turn around when I sensed a purple emanation through the tinted glass and he rolled up to the light beside me. I lowered the brim of my hat and stole a glance. He'd unwrapped his Whopper on the steering wheel and was quickly pushing fries past his lips. His polarized sunglasses shaded from yellow to red.

The light turned green, and we had to drive side by side for a while before I could sneak into the lane behind him. He was heading into the mountains and the smoke was getting denser. Soon the road narrowed to just two lanes walled with stone. Evacuees jammed the lane in the other direction.

I hung way back, the truck a distant purple smear in the smoke. The sky was drawn—nothing cast a shadow—as he led me up into the afternoon dusk.

5.

We'd been ascending for half an hour when he finally turned off the road. I zoomed past, watching the truck disappear down an unmarked drive-way. On the gravel shoulder, I found a place to park the Jeep and put on my respirator mask. The air stung my eyes when I got out of the car, but I could breathe.

I squatted in the brush, my piss hissing on the forest floor. It occurred to me that this would be a good time to call Gordon Stone. But when I flipped my phone open, I couldn't get a signal on the mountain.

I walked along the slanted road. White fumes crawled over the asphalt and somersaulted when a car sped by—evacuees from the higher mountains, the trunks of their SUVs loaded, pets in passengers' laps.

The driveway was a track of packed dirt through the forest, dark as a tunnel with the smoke. I followed the impressions of the tires. Away from the road, the silence was unsettling, lacking even birdcall. I knew that the man—the ghost, Rainer, whoever—could emerge at any moment. Unless I heard him coming, I wouldn't have time to hide.

Just where the driveway curved ahead of me, I discerned a figure in the shifting dark, coming my way. I jumped behind a tree and pressed myself against it. A deer trotted out of the smoke and paused, put its nose in the air, almost two-dimensional in its stillness. Then it raked a hoof across the dirt and loped into the woods.

I started walking again. At last the tunnel broke onto a clearing where the haze thinned somewhat, revealing two structures—a house and an outbuilding—on a roughly circular field of dead grass ringed with pines. I kept to the perimeter, not wanting to leave the cover of the trees.

The house comprised five or six glass cubes on an elevated stone foundation. All the lights were on, as if it were night. Even through the dimming smoke, I could see into a living room and kitchen and up a staircase to a bedroom.

The man had parked the Common Dreams truck at the outbuilding, a flat, windowless construct that looked cheap and hasty beside the house. If it hadn't been so large, I would've thought it was a shed, just squat concrete brick with one metal door.

I hid in the smoke for a long time until I thought I detected movement in the house. I hurried along the edge of the clearing and found a better view. I don't know whether it was the air quality or the elevation, but I felt breathless after just this slight exertion. I lay on my stomach on a bed of needles and peered through the binoculars, steadying them against my heaving lungs.

Inside the house, the man was mounting the staircase, still wearing those red-yellow sunglasses. When he entered the bedroom, I saw him twice, both standing by the bed and in a nearby mirror. Dr. Kriss stepped into my circular frame. She was wrapped in a towel, wet hair clinging to her shoulders, and she sat on the edge of the bed, leaning back on her hands. As she listened to the man talking, I discerned that cross, impatient look, the last face seen by her many fired employees.

Now I was almost certain this was Rainer, the Rubicon technician, the one she disclaimed any relationship with, because, to my surprise, she put a hand on the crotch of his jeans, felt him through the denim, and unclasped his belt. Without pulling his pants down, she reached into his underwear, removed his cock, and let it dangle, half-hard. I changed angles again and saw Dr. Kriss grip the cock—it wasn't very large—at the base of the shaft and take the whole thing in her mouth.

I put the binoculars down, embarrassed. Smoke peeled off the tips of the pines.

I decided to watch them in the mirror, as if that made it less invasive. Rainer never moved, like a statue with just this one living appendage. Only when he suddenly reached for a fistful of her hair did she pull back. I don't think he'd come. She wiped her lips with the towel, gave him a little pat on the ass, then nodded at the cock still bobbing loose, searchingly, unfinished. She'd already gotten up and exited the frame by the time he'd stuffed it in his jeans and cinched the belt.

They disappeared into another room. I followed the edge of the trees, sometimes squatting and waiting for a gust of smoke to dissipate, but no matter what angle I tried, I couldn't find them.

Then I heard a door slam and had to hurry to the other side of the house, trying to be light so the forest floor didn't crack beneath me. There I saw Dr. Kriss and Rainer heading for the outbuilding, carrying tent poles, duffel bags, and a filthy blue tarp. They set the gear on the ground by the Common Dreams truck.

I lay on my stomach again and looked through the binoculars. Dr. Kriss had climbed into the back of the truck and was lowering a stretcher to Rainer.

It was when she stepped down that I saw him point toward the woods, toward me. She followed his outstretched arm and her eyes touched mine through the lens. I couldn't move. They took a few steps in my direction. Dr. Kriss squinted. I knew I should run, but I just flattened myself against the needles.

It was two fawns. They almost walked right over me, probing the dead ground with black noses, taking uncertain steps on their gangly legs. They entered the clearing with wide eyes, ears pressed back, and I saw Rainer shape his fingers into a gun and bend his trigger finger at them. Dr. Kriss shook her head and turned away.

There was a keypad for the outbuilding door, but I couldn't see the code she entered. They wheeled the stretcher inside, emerging a few minutes later with the unmistakable shape of a body wrapped in a tarp. Dr. Kriss clambered into the truck and they hoisted the stretcher in, then Rainer helped her bring it back down, empty, the tarp flapping loose.

They were rolling the stretcher to the door, and he'd already turned to enter the code, when the tarp caught in the wheel and jammed it. Dr. Kriss crouched down and fiddled with the wheel, and Rainer, not releasing his grip on the stretcher, had to reach all the way out to touch the keypad, giving me a view of the code.

I still recall the rhythm of those numbers, *1488, 1488*, beaten into my memory.

6.

Soon they brought another body from the outbuilding, and after loading in the camping equipment, they got in the truck and disappeared up the driveway.

I stepped into the clearing, the fawns still picking at the grass, and checked my phone. There was service, enough to place a call to Gordon. The ring got choppy and I thought the signal would die, but he answered.

"Hell—"

"Gordon?"

"—ney?"

"I want to tell you where I am."

"Where—"

"Gordon?"

"Whit—"

"Just listen." I explained as best I could: the road from Arcade, the driveway, the house and outbuilding. I hoped some of it got through. "Hello?"

I looked at the phone. The call had ended, the service whisked away on a changing wind.

I entered 1488 into the keypad and turned the handle. It was pitch-black inside. I felt along one wall, then another, and found the switch. Rows of fluorescent lights shuddered on, except toward the very back. By now my respirator mask was wet, and I was relieved to take it off and inhale crisp AC.

The building contained one large room, concrete walls and concrete floor, roughly divided into three areas. Near the entrance, an industrial fridge loomed beside a laboratory bench. In the middle of the room, something was surrounded by a white privacy screen of the sort you'd find between beds in a hospital ward. Beyond that, drab shadow cloaked the back.

If this was where Dr. Kriss had manufactured the solution—the closed quarters of her trade secrets—there wasn't much left of the operation that had churned out enough white blood to keep three trials supplied. The fridge was humming, and when I opened it, I saw about a dozen bags of solution on mostly empty shelves. Others were heaped in a stainless steel sink, squeezed dry.

From the impressions on the floor, I could tell that laboratory benches had once stood all around, but now just one remained. In cardboard boxes stashed beneath it, I found piles of broken glass. Some shards had printed measurements; I assumed they'd been beakers and flasks. She'd gotten rid of almost everything.

I took out the camera and snapped pictures. Sneakers squeaking on cool concrete, I approached the privacy screen. It rested on black plastic wheels. When I rolled it aside, I was smacked with the reek of blood, sickly metallic, and had to turn away. Holding the mask to my mouth, I breathed deep and faced the wooden table.

Blood slathered the surface, coursed down the legs, and emptied into a drain in the floor. Some of the blood had dried, but in spots it was still sticky. A couple IV stands flanked a trolley carrying heavy-duty saws and serrated blades, unwashed, bits of flesh caught in the teeth, black hair stuck to the metal.

I clenched my stomach and took photos. When I stepped back, I realized I'd planted my foot in blood and imprinted a Nike swoosh on the floor. I took the sneaker off and washed it in the sink, then wet my hands and hurried back to the stain, effacing it with my fingers. The blood browned and pulverized on my hands. I rinsed them off, water pattering on the empty sacks in the sink. White residue curled down the drain.

I wheeled the screen back in place then crossed to the rear of the room, where the fluorescent tubes had been unscrewed from the fixtures overhead. I found a standing lamp, and when I switched it on, I saw the holes.

There were three of them, dug in the concrete floor. One was still covered by an antique wooden door, the paint peeling, the knobs brass, but the doors to the others were swung open on their hinges. The holes were maybe seven feet long, two feet wide, and deep. I could see pale worms in the earth below.

That's when I should've left. I'd already seen enough. But at that moment, the camera in my hands, I needed to know everything, ball it all up and unfold it in the story.

I pulled on the handle of the door over the covered hole. It met resistance. I pulled again and saw it was locked. I slid the bolt and yanked the handle.

There was a body. Naked, hairless, white. Black nylon wrapped around the man's ankles and bound his arms to his torso. He was blindfolded, but blood had soaked through the fabric. His stomach looked like some misshapen pregnancy. Pink growths had burst through his fingernails and split his hands open, the shocking white of raw knuckles. His testicles had bloated pink and broken through the skin. He wore that chewed-up smile, the face half skull.

Even as the reek of waste escaped in waves, I didn't look away. But I must've said something, like "Jesus" or "Fuck" or "No," because the body responded, his mouth opened with a burp, blood sputtered on his chin. Gobs of plastic fell and hung and he made wet sounds, bubbling air, his brow furrowing and wringing more blood from his eyes.

I ran for the door, bursting out into tatters of smoke just in time to see the purple truck arriving.

I locked eyes with Dr. Kriss. Rainer was already getting out. I broke across the field. Though I was dizzy, purple dots swarming in my eyes, for a moment it seemed like I could make it to the woods, but Rainer tackled me, I hit the ground, the wind shot from my lungs. He straddled me, I tried bucking him off, and he gave just enough for me to turn over and catch sight of the gun in his hand, the butt held high before it swooped.

7.

The pain woke me up. Every heartbeat sent it throbbing through my skull. But I couldn't touch my head. Nylon bands bound me to the chair.

I was beneath one of the empty light fixtures at the back of the room. I could see the doors closed over the holes. I was feet from the body I'd seen, just a wooden slab between us. Dr. Kriss stood at the sink, squeezing out bags of solution while listening to her iPod. I heard the milky stream ringing off the basin. Every time she'd twisted out the final drops, she ran the faucet to wash it down, then chucked the empty bag on the pile.

I didn't say anything, just watching her work. She was singing "Ray of Light." When she noticed I was awake, she pulled out the white earbuds.

"I hate doing this," she said, finishing one off. "This is the final batch."

She picked up a full bag and came over to perch on a stool in front of me. This would be our last interview, no notebook, no recorder.

Dr. Kriss tossed the bag in my lap. It jiggled on impact and settled.

"I was this close to getting it right." She stared at the bag. "This batch is the product of countless reformulations, all based on the trial's data pool. It's that much closer to the real thing. Maybe it is the real thing. We'll never know, thanks to you."

I could barely hear for the rush of blood in my head.

"Do you realize what you've done?" she said. "The number of lives we could've saved?"

"You still expect—" A heap of phlegm clogged my throat. I spat, but the wad didn't clear my leg.

Dr. Kriss looked on with disgust.

"You still expect me to believe you care about saving lives," I said.

She planted her feet, leaned forward from the stool, my frustrated instructor. "Everything great is built on this," she said with finality.

"On what?"

"Lives—someone's, somewhere. No one cares, you understand? No one cares who died carrying stones for the cathedral, or who's buried in the diamond mine—"

"Or whose house burned down."

"If the solution worked, no one would even ask. The story would've been true by the time you told it. I only needed a few more months, maybe weeks."

I told her that would've been of little comfort to her subjects, and she said, as if with pity, "You looked in the hole."

"Yes."

"Brave of you."

"There must've been some other way," I said. "Why did you need to rush like this?"

The impact of the question surprised me. Dr. Kriss looked about the room with dismay, as if she could see all her failures at once.

"I told you about my father," she said.

"So?"

"I told you I promised to make his life count for something, that I built my entire career on that. I had to fight for every inch. I was a woman, I didn't have money, I had to work twice as hard—"

"You're not answering."

She seemed startled, severed from some daydream. "I am."

"No, you're not."

The doctor stood.

"You can't, can you," I said. "You don't have an answer."

Some interplay of rage and fear almost choked her off. "It doesn't matter if you understand anymore."

The door opened and Rainer entered. He glanced at the bags still full on the bench. "There isn't much time, Eva. I have to strip him. If you don't want to be here for this, you'd better hurry up."

Dr. Kriss wheeled an IV stand to my chair.

"What are you doing?" I said.

She prepared the needle and swabbed my forearm with alcohol. I began struggling against the nylon. The bag of solution flopped to the floor.

I cried out.

"Rainer, come hold her."

He crouched behind the chair and hugged me from behind. I couldn't move my arms.

"Don't."

Dr. Kriss applied the tourniquet. I watched the needle break my skin.

"Please don't."

She picked up the bag. I would be the last subject, her final attempt to discover if it worked, if it was real.

"Eva, please."

"Relax," she told me, and hung a bag. The liquid was perfectly clear. It dripped into the tubing.

I think it was morphine. At first I felt nauseous, as if I might puke down the front of my shirt, but then I experienced an overwhelming inner contentment, a godly flow.

I could hear Rainer saying something in a low voice.

"That's out of the question," replied Dr. Kriss. "They'd come for her."

"Who?"

"She has a name, Rainer. She's not a nobody."

"But the story."

Dr. Kriss was petting my forehead. The pain was gone, the very concept of pain was gone.

"She won't tell anyone," she said. "She's mute."

When Dr. Kriss left, Rainer tied an apron behind his back, wheeled a stretcher to the hole, and unearthed the last subject. Black dirt crumbled off his back as Rainer hauled him up. The blindfolded face slumped in my direction, the smile hideous as Rainer pushed him to the wooden table behind the screen. For a few minutes there was silence. It must've been the silence of Rainer putting him down, a fatal dose in the drip.

Then came the sounds of Rainer ripping out the plastic. Whoever discovered the bodies couldn't find the pink stuff melted with the flesh, so he stripped it out like wires from a wall. I heard the grinding saw, snapping sounds, and his exertions as he pried something open with a crunch. I saw him rush to the sink and wretch, dry, his apron black with blood. But with the morphine icy in my veins, everything had a farcical aspect. These were sound effects, and Rainer was a cartoon, and when he saw that I was laughing, he said, "You're a sick bitch, Whitney."

"No I'm not." But still I laughed.

I fell into a flying dream, soaring over treetops in the coolest rain. When I landed, two nurses argued over my body, because I was so happy.

"We need to start it soon."

"But when will she wake up?"

"There will be time."

"If something happens—"

"Then it happens."

I was grinning.

"You're so kind," I told them, unable to open my eyes. "Do you really love me?"

"Yes, Whitney," the nurses said. "We really do."

My heart thrilled with joy.

8.

I surfaced to the moan of the wind. My eyes adjusted to the dark. I'd been untied. There were two faint windows and I felt my way toward them, grasping out, then pushed through the door and fell to the grass. The drugs had worn off and my head throbbed again.

I'd fallen from the back of the purple truck, which was parked by the outbuilding. Wind ripped over the field, debris spitting through the air. Smoke forced its way down my throat and I coughed. I stuffed my face in the crook of my arm and looked around, confused.

It was nighttime, of a sort I'd never seen. The sky was blood red and the tips of the pines stabbed into it, black. I heard a tree crash, and a still-burning ember came weaving toward me on the wind. The fire was close, and Dr. Kriss and Rainer were gone. I had to get off the mountain.

I couldn't risk trying to get back to the Jeep on foot. I looked inside the cab of the truck. There were keys. I started it up and bounced over the grass. Now the driveway was bright, live flames seething on the forest floor. Embers floated toward the truck and exploded into sparks on the windshield. I accelerated through them, branches raining from the canopy, but had to hit the brakes when I saw that a tree had fallen over the drive.

My first instinct was to get out and try to move it. As I hurried to the tree, I could feel the heat of the fire exhaling. The tree wasn't especially large and it didn't appear to be smoldering. I knew I could lift it. But in fact I couldn't, either because the drugs had weakened me or because it was just too heavy. Coughing, choking, I got back in the truck.

I slammed the door and spent a crucial minute hacking. There was no choice. I backed up, gathered momentum, and aimed for the tree's narrow tip. My head smacked the roof as I thumped over, then I yanked the wheel to avoid a crawling flame. The driveway spat me onto the road.

Fire poured around me into towers of smoke. There was no one on the mountain anymore; the evacuations must be complete. I could feel myself cooking in the truck, the windows getting hotter. My eyes gushed and I had to squint through swarming embers as I drove straight down the middle of the road, straddling the yellow line, flames sweeping overhead.

Then I saw the pine. Its upper half had ignited, the pitch boiling inside. As I neared it, I had a premonition of its falling and planted my foot on the gas. It was like a huge hand of white flame, waving and faltering, then the trunk snapped and it all came streaking down. I shot into the road's closing eye as it plunged. Branches smashed the back end of the truck and I spun out of control, fanning across the lane and then swerving to the side. I was about to hit a wall of orange flame when the truck suddenly skipped over a bump and hurtled back onto asphalt. I regained control and never touched the brakes, soaring down the road.

There came something like actual night. The massive stones along the road were like boulders of ice. Soon I saw the sirens spinning at a checkpoint.

A fireman lit up golden yellow in my headlights and waved me to a stop. I rolled the window down.

"Jesus, you're late," he said. "Got anyone back there?"

I shook my head.

"Thank god. Everyone's checking in at Ascension. Make sure they know you're safe, okay?"

I forced it out. "Okay."

They let the purple truck through, but I didn't take it to the hospital. I drove straight to my hotel and parked it down the block with the keys in the ignition. The purple paint had bubbled off.

When I got back to my room, I used every lock on the door and window, stripped off my clothes, and stepped into the shower. The runoff was black, soot in my snot. I could barely stand anymore, so I kneeled in a corner of the stall and let cold water pour over me.

I held my head in my hands, the day's images all out of order. I could've stayed in there for hours—my body screamed for it—but I toweled off, sat at the desk, and wrote up my notes.

THE FATHER

1.

There's nothing for me in my condo. Nothing on the glass walls, where I can't hang paintings, nothing to make with the steel appliances, nothing in the stack of hardcover novels that only vex and bore me. The wound in my arm tingles and calls, almost like a sexual organ.

I let my hair down; it swings almost to the backs of my knees. I pour a glass of wine and put a frozen dinner in the microwave, chicken in wine sauce with roasted red potatoes. I stand there, drinking, until the timer counts down, and then sit before my laptop with the food.

I'm startled to find an e-mail from Gordon Stone. I can't recall the last time we corresponded. Besides composing the foreword to *The Complete Bystander*, Gordon has kept busy writing slender books about the famous food regions of Europe. Evidently the journalist from *Vice* contacted him and mentioned her plan to interview me.

She's excruciatingly earnest, don't you think? I wanted to disillusion her as a matter of principle. But it occurred to me that I hadn't heard if you were coming

*to the launch. In fact, I didn't even have your e-mail. I had to find it through your
company.*

I feel a pang of shame that Gordon knows what I do for a living.

*I ran into your old friend, Annette Cale, at a function recently. She told me
she'd seen you on 6th.*

I remember the flicker in her eyes—"Whitney?"—as she took in the
fingernails, the wilding hair.

*I was very jealous, it's been so long since I saw you. Please, Whitney, come to
the launch. I'm attaching the invitation. You can't ignore your family.*

Gordon doesn't understand, and somehow my years of silence haven't
conveyed it. I have no family, not really. Even my mother was a stranger in a
mother's skin. I've begun to look like her lately—a little harder, a little meaner,
as if the nutrients have drained from my face—and it's given me a clearer
vision of her. Now I recognize her not as a lonely woman, not at all, but lonely
around me.

I visited her occasionally after that day in Los Angeles. I'd had to admit
she was right, the solution was impossible, it didn't exist. "It sounded like
science fiction," she told me, and never mentioned it again.

And I was there at Cedars-Sinai when she died, surrounded by the gang,
her loyal group of friends. I used to wish Mom had given me the tools with
which she'd built her friendships. The gang knew her in ways I never did,
and now, on her deathbed, she rested, cloaked in intimacy. When I surveyed
my life, I found nothing like that—no shelter, no history—like I'd passed
through time on an empty wind.

But since her death, I've come to loathe, rather than envy, that kind of
friendship, all that emotion bursting through the surface. I look back on how
the gang wailed and moaned at her bedside and it all seems false and ridiculous. I think words perish in the open air. Only what's sealed inside is real.

I crush a potato with the fork and rub it in the sauce. I delete Gordon's
e-mail.

2.

The morning after the forest fire, I caught the early bus to Denver. With smoke stacked up in the sky, I thought of how the fire had probably swept over the house, engulfed the outbuilding, incinerated the bodies where they'd dumped them. If anyone found human remains, they'd discover the burnt tent poles and tarps I'd seen Dr. Kriss and Rainer carry, and the bodies would seem like more of those nomads from the Tomahawk. Over the following weeks I kept a close eye on news of the wildfires, but the *Ledger* never reported fatalities. When I called Colorado's Wildfire Resource Center, they said no, there had been no deaths near Arcade.

I had more than enough, now, to write the story, but as the bus neared Denver, I knew my reporting wasn't over. Not quite. There was still one note with a question mark, the name I'd found in Lane Porter's papers—*A. Kriss* of Everett, Washington.

I booked a flight to Seattle, but before I could fly, I had to calm the manager down at the car rental outlet. He couldn't believe I'd lost another Jeep. As he dealt with me, he kept pawing through what little hair remained. I filled out a booklet of forms and he said, "This could get dicey," as he got on the phone with regional headquarters.

I sat in the waiting room, where I could hear his submissive muttering, and called Gordon Stone to tell him I was fine. He said my package from Tampa was waiting for me at the office.

Finally the manager set the phone down and said, "You're clear."

"That's good news."

"Never rent another car in the state of Colorado."

3.

I landed at Sea-Tac and was surprised to find I could rent an Acura Integra, no questions asked. My plan was to drive up to Everett, interview A. Kriss, then head back to the airport for a red-eye to New York.

It was a day of drifting rain, the sky low. I remembered when I first moved here, how I'd felt like a desert woman finally taking water to the core. A lot of people got depressed in the Pacific Northwest, but I loved the slick streets and crawling mist. As I passed through Seattle on my way north to Everett, my years at the *Post-Intelligencer* didn't seem so distant. In this particular rain, as if it had been falling from the day I left for New York, I felt as if my whole life were preserved here, untouched.

I couldn't resist it. I parked on Elliott across from the *P-I* building and ate lunch in the driver's seat, rain running off the windshield in cool rivulets. I crept with an old picture of myself hurrying in the early morning, coffee in one hand, umbrella in the other, aping my idea of a professional journalist. I'd been so proud of the globe that sat atop the building, as if its glory redounded to me. IT'S IN THE P-I wrapped around the aquamarine orb in classy red lettering, and a golden eagle spread its wings at the northern pole.

At once I felt the need to go into the *P-I*, find my old colleagues, tell them everything I'd done—relief.

My phone rang. I placed the lox-on-bagel on the dash and sucked some cream cheese off my thumb.

"Hello?"

A woman's voice came through. "Is this Whitney?"

"Yes?"

"It's Louise, Lane's mother, do you remember?"

"Of course," I said, sitting upright. "How are you?"

"I hope you don't mind my calling you. I asked for your number, but I didn't want to bother you."

"It's no bother, really."

"It's my son's work," she said, "his notes for your book? I wondered if you were ready to return them. I've been trying to keep everything together, and it's been making me nervous knowing you have all those papers, because you're so busy, and things get lost."

"Don't worry, I'm on a reporting trip at the moment, but when I get back to the city, I'll send them to you right away."

"That would be wonderful, Whitney, thank you. Do you have a pen?"

I took down her address. She sounded determined, as if reclaiming his body from a foreign country. I wasn't sure what I'd do.

"How is the book?" she asked.

"It's only a proposal," I said, "but it's coming along, thanks in no small part to Lane's notes."

"He told me you made a great team."

"We did."

"He left a lot of work unfinished," she said, and I heard her take a shaky breath.

But something had changed. Just a few days before, I would've held the phone away as she cried, and as the raindrops combined on the window and slid. Now I pressed the phone close, pressed hard until my ear was hot and red and her voice filled up my head.

4.

I arrived in Everett in the early afternoon and found the address. It was a modest, two-story home in a neighborhood fizzing with rain. A rusty bike was locked to a low chain-link fence around a front yard choked with dandelions. When I opened the gate, I heard a dog bark inside the house. It caught the attention of some men across the street who'd been fiddling under the hood of a pickup. They straightened and stared at me.

The front curtains wavered as I opened the screen door and knocked. A middle-aged woman came to greet me in a long denim button-up shirt over jeans, her reading glasses on a strap. She had bright-blond hair, shallow eyes of powder blue, and a face wrinkled like paper that's been bunched up and flattened out. Between her legs, the barking German shepherd tried nosing through, and she kept pushing his head away.

"Yes?"

I introduced myself and, not knowing who she was, simply said, "I'm writing a story about Eva Kriss."

"Really? Eva?"

"Are you—"

"Her mother, April. It's okay, it's okay," she cooed to the dog, scratching beneath his collar.

She invited me into the wood-paneled living room. Beside the recliner, a king-size cigarette burned in a crystal ashtray, the smoke mingling with cherry air freshener. *The 700 Club* was playing on TV. April muted it.

She said, "Will you hold on a minute?"

"No problem."

She hurried upstairs. The German shepherd sat and regarded me from the doorway.

I took out my notebook and glanced over the photos on the wooden mantle. I found Dr. Kriss's graduation portrait from the University of Washington, a shining purple sash about her shoulders.

April came back downstairs. "Eva was the first Kriss to go to college," she said when she saw where I was looking. She picked up the photo, frowning at how dusty it was. "We weren't against it, but we wanted to keep her close."

"So she grew up here?"

"Eva lived right in this house until the day she went to college."

April indicated a display by the television, a kind of military shrine, glowing with electric candles. I saw a photo of Dr. Kriss in her navy uniform, standing against a desert background, along with portraits of several other soldiers, all men, from the Second World War to Vietnam. Two flags were folded in triangular cases of mahogany.

"My father and brothers all served," April explained, "so I was very proud when Eva enlisted. This may be hard to understand, but she was both daughter and son to us."

She didn't say anything more until I wrote this in my notes, then she pointed to a framed white T-shirt on the wall above the display. It said OPERATION DESERT STORM: VICTORY over a map of Iraq and a caricature of Saddam, a bald eagle swooping down as if to pluck his head off. Signatures were scrawled all over in black marker.

"Eva marched in DC with the returning troops," April told me, "and I wore that shirt at the parade. I got it signed by a member of every branch of the service."

She climbed back into the recliner and lit a fresh cigarette. I sat on the sofa beside her, notebook in my lap.

"So you come from New York," she said.

"Yes. Have you ever been?"

"No." April screwed up her face. "I don't think I'd like it."

"Why not?"

"I didn't like DC. Too busy, too many drug dealers, and then the attacks. But you understand, I'd live on a base if they'd let me, or I might be happy in Idaho."

She fished a photo album from under the coffee table. When I edged closer on the sofa to watch her turn the pages, the German shepherd barked once. The sound went through me like a shot.

April shushed him. "He's bored. See Eva?"

She tapped her pink-lacquered nail on some shots of Dr. Kriss as a child. The girl had her blond hair cut in a wedge and wore the same clothes as her parents: plaids of red, yellow, and green, blue jeans, army surplus coats.

The album largely showed the family outdoors, their interchangeable outfits bright against a dark-green wall of pines. From this rugged Pacific

Northwestern setting, Dr. Kriss's self-invention seemed so unlikely, ranging in whites across the tennis court, golfing at a Colorado country club.

April indicated one shot in which the father was shirtless, the sun lighting up his chest hair as he brought an ax down upon a hunk of wood. In another, the future Dr. Kriss placed a hot dog in a bun with two fingers, her face pinched with disgust.

April was always smiling, always aware of the camera. She looked like she hoped the photos would turn out well. By contrast, her husband and daughter wore expressions more common in nineteenth-century photography, before subjects knew how to put on a face, ghostly eyes gazing through the lens, jaws set, as if nervous about what will happen when the shutter blinks.

There weren't many photos of Dr. Kriss and her father together. I saw one of the girl running away from his outstretched arms, another of her pointing a toy rifle at his back.

"She was always very headstrong," April said as I lingered on that last photo. "By the time she was ten—you can write this in your magazine—she was smarter than the two of us put together. We were only along for the ride."

I duly put her words in the notebook.

Beside the ashtray was a cup of marbles. April picked out two large ones, ruby and amber, and began grinding them together in her palm. The dog watched the marbles, ears pert.

"So what did Eva do to get into a magazine?" she said.

"I'm writing about her work in medical science."

Her mother made a small knowing sound—"Ah"—but I didn't think she understood what I meant.

"I'm not sure how much she's told you," I added.

"Oh, well." April kept rolling the marbles, as if embarrassed that she couldn't give an answer. "It's been a little while since Eva visited, and she doesn't get a chance to call very often."

"I understand."

A brief, anticipatory silence fell between us, and I realized it wasn't April who had something to add. She wanted me to give her news of her daughter. I considered how to break it to her. But I was already thinking about the integrity of the story I'd compose, and it occurred to me that this interview was more valuable if April remained ignorant. I'd keep the widow in a kind of quarantine, so the innocence of her words could rub against the story's darker truths and set them off. *We were only along for the ride.* It wouldn't matter to readers that our interview took place after everything I'd witnessed. They wouldn't be able to discern the order of events unless I told them. I could act, here in Everett, as if I were crafting the profile I was originally going to write. This wasn't the creep, but simply the art of the magazine feature—to experience the present refracted through a future piece of writing.

And so I gave April a kind of truth. I told her about the solution, I told her about the trial, I told her about the purple trucks of Common Dreams. I painted a picture of Zeke walking off in the Florida sun, his new blood coursing freely, and amazed her with an image of the jets that bent toward Wigwam Deck. "I owe the trial my life," I said, quoting Pavel Firea.

All the while, April passed the marbles between her fingers.

"I want to stress how much you mean to her," I finished. "In particular, Eva has always identified her love for her father as essential to her work."

I knew I was venturing into a sensitive area, but I had to go there.

April said, "I wish Amos could hear you say that."

I wrote the name in my notes.

"If you don't mind," I said, "when did he begin getting sick?"

"Eva told you about that?"

"Yes."

April plunked the ruby marble back in the cup and chose a green like pond scum, which she clicked against the amber in her palm.

"It was around the time she went to school," she said. "Eva started noticing problems with his nerves. I couldn't really tell what was happening, I couldn't see what she saw, but Eva could always see more than me. Anyway, it was very sad, because she tried all sorts of things, and it only got worse. When it got worse, I could see that."

"When did he"—in the glow of *The 700 Club*, I chose my words carefully—"pass on?"

Now she held the marbles tight. I could hear the rain outside.

"What do you mean?"

"Sorry. If you'd prefer not to talk about it, I understand. It's just that Eva has always spoken of his passing as a transformative event, kind of like a crossroads in her life. It's what made her the person she is today, it's why she's done everything she's done."

"Pass on," she said. "You mean die?"

"Yes."

April showed a row of gapless teeth, like a mouthguard. "You've got your facts mixed up," she told me. "Amos didn't die."

"What?"

"He's upstairs right now."

I was off the couch, nearly tripping on the dog. He growled as I took the stairs two at a time, April calling after me: "Wait a minute."

I saw a bathroom, a bedroom, and one closed door.

"Don't go in there."

I heard the dog's nails scramble over the floor. He yelped as April snatched him by the collar. I opened the door.

A man lay on a single bed, facing me, his knees drawn to his chest, a thin wool blanket pulled up to his neck. Snowy stubble frosted his cheeks, which were collapsed as if he were sucking something. I could see the tremors. It was Amos, alive.

I told you about my father.

An old-fashioned radio in a wooden case played some classical music, and two sabers with golden tassels were crossed beneath a Confederate flag push-pinned to the wall. A reek, like a shoe rotting on a foot, rolled off the bed. The father kept shaking in the blanket, but his eyes didn't flinch as I stood in the doorway, the dog pulling April toward me. Sick or insane, I don't know, but he wore a smile of perfect serenity.

The German shepherd flashed his teeth and April could barely restrain him.

"You better leave," she grunted, leaning back.

I stared at Amos, Dr. Kriss's last story voiding.

"I'll let go of this fucking dog if you don't leave right now."

THE MUTE

1.

I flew home and slept for days. At first the dreams were unbearable. Or they weren't exactly dreams—in the deepest pit of sleep, there was nothing—more like memories that, when I'd briefly rouse to roll over or shoot awake at a car horn's blast, would surface in weird combinations. I'd see wildfire sweeping through Manhattan, the German shepherd gnawing its legs, Lane in a hole, blindfolded.

I found a very old stash of pot in my medicine cabinet. It was dry and harsh, and my lungs were already wrecked, but it helped subdue the dreams. Stoned in bed, I'd focus on a kind of humming green at the back of my mind and sleep through the morning. Then I'd take a long shower and order something in.

My first piece of business—I was technically still on leave—was to send a package to Lane's mother. I spent an absurd afternoon printing off copies of my work from the *Seattle Post-Intelligencer* and arbitrarily underlining sections in red and blue, adding the occasional question mark, exclamation point, and coffee stain for verisimilitude, just like I'd done when fabricating notes. I'd only chosen articles that hadn't made it into Lane's original dossier, like my piece about the igloo, and by the end of the process it almost felt like it could make a decent book after all.

When I ventured out to courier the package, I finally registered that the scaffolding was gone. The restoration was complete. As promised, they'd painted the building. It was only a matter of time before the neighboring buildings matched it, and the new aesthetic would spread.

I stood outside in the early September air, unsettled by the paint job. They'd slathered the white so thick, you could hardly tell the facade was brick. I put a hand to it, as if communing with the building trapped within, and the paint was smooth and cool, like plastic.

2.

I started work on the story. As I sketched my outline, I kept tripping over what Dr. Kriss had told Rainer in the outbuilding: *She won't tell anyone, she's mute.* I didn't understand, but I sensed that's why she didn't have Rainer kill me on the spot, why she'd given me a chance to get off the mountain. In moments of self-doubt, I thought she knew: I was like her, a fabricator— two women given over to the creep. A liar couldn't tell the story of a liar.

But that wasn't me, not anymore. The outline issued effortlessly, as if on a sheet of tracing paper placed over my mind. No matter why Dr. Kriss had spared me, I was going to write this story. More than ever before, I felt loyal to the unadorned truth. It didn't matter what I was or what I'd been. The story was mine. I was going to tell it.

The writing came easily, trancelike and time-annihilating. I opened with Zeke's stabbing, an emergency to snag the reader's attention, and the strange white blood transfusion. Without going into too much detail, I gestured toward the significance of the solution, *the Holy Grail of medical science.* And then, to complete the introduction, I cut to an image of Zeke in the tub at the House of Brothers. The friction between these elements would spark the central mystery.

Despite the data being shown to corporate executives and top military personnel, I wrote, *the solution was a catastrophic failure, an elaborate deception that's left a trail of gruesome fatalities from one coast to another.*

I set about dismantling the fiction, piece by agonizing piece: Jules's eaten face, Ray and his dogs, the burned-down homes and the new developments, Rainer posing as Pavel, the holes, the bodies, and Amos, trembling beneath a Confederate flag.

The piece unspooled unlike anything I'd written before. But at the same time, I felt the presence of an alternate narrative, a shadow side to the story filling my pages. I'd experienced so much in the course of my reporting, I knew I'd be left with countless impressions that would never be written, that would never resolve. Even the shooting, even the wildfire, didn't belong in print. And then there was Lane. No matter how the piece turned out, I'd have another story on the tip of my tongue forever.

3.

While composing the draft, I got a call from Gordon Stone.

"I know you're on leave," he said, "but is there any chance you could come into the office today?"

"What's going on?"

"Have you seen the *Times?*"

There was only one story he could be talking about. On the front page that morning, a report by Michael Gordon and Judith Miller had appeared, stating Saddam Hussein had *stepped up his quest for nuclear weapons* and embarked upon *a worldwide hunt for materials to make an atomic bomb.* The report centered on the purchase of aluminum tubes, which, the reporters wrote, American officials had identified as components of centrifuges to enrich uranium.

The piece seamlessly transitioned into the case for war. Certain *hard-liners* were quoted as saying Washington shouldn't wait until evidence of Saddam's program was verified. *The first sign of a "smoking gun," they argue, may be a mushroom cloud.*

Even in the midst of my writing, I'd been shocked by the article. All the talk about Saddam's weapons had seemed like hearsay to this point. But it was right there, page one, the *New York Times.*

"Rice and Cheney have already been on TV," Gordon told me. "Condoleeza lifted the mushroom cloud line right off the front page. It's total chaos over here. Mort's doing something, well, quite drastic."

"What is it?"

"He's rushing out another issue. We've already produced and shipped this month's, but he says the *Times* allegations can't wait to be investigated. We have a lot of work to do, Whitney. It's all hands on deck, I'm afraid."

I'd never seen the office like this. A few writers, whom Mort had tasked with probing the *Times* report, seemed to know what they were doing, but everyone else was clueless, and the man who ought to be guiding us through the situation had retreated to his office. I could see Mort with his head in his hands, staring at something on his desk. To make it all more miserable, a urinal had overflowed in the men's room, and water of unknown composition was running down the hall. Everyone was using the women's, and there was piss all over the seats.

After Gordon gave me the package I'd couriered from Tampa, I asked, "What do you need?"

"Do you have the courage to talk to Mort?"

"Sure."

"He said to give him an hour and it's been three. After he went apoplectic this morning, everyone is spooked, myself included."

"What do you want me to ask him?"

"In brief, what the hell is going in this issue? And is a plumber on the way?"

I knocked on Mort's door and gently opened it. I could feel my colleagues' eyes on my back.

Mort glanced up. "Whitney?"

"I'm back," I said. "I'm feeling a lot better."

He just blinked.

"The story's going well," I added. "You'll have it soon."

Mort smiled but made no reply. I looked at the paper on his desk, which I realized was a financial ledger. The cost of printing a second issue must've been astronomical.

"The staff is wondering what's going on," I said. "Is there something I can tell them?"

Mort sighed. "Tell them we'll make this work, somehow."

"Alright. Anything else?"

He pushed his upper lip with a pencil. "Tell them there won't be a culture file in the issue. If these guys aren't stopped, there won't be a culture to file on."

"Okay, I'll tell them," I said, trying to stay upbeat. "And I'm going to call a plumber too, unless you've already done that."

"Plumber?"

"Jesus, that bad, huh," Gordon said after I'd relayed the directives. "I'm sorry for calling you in."

We both looked through the window of Mort's office. He had his head in his hands again.

"I wonder what he'll do if the *Times* story turns out to be true," I said.

"I'm not sure it matters," said Gordon, and whether he was speaking of the country or the magazine, I don't know. "It's already written."

4.

New York was on orange alert on September 10, 2002, when I finished a rough draft of the story. It came in at over twenty thousand words. There would be cuts, but I trusted Mort to do the right thing and run it long. After all, he'd started the *Bystander* for stories like mine.

My plan was to read it after lunch and then send certain relevant sections to Kenneth Sample, the CEO of Rubicon, for comment. I was positive I had my facts straight, but for legal I needed the corporate reaction.

I left the office, but with the Donut Shop closed, I wandered aimlessly, sometimes looking into windows or even stepping through doors but never connecting with what I saw or smelled. Eventually I was so hungry I went to the Corner out of sheer desperation.

The Corner was a diner equidistant to the offices of various newspapers and magazines that had become, over the years, a semi-famous media haunt. But it was more for tourists than anything else, people expecting to see journalists with press cards in fedoras. I recognized a few faces, but squeezed in alone at the counter beside an obese middle-aged guy reading the *Wall Street Journal* and eating steak and eggs. The greasy air made me famished and I ordered a burger and fries, extra patty. I really laced into the thing, letting the juice run down my wrists. It was a celebratory feast. In my head, I carried a brilliant secret, the story.

"Whitney Chase?"

A woman straddled the spare stool beside me. She wore a red suit and white blouse, and leaned hazardously close to the burger I was ripping into like a lion.

Through a big mouthful, I said, "Yeah?"

"Sandra Hart." Instead of a handshake, she latched a pinkie finger onto mine and gave a little laugh.

I assumed she worked for some publication or another.

"How's life at the *Bystander*?" she asked.

"Good, thanks."

"Really?" Her eyes flashed, the kind of look you have to practice in a mirror. "That's surprising."

"Why?"

"I've heard there's turbulence."

"It's been a difficult week."

"I think there are going to be a lot more difficult weeks," Sandra told me.

I swallowed, dabbed my lips with the napkin, and said, "Who are you, again?"

She took out a business card: SANDRA HART, DIAMOND COMMUNICATIONS, A GLOBAL CONSULTING FIRM.

"I'd love for us to get together sometime," she said. "If you're ever looking to make the transition, I can help."

As the industry had begun to sense decline, many people had been switching over to more lucrative positions at communications firms like hers. But I'd never felt more like a journalist than I did that day.

"Thanks, but no thanks."

No rejection registered on Sandra's face. "Just want to keep my name in the mix," she said.

"Well, you've done that."

When she got off the stool and left the Corner, the man beside me said, "I like how you handled her." He had bushy orange hair and a red bow tie. "These consultants are growing like weeds, choking out the profession."

"I guess so." I asked for my bill.

"Journalists have to stick together, stay the course. We've got to keep the faith. So you're at the *Bystander*."

"Yes."

"Fine magazine," he said, "very fine."

He looked at me until I said, "I assume you work in media?"

"Retired. That's Dow Jones for you, the mandatory ax at sixty-five, no exceptions. I was at *Barron's* for thirty-nine years. I worked my way up from the mailroom, no kidding. I can do it all. I can write features, set the type, fact-check. I can toss a paper to your doorstep like Johnny Unitas."

"It's good to be versatile," I said, counting out the tip.

"I still have a lot in the tank. That's why I like to mingle with my colleagues here, keep my ears peeled, you know, in case something opens up."

The Corner was almost empty. The waiter was wiping the counter around us.

"I'd better get back to work," I said, and for some reason pocketed Sandra's card.

"Wait." He quickly wiped his hands on his pants. "I'll give you my number."

"That's alright."

"But you don't even know my name."

I pushed the door twice and then saw it was a pull.

5.

A few days after reaching out to Kenneth Sample, I got an urgent message from his assistant on my cell. I'd only listed my *Bystander* extension in the e-mail but didn't have a chance to ask how she'd found this number before she asked if I'd be able to interview Mr. Sample soon, "maybe this afternoon?" We could meet at the headquarters of Rubicon's parent corporation, Inland Medical.

For the last time in my life, I packed my notebook and recorder, along with a copy of the story. I took the subway to 51st and found Inland's address on 3rd Avenue. The tower was sheer glass, wavy with blue reflections, and the revolving doors were flanked by Union Jacks.

I swung into a vaulted marble lobby and gave my name to the security guard. He called upstairs, and in a few minutes a woman came clicking across the floor in silver pants and a black turtleneck, hand extended all the way. With a British accent, she introduced herself as Nahid, and as I stood in the elevator beside her, breathing in her perfume, I reflected on how she had no idea who she was conveying, or how the story in my bag would bring this whole tower down.

"How long have you worked for Rubicon?" I asked.

"I'm with Inland, actually."

"You don't work for Mr. Sample?"

"No." The doors opened. "Right this way."

Nahid led me through a strangely empty office, cubicles abandoned on a Friday afternoon. At the end of the hall she opened a door to a boardroom and, when I stepped inside, closed it behind me.

At the long, slightly curved table sat two men I didn't recognize. Only one stood to greet me. He was in his forties, eyes friendly, no eyebrows. Boardroom light glared off his shaved head and there was rosacea on his cheeks.

"Jeff Sloan," he said, shaking my hand, "CEO of Inland Medical. And this is my associate."

The other man wore a blond goatee and was seated with a briefcase in his lap. He didn't nod or smile.

I said, "I was expecting Mr. Sample."

"Ken's no longer with the company," Sloan told me. "Please, sit."

I took one of the ergonomic swivel chairs along the polished table, and Sloan sat a few seats away from the associate. I could see people in the office building across the street. They were still at work, waving papers in the air, phone cords at maximum reach.

"We're relieved you could make time for us on such short notice," Sloan said. "I'm sure you understand why."

I brought out my notebook. "Do you mind if I record?"

"If you like."

I set the tape running.

Sloan said, "I've had a chance to read what you sent me. It's terrifically written, very engaging."

This was the first reader response I'd received.

"If you can believe it, there was a time, long ago, when I wanted to be a journalist myself. But I never had an eye for a good story, not like you, Whitney. You've shown me once again all the talent I don't have." He smiled, teeth blunt, as if filed down.

"I suppose I should say thanks."

"Don't mention it," said the CEO. "You came here for a comment from Ken. Tell me, does that mean you've given us a first look, so to speak, and that you haven't yet shared this widely?"

"Yes."

"So no one else has read this stuff?"

I hedged by saying, "Not in its most recent form."

Sloan glanced at the associate, who inclined his head.

"The story is coming out," I added, "and whether anyone has read it yet is beside the point."

"Off the record?"

The skin flexed where his eyebrows should've been. I said nothing.

"Or on, it doesn't matter." He laughed. "Here's the truth, Whitney. I had no idea what was happening at Rubicon. As it turns out, neither did Ken."

I began taking notes. The associate watched my hand.

"Of course, he had to fall on his sword. A lot of people had a stake in Rubicon, and they're going to be very disappointed. It was a high-risk, high-reward venture, and for a while there it really looked like it would pay off."

"People will be more than disappointed when they read my piece."

"I'm sure you're right," he said quickly.

Was this the eerie calm and acceptance of someone who knows his corporate days are numbered, that people close to him are going to jail?

"You're pretty casual about this," I observed.

"Don't think I'm not concerned," Sloan said, "and don't think I wasn't moved. Like I said, your claims are substantially documented, and compelling."

"And they're true. People lost their lives."

Sloan said nothing, but his eyes said yes.

I looked at the recorder. It was running. I made a note.

"When Ken forwarded what you sent him, he had more news to report," Sloan continued. "Apparently Eva Kriss sold off her stock in Rubicon and disappeared overnight. I don't recall the exact figure, but suffice it to say she sold high. At the end of today we're issuing a press release, announcing that Ken has stepped down and Rubicon is dissolving. You can expect the market to react accordingly."

It was a classic news dump, disclosing embarrassing or incriminating information on a Friday afternoon, hoping it would get buried over the weekend.

"This is not how a man of Ken Sample's stature wants to end his career," Sloan said. "Not that I feel sorry for him, between you and me. There was incredible negligence here. I was especially shocked by the allegation that these experiments were tolerated by municipal governments as part of some urban clearance initiatives. You really believe that?"

"Yes."

Sloan clucked and said, "Outrageous."

"You might be able to spin this for a few more days," I said, "but what will you do when the story comes out?"

Sloan again looked to the associate and the clasps on the briefcase shot open.

"As it happens," Sloan told me, "Ken did hear from Eva Kriss one last time before she went off to God knows where, Vienna or Montpellier, they seem to think. She sent him a package, and Ken's last task at Rubicon was to confirm its veracity, as well as its significance. And with that, Whitney, I'd like to wish you a restful weekend."

The CEO stood and started coming around the table.

"Where are you going?"

"My associate will have a word with you now."

I laughed in disbelief. "This is ridiculous. Don't you realize how this interview will look?"

His associate slowly reached across the table and stopped my tape recorder.

"There is no interview," Sloan said, quietly and evenly. "You were never here."

"But the tape."

"Goodbye, Whitney."

The door clicked shut behind him. I was alone with the associate.

I didn't set the tape running again, but even if I had, what happened next would've remained obscure, off the record, a space for anyone's conjecture.

The associate did not spare a word for me. In the hum of central air, he said nothing at all. He only withdrew a manila envelope from the briefcase, slid it across the table, and exited the boardroom.

A Post-it Note was stuck to the envelope: COPIES. I shook out the photographs. I felt like I'd leaned over an edge.

It was Whitney Chase, staff writer at the *Bystander*. Her face was clearly discernible, incontrovertible, eyes checking first to one side and then, in the next photo, to the other. Rain drooled off the awning above her. She hugged a file folder. That's my face on the night of the storm, my face when I fled Lane's apartment.

I was no danger, no journalist. It didn't matter what I knew. Rainer, the ghost, had followed me that night, and that's why Dr. Kriss could spare me on the mountain. She knew she had me, forever, in photographs. She knew I'd never say a word.

6.

After all these months, I had to tell Mort the story had fallen through. I could see the disappointment flicker on his face, though I was pretty sure it was more about the money I'd wasted.

"What happened?" he said.

I invented a story about how the doctor discovered complications during the trial and had withdrawn participation until they could be solved. I was careful to make the excuse not interesting enough in itself to write about.

"So it's still ongoing," he said.

"In a way."

"Maybe it's something you can write about later."

My eyes ranged over the mementos on his bookshelf—the Nixon caricature, the photo of the Black and White Ball. They struck me now as the keepsakes of an old fool, relics of an empire that would never rise again.

"Maybe, yeah," I said.

"Well, keep your notes, okay?"

I'd already destroyed everything, fed my work to the city in shreds, like Lane's files.

"I will." I turned from him. "Thanks, Mort."

"Don't be so glum," he told me. "These things happen, Whitney. Just be patient. The time will come when you can tell it."

.

I stayed at the *Bystander* for another few issues. I didn't take on assignments, I just helped out where I could, writing captions and headlines like an unpaid intern. When I finally tendered my resignation, Mort wasn't in a position to grieve it. He knew the magazine was close to folding. In a year's time the writers he'd so carefully collected would be scattered across New York and London. The magazine would become a rumor, as if it never was, until *The Complete Bystander* bound it back together. And by then, he was dead.

When my money ran out—I'd insisted Mort keep the withheld check, pathetic recompense for all the company dollars I'd squandered—I called Sandra Hart at Diamond Communications and made the transition to my journalistic afterlife. Since then, I've stood by and watched the wars never ending, the markets collapsing, the summers getting hotter and hotter.

Every now and then, unable to resist, I've spied on the story through the Internet. The cities I visited in pursuit of Dr. Kriss were among the hardest hit by the housing bubble's bursting. In the case of just one house at the Glades, you can trace its fate through public records, as JPMorgan Chase foreclosed on it and sold it to BNY Mellon before ownership passed from Countrywide to Bank of America to Nationstar. Today, you can buy it for practically nothing. There's a silence over the Tomahawk. Traffic pours over Mimico.

I've never found a trace of Dr. Kriss, but sometimes I creep with her. She's wrapped herself in a blanket and sits out on the balcony. Sparkling water fizzes in the glass, a falcon floats above her. She peers across a glacial lake. There's the smell of pine, a splash of oars. In another minute, the doctor will go in. The subject is waiting on the table.

7.

The other day, I passed through the underground garage. All the units in my building have sold, but hardly anyone actually lives here and the garage is always empty. I don't know whether the city cut a deal with the building, or whether the workers just found a way to sneak down there, but ever since winter hit, they've been plowing snow off the streets and down into the garage. Now, in the center of the lot, there's one tall berg of hard, blackened snow.

I'm seated on my couch, all hair and fingernails. I could open the seam on my wrist, let the story perish in the air. It would all be over in minutes; there is no solution. But after last time, I don't trust myself to let it run. I know I'll call for help.

I think instead of the snow's cold weight and I'm up from the couch, through my door, heading down the hall toward the elevator.

The building isn't made of the best materials. Look closely and you'll find premature cracks, unexpected stress. Measurements weren't double-checked before cuts, the carpet runs out before the end of the hall.

I press the button for the basement. The elevator falls. When the doors open, I cross the rubber-stained concrete of the underground garage.

Would it have been different in the telling? A telling not like this, words mute on the gag of my tongue, but out loud—a historical scream. Or would the dead still be here, forever inside this body until I die, or until I, the killer, kill it?

Fluorescent light silvers the ridge of the berg. I stab my nails in the snow and start ripping out fistfuls, flinging hard, dirty hunks behind me. They shatter and spread on the lot. Soon I can't feel anything up to my wrists, but my hands keep clawing until they meet a wall of ice. I smash through it to the soft inner core, then get on all fours and begin to tunnel, furious, panting, desperate.

Soon my legs are numb, my hair is filled with ice, and I've scooped out a pocket deep inside the mound. I look back at the misshapen mouth of the tunnel. The light doesn't penetrate. I smell car exhaust, there's salt on my lips, the filth of the city.

In the dark, I curl up in the cocoon of my hair and the dead lie down beside me. Within these walls, the story creeps out toward obscurity. One moment to the next, we are free of what happened, there's a glow instead of memory. We can sleep, here, in permanent silence, we can seep into the snow.

MICHAEL LaPOINTE has written for *The Atlantic*, *The New Yorker*, *The New York Times* and the *Times Literary Supplement*. He was a columnist with *The Paris Review*. He lives in Toronto.